He wante

Ellie could sense it. An[...], as if a wall had fallen away and she'd realized it was possible to touch.

Dear heaven, how she wanted to. She wanted to step closer, take Ryan's face in her hands and kiss him. Softly the first time, hard and deep the second time. To find out what all those lean muscles felt like under her fingers. She wanted to wrap herself around him, experience what this cowboy had to offer and for one brief moment just feel and not think.

But it wasn't possible. That was what had gotten her into this situation, and she'd been stupid to let herself meander along this path. She was pregnant. She was leaving. She couldn't toy around with this guy—it wasn't fair to either one of them.

Ellison stepped back.

was about fifty years behind the times… Well, it seemed like a good opportunity to change scenery and help them out at the same time."

A long silence met her words. Kate had known Ellie since they'd first been assigned as bunkmates at boarding school seventeen years ago. Changing scenery was not something Ellie had ever been concerned with.

"Ellie…" There was a soft note of desperation in her friend's voice, one that made Ellie come very close to confessing.

Not yet. Not until she had some kind of plan in place. Not until she'd come to terms with everything. Telling her aunt the truth had been ridiculously difficult, and she was not ready to repeat the experience. And then there was always the chance that she wouldn't have to confess—which was why she hadn't yet told her mother.

You're only six weeks along. Sometimes…things… happen.

Her aunt's words had given her a smidgeon of comfort two weeks ago when she'd simply had to tell someone the devastating news. How horrible was she that she kind of hoped something would happen? That the pregnancy would end itself naturally before the first trimester; that she could go back to her old life and never, ever make a mistake like this again?

Really horrible.

So she had that to deal with, too.

"Kate…my decision is made. I'm going to Montana. It's what I want to do."

"I don't believe you," Kate replied. "Quitting your job, moving to a foreign environment, holding out on your best friend…. You don't have a dreaded disease, do you?"

"No disease. Just a need for a change. And some privacy."

Kate sighed into the phone. "All right," she said sullenly. "Go to Montana. Keep me in the dark."

"It isn't like I won't be back," Ellie said, relieved that her friend was finally showing signs of backing off. "I have to finish packing. I'm running late and I won't make my flight if I have to keep answering calls."

"No more calls."

"Thanks."

"It's okay."

Her words were followed by an awkward silence as if they were both waiting for the other to hang up first, and then Kate said, "You know I have your back."

"You always have," Ellie replied, forcing the words over the lump forming in her throat. Stupid hormone-induced emotions. "I'll talk to you soon." And then she did hang up. Fast.

For a moment she stared down at her suitcase, blinking against the tears, before she regained control and started packing again, her movements quick and automatic.

Her new job was bogus—or at least it had started out that way. When her aunt had first suggested that Ellie go to work for them at their new ranch in Montana, her initial instinct had been to say no. It had been more than obvious that Angela was trumping up a way to rescue her niece from the consequences of her actions—something Ellie's own mother would have never done. Besides, Milo had a ranch consultant coming in later that summer to evaluate, so why would he need her? Easy answer. He didn't.

But for the first time in her life Ellie had no plan, no idea what her next move would or should be. After several days of considering her alternatives— paying rent from savings while she looked for another job in a tight market, trying to find a position that would work with single motherhood, coming to terms with her pregnancy—she'd realized that she was damned fortunate to have this opportunity. It gave her time, although she hated admitting she needed that time.

So three days ago she'd called her uncle Milo and hammered out a deal. She'd travel to Montana and familiarize herself with the ranch, which was still being managed by the original owner, before the consultant arrived. Milo had seemed relieved, saying that while the consultant came highly recommended, he'd feel better if he had another set of eyes there—Ellie's eyes. The person he was most concerned about was the former owner, now the un-communicative ranch manager. On the one hand, he didn't want to let the guy go if he was the best man to run the place, but on the other, the guy was hell to deal with.

Ellie assured Milo she'd take care of matters. That was what she did, after all—take care of matters, evaluate staff, make hiring and firing decisions. Between her and the consultant, they should have the ranch in decent shape by the time Milo retired.

She closed her suitcase and locked the latches. This was not going to be an escape. It was going to be a mission.

THE ARENA WAS muddy as hell. Ryan Madison shook out his loop, found the sweet spot and gripped it tightly as he urged his black gelding, PJ, into the roping box.

"Come on, Ryan. You can do it!" A female voice broke through his concentration, but he instantly tuned her out.

Focus.

PJ's body tensed as the calf was pushed forward into position. Ryan sent up a quick prayer, then nodded. The chute clanged open, the calf shot out and after that it was autopilot.

PJ caught up with the calf and squeezed in on him as Ryan dropped the loop over the animal's neck and dallied around the saddle horn, dismounting almost before PJ had skidded to a stop in the mud. He flanked the calf, a heavy, squirming heifer, dodging a foot as the calf hit the ground before grabbing that same foot, holding it with the two front feet with one hand and making his wraps with the other. Two wraps and a half hitch.

Ryan jumped to his feet, hands in the air. PJ eased forward, slacking the rope stretched between the saddle horn and the calf. He held his breath as the calf squirmed and bucked, and then the judge dropped his flag.

Ryan bent to loosen the rope on the calf's neck before releasing the animal's feet from the wraps of the pigging string. The calf jumped up and loped to the far end of the arena as Ryan remounted the gelding, coiling his muddy rope.

He was vaguely aware of the announcer giving his time—the best that day so far—and cheers from the crowd as he exited the arena; he nodded at some of his acquaintances. Smiled even though he didn't feel like smiling, despite a decent run.

Somewhere in the warm-up crowd was his half brother, Matt Montoya, who had every intention of stealing this purse away from him.

Have at it, Ryan thought as he rode through the crowd and then headed for his trailer. His run had been pretty damned close to perfect, especially in a muddy arena.

Once at the trailer, he tied PJ and pulled the saddle off. The horse was done for the day, but Ryan wasn't. He had a mission ahead of him that he was not looking forward to, but one that couldn't be avoided. He needed to talk to his father.

It was a good-size rodeo, but Charles Montoya tended to show up in the competitor's area to congratulate his legitimate son after a good run. Ryan had purposely parked his trailer within sight of his brother's, although under normal circumstances, they avoided any proximity with one another. In fact, they'd never actually spoken since the fistfight in the rodeo grounds' bathroom just after he'd turned fifteen.

After PJ was taken care of, Ryan sat on the trailer fender where he had a decent view of Montoya's trailer, and began his vigil. Matt would make his run within the hour and then, hopefully—

Score.

Charles Montoya was a tall man with a full head of silver hair. Hard to miss in a crowd, and even harder to miss as he headed for Matt's trailer. Ryan, vaguely aware of his heart rate bumping up, just as it did when he was about to rope, pushed off the trailer and started toward the man who, after finding Matt's trailer deserted, reversed course toward the stands. Ryan knew he probably wasn't going to have another semiprivate opportunity such as this anytime in the near future, so he started to jog after him.

"Excuse me," he called, when he really wanted to say, "Hold up, asshole."

Charles Montoya stopped walking and glanced over his shoulder, a stunned expression forming on his face when he recognized just who had hailed him.

Yeah. It's me. Surprised?

Ryan's mouth clamped into a hard straight line as he slowed to a walk, and damned if Charles didn't take on a polite, distant expression.

"Can I help you?" he said.

"Yes, you can. Stay away from my mother," Ryan said as he came to a stop.

"Excuse me?"

And this was when the bluff came in, because although he knew from Cindy, his mother's best friend, that Charles had been in contact with his mom—and that she'd been in a deep funk for days afterward—he didn't know the nuts and bolts of the situation. As always, Lydia Madison was protecting people. Ryan. Charles. Everyone but herself.

Ryan took a step forward, putting himself close enough to his father that the guy knew he meant business. "Leave my mother alone. No contact. Understand?"

A fierce frown formed between Charles's heavy white eyebrows. "I don't know what you're talking about."

"Don't bullshit me. You called her, you threatened

her, and if you do it again, the era of 'don't ask, don't tell' is over. Forever."

Charles drew himself up in a way that told Ryan he wasn't used to being challenged. Tough shit.

"Don't threaten me," he rumbled.

"Or?" Ryan asked calmly. "You'll tell the world the truth?"

The older man's face went brilliantly red and then, apparently unable to find a reply, he turned on his heel and stalked toward the stands. He'd made it only a few steps before he stopped dead in his tracks.

Ryan's first thought was, *What the hell?* But he quickly saw exactly what had brought his father to a screeching halt. The golden son, Matt, stood about fifteen yards away, blocking Charles's escape between two trailers.

Cool. A twisted family reunion.

Ryan started walking before he had a chance to think things through. He had a few words for his brother, too. Matt also moved forward, while Charles stayed planted, one son approaching from the front, one from the rear. Trapped.

Matt's face was a blank mask when he stopped in front of his father, his gaze raking quickly over the old man's face before moving on to Ryan.

"I was just explaining to *your* father how much his recent phone call to my mom had upset her," Ryan said.

If he'd had any question as to whether or not Matt

would automatically back his father, it was answered when his brother shot Charles a fiercely angry look.

"If it happens again," Ryan continued, "I'll make a call of my own." If his mother was being harassed, then Montoya's mother could join the fray.

"Do that," Matt growled, "and I'll beat the shit out of you."

"Or try?" Ryan asked flatly before he turned his attention back to Charles, who appeared to be on the verge of a stroke, he was so red. "No more calls, you son of a bitch. Leave her alone."

Then, having had all the family reunion he could handle for one day, he turned and stalked back toward his trailer. Neither Montoya followed him. Good thing.

He loaded PJ, locked the tack compartment, pocketed his keys. Now that his mission was accomplished, he had to stop by the rodeo office and then grab a hamburger for the road before he put a couple hundred miles between himself and his old man. If he could choke a burger down. Talk about a bad taste.

"Great run, Ryan!" a young voice called as he approached the rodeo office.

Ryan smiled and nodded at the boy dressed in chaps and carrying a red, white and blue rope. "Thanks, bud."

He conducted his business in the rodeo office,

which took about fifteen minutes longer than it should have, and got into the concession line.

People stopped and said hello as he waited, congratulating him on his run—still the winning time—and Ryan chatted with a few of them even though he wanted nothing more than to get the hell out of there. He'd just made it to the counter and was about to give his order when a collective gasp went up from the crowd, followed by silence. The nasty kind of silence that indicated something bad had just happened. Ryan's gut tightened as he waited for the hubbub that would erupt when the injured cowboy got back to his feet. The crowd remained stubbornly silent.

"Oh, no," the elderly lady in the booth gasped, craning her neck to see, but the solid gate panels blocked the view.

"Our medical team is on the scene, taking a look at this cowboy," the announcer finally said in a re-assuring voice. "As you know, these guys are the best in the business." The ambulance rolled past the concession stand then, and the wide arena gate swung open to give access. The lady gasped again and Ryan instantly understood why.

The sorrel horse with the distinctive white spot on his side standing near the crouched group surrounding the downed cowboy belonged to the crowd favorite.

His brother. Matt Montoya.

JUST WHEN ELLIE was beginning to think the dusty single-track road was never going to end, she rounded a corner and a rustic ranch spread out in front of her in postcardlike perfection. She pulled her leased Land Rover to a halt, taking in the large red barn and several smaller outbuildings on the edge of green fields. The single-story, shake-roofed house with a porch surrounding it on three sides nestled close to a stand of evergreen trees. Cows and horses grazed in the pastures and a pair of large birds flew in lazy circles over the pond at the edge of one of the fields.

Milo had bought the place eight months ago and since then had spent a grand total of one week there, shortly after the purchase, but didn't seem to be able to stop talking about "his ranch" to anyone who would listen. Now Ellie understood why. It was gorgeous.

Gorgeous and really, really close.

After fifteen hours of travel Ellie was more than ready for a hot bath and a bed. Ten minutes later she parked at the end of the flagstone walk, not liking the fact that the place felt as deserted up close as it had appeared from a distance. Had Angela or Milo told the staff she'd be arriving? A question Ellie hadn't thought to ask. Ellie, who always thought of everything.

She'd been rattled lately. Disorganized. Not herself.

Ellie rang the bell. After the second ring she

knocked, then, after a suitable amount of time, tried the handle. Locked. Okay. She set down her handbag and stood for a moment, hands on hips, surveying the ranch, watching for some sign of movement around the barn and outbuildings. Nothing.

Great. Her feet hurt and the small of her back ached from sitting for too long and she wanted to get inside. Now.

She started walking around the house, her heels clunking hollowly on the wooden porch, looking for another way in and wondering if she was going to have to call Angela to get the number of the caretaker. She tried the side entrance, the back entrance, the sliding door. No luck. She'd just pulled her phone from her jacket pocket when she heard the sound of an engine.

Salvation.

Ellie rounded the corner of the house in time to see a woman with long dark hair scramble out of the open Jeep.

"Miss Bradworth?" she called as she strode up the walk, her long flannel shirt flapping loosely over very worn jeans.

"Hunter," Ellie called back. "Mrs. Bradworth is my aunt."

"Oh." The woman quickly crossed the distance between them, taking the porch steps two at a time. "Sorry about the wait. I didn't know you were coming until half an hour ago."

"Really?" How was that possible?

The woman held out a wad of keys and then, after Ellie automatically took them, shoved her hands into her back pockets. "I was in town when Walt called and got here as quickly as I could. I hope you haven't waited for too long."

There was nothing about the woman's tone that was impolite, but there was nothing that was particularly friendly, either. Ellie felt rather like an interloper. Well, she was an interloper related to the owner of this place.

"Thanks for hurrying," Ellie said, holding out her free hand. "Ms...."

"Garcia. Jessie Garcia." Jessie met her gaze directly as they shook hands and Ellie was struck by how really gorgeous the woman was, with high cheekbones and amazing dark eyes.

"I'm Ellison Hunter. Milo and Angela's niece."

"Will you be staying long?"

"My stay is open-ended."

Jessie pulled her mouth into a polite smile, yet Ellie sensed she was not pleased with the answer. Why?

Probably because life was easier when the staff had the place to themselves.

"I hope you enjoy your time here," Jessie said coolly.

"I'm sure I will."

"There's no fresh food in the house, but you

should be able to find some things in the freezer and pantry."

"Thanks."

Jessie smiled slightly then started back down the steps.

"Excuse me," Ellie called, waiting for the woman to turn back before she said, "How can I get hold of Mr. Feldman?"

"Walt?" A shadow crossed Jessie's face. "It's Sunday."

"Yes."

"It's his day off."

"I see. And after that?"

"I'll have him give you a call. Okay?"

"Thank you."

Ellie had the distinct impression that Jessie wanted to escape and was getting annoyed at the prolonged conversation, but her tone was courteous when she said, "Anything else?"

I want to meet with the staff... . But she'd pass that along through Mr. Feldman when they got a chance to talk. "Not right now."

"Well, have a good one."

The woman climbed into the Jeep. It coughed once, then the engine caught and roared to life. Jessie raised a hand then turned the Jeep into a tight U and sped back down the road in the direction from which she'd come.

Ellie held up the ring of nine keys, frowned a little

and then picked one at random. Surprisingly, it slid into the lock and the mechanism clicked open. A bed and a bath awaited.

Maybe her luck was changing for the better.

CHAPTER TWO

RYAN HAD HAD his share of knocks in life, but he was having a hard time recalling a day where he'd had two big emotional wallops back-to-back like this.

Right now he had no idea where his father was, what he was doing or thinking or planning—although it had better not involve his mother—but he knew exactly where his brother was: lying in a hospital with a career-ending crushed leg. Ryan was more shaken by the accident than he wanted to admit.

For almost two decades, Matt had been his fiercest roping competition, and for fifteen of those years, he'd known they were half brothers, thanks to a painful heart-to-heart with his mother after that fistfight in the rodeo grounds' john. That conversation had explained why Matt hated him so much—because he existed.

Well, Ryan was pissed at the situation himself. They shared a father, but Matt had been the son with a father in residence. Matt had been the son with the fancy horses and trucks and trailers. He'd enjoyed the kind of easy, charmed career that money made possible—right up until a few hours ago when that charmed career had come to a screeching halt, leaving the way wide open for Ryan to take his place in the National Finals.

Ryan didn't feel good about that at all. The short visit to his highly doped-up brother in the hospital before he'd started the drive home hadn't helped. All Matt had been concerned about was that Ryan not call his mother.

As if.

He needed a tall beer and about ten hours of sleep. Then maybe he'd be in better condition to deal with all the shit that had gone down today.

He turned down the two-mile-long driveway leading to the Rocky View Ranch, where he'd lived and worked since graduating high school. At one time, back in his great-grandfather's day, the ranch had encompassed more than two sections and employed a dozen people. Most of the hands had lived in the bunkhouse, but there were two staff houses with their own corrals and outbuildings located half a mile from the main house, which gave the residents some privacy. The ranch manager and his family had lived in one house and the rural schoolteacher had stayed in the other for nine months out of the year.

Now the ranch was smaller by a section, the school had been bulldozed thirty years ago, and Ryan's friends and coworkers, Jessie and Francisco Garcia, lived in the schoolteacher's house. Walt Feldman, who'd owned the place up until a year ago, lived in the manager's place next door. Most of the time, he was okay with that.

Most of the time.

Ryan still lived in the small three-room homestead house behind the barn on the main ranch that he'd moved into the week after graduating college with his degree in range management. It was hot in summer, cold in winter, way too cramped and right now he wanted to get there like nobody's business.

Jessie and Francisco's place came into view, lit to the max. Walt's house, an eighth of a mile away, was dark. Ryan had barely registered how much he didn't like that when Jessie stepped out of her house and waved frantically at him before trotting down the steps as he slowed to a stop.

"We have a problem," she said as soon as he rolled the window down. "One of the family is at the house. She came this afternoon. Walt didn't even tell me until she was already on the property. He called me from town and I was lucky to get the keys down to her."

Well, shit.

"Do I need to go looking for him?" he asked.

Jessie shook her head. "Francisco called just a few minutes ago. No surprise that he found him in a bar, but I'm afraid if he brings him back here, Walt might try to go to the house. Scare the lady… get himself fired."

Ryan pressed his fingertips to his forehead. It'd been one long friggin day and he'd been looking forward to that beer and some sleep.

"All right," he said just as a loud "Ma-a-a" sounded from inside the small house. Jessie ignored her son's plaintive call, her dark eyes holding on Ryan's face as she waited for him to tell her how they'd handle the situation. One thing was for certain: he didn't want Walt anywhere near the main house while he was drunk. Sometimes Walt didn't remember who owned the place—or that he'd basically been sold with the ranch, along with the rest of them. Once, Ryan had found him asleep in the master bedroom after one of his benders. That would never do while the family was in residence.

"Ma-a-a!" Four-year-old Jeffrey stepped out onto the porch holding his bear by one ear. "I *need* you!"

"Sounds like you're needed," Ryan said as Bella and Emmie toddled out onto the porch behind their brother, one taking hold of Jeff's bear, the other his shirtsleeve, before they simultaneously put their thumbs in their mouths. "I'll take care of things and see that Francisco gets back home."

"Thanks, Ry. It's bath night."

Jessie stepped back and Ryan put the truck into low gear, easing the horse trailer forward as he pulled his phone out of his pocket. He punched the number three with his thumb and Francisco answered almost immediately.

"Found him."

"Drive him to my mom's," Ryan said. Lydia would keep Walt contained until he sobered up. "I'll take it from there."

"If I can get him into the truck. He can barely walk."

"Want me to call Mitch?" Ryan asked. His bull-riding friend had helped contain Walt on a previous occasion.

"I'll get someone here at the bar to help me."

"All right," Ryan said. "Let me know if you have any trouble." As soon as he hung up, he punched his mother's number and explained the situation.

Lydia Madison responded with a heavy sigh, which Ryan read more as resignation than annoyance. "The extra room's ready for him."

"Want me to come back to town, help you with him? He's upset about the new owners coming to stay at his house."

"Get some sleep," Lydia said. "He'll be okay in the morning. I'll feed him some ham and eggs, keep him here until you or Francisco can come and get him."

"I'll see you then," Ryan replied. "Thanks, Mom."

"Get some sleep!"

He'd do his best because tomorrow was probably going to be one hell of a day. The owners would undoubtedly want to talk to Walt—they always did—

and Ryan needed to make sure the guy was in decent shape for the meeting, which was never an easy task.

The hell of it was that he had no idea how long the owners planned to stay, and he was only going to be on the ranch for a few days before he had to leave again for the next rodeo halfway across the state. He didn't want to add more to Jessie and Francisco's workload, but the chances of Walt coming to terms with his demons by the weekend bordered on nonexistent.

Sometimes he wondered if the old man was ever going to get over having to sell the ranch. Would ever forgive himself for overextending, borrowing recklessly and then having it all come crashing down on him during a perfect storm of drought, wildfire and recession.

Enter the rich people.

If there'd been any way for Walt to support himself other than staying on as manager, Ryan would have quit and gone with him. But no one wanted to take on a seventy-year-old cowboy who'd lived on only one property for his entire life—a guy whose management methods had been behind the times until recently, which hadn't helped when he'd started to get into trouble.

Walt blamed only the times.

Ryan never argued with him, though he had cause. Walt had been the closest thing to a real father he'd had.

Ryan rounded the last corner before the main house and, sure enough, the lights were on…seemingly all of the lights. The house was long and low, with a roofed porch on three sides. Walt's grandfather had built the place and his father had added on. It was spacious and comfortable and Walt had always been so proud of his house—so of course Mrs. Bradworth had plans to gut the place before they took up permanent residence.

If they took up permanent residence. And lasted. Most rich transplants stayed an average of five years before the brutal Montana winters convinced them to use their hobby ranches as summer getaways and hunting camps.

Ryan rolled to a stop next to the barn. He'd already grained PJ and rubbed him down before starting the long trip home, so all he had to do was unload him and put him out into the pasture with his buddies before collapsing onto the sofa with a beer. Maybe get that sleep his mom had spoken of.

Ryan waved the horses back and led the big gelding through the gate and released him. PJ put his nose down, blew at the grass then ambled off as Ryan coiled the lead rope.

Normally he would have left the truck right where he'd parked it, but not tonight. The Bradworths had requested that there be no parked equipment in sight while they were in residence, and since Mrs. Bradworth was a bit of a stickler for rules, he didn't want to do anything to set her off—even if he'd probably have the truck moved by the time she rolled out of bed. During the week they'd stayed, shortly after purchasing the place and saving Walt's financial ass, he'd never known them to show signs of life before 9:00 a.m.

Ryan parked behind the barn, with only the nose of his truck offending the Bradworths' view. He walked toward his dark house, his steps slowing before mounting the one step leading onto his porch as he caught sight of a shadow moving across the curtained bay window of the main house. A second later the shadow, obviously female, crossed again, going in the opposite direction.

Ryan stopped at his porch and stood, the rope and halter hanging from one hand, watching as the shadow moved back and forth. Back and forth.

He had a bad feeling about this.

A pacing woman was never a good sign.

THE SOUND OF the engine, followed a few minutes later by the hollow clang of a metal horse-trailer door opening, had come as a welcome relief after hours of silence. Less than five minutes after the truck had pulled in, the night was once again quiet, but Ellie felt better knowing that there was another human being within shouting range. She'd thought she'd been prepared for isolation when she'd embarked on this trip, but she hadn't realized just *how* isolated she would feel in the big house surrounded by nothing but trees and fields and strange noises. The satellite TV wasn't hooked up yet, so she had nothing to watch. The internet service was also disconnected, and her phone only worked in certain parts of the house.

Alone.

With her thoughts.

But worse than being alone, she felt disoriented. Unfocused. The only other time in her life when she'd felt this unsettled had been when her mother had dropped her off at boarding school with the clipped assurance that she'd like it there and she would make friends. Her mother had been right. She'd met Kate and bonded within a matter of days, but here she didn't foresee any bonding occurring— not unless Jessie Garcia turned out to be a lot friendlier than she first appeared.

You didn't come to the ranch to bond. You came to get a grip.

But here she was in her new sanctuary, where she'd assumed that the peace of the surroundings, the distance between her and Nick—the now happily married father of her baby—would give her some perspective, yet she felt exactly the same in a different environment. Angry, scared, unfocused.

The situation still seemed unreal. And the baby who had so disrupted her life seemed equally unreal. So far she'd had no symptoms of pregnancy other than sore breasts, but she'd been assured that the baby was real by trained medical personnel. Twice.

When would it *feel* real?

Soon, she assured herself. Everything would fall into place and she'd know what to do. She just had to acclimate to her new surroundings and then make a plan. Once she had a plan, she would feel better. More grounded and able to make decisions about the next steps in her life.

But her brain wasn't listening and her thoughts continued to tumble over one another.

When she couldn't focus, Ellie moved, but there was no treadmill at the ranch, so she couldn't run until she was exhausted as she'd sometimes done in her town house when work pressures got to her. She ended up walking the floor, focusing on making slow, even steps, clearing her mind, ordering her thoughts.

The house was sparsely furnished, so pacing was easy—she probably could have jogged if she'd wanted to. When Milo had bought the ranch, the owner had become the manager and had moved his belongings to the small staff house that Ellie had passed on her drive in. Angela had bought some bare-bones furniture to see them through their first visit—bare bones to Angela anyway: two expensive leather chairs, a pecan dining-room set, a bureau and a bed with a wrought-iron headboard for each bedroom. Most of the linens were still in their original wrappers and the towels had price tags on them. Angela was no cook, so the kitchen was also bare bones—to the point that Ellie wondered how'd they'd eaten during their stay. There was, after all, no takeout close by.

Earlier in the day Ellie had busied herself making the bed, taking an inventory of her food supply, familiarizing herself with her deserted surroundings, although she didn't stray too far from the house and its untended yards. Frankly, she'd expected the house to be prepared for her when she arrived—and was certain that Angela had, too—but something had gone awry. She could live with that. People made mistakes. The lack of communication between Mr. Feldman and Jessie might have an easy explanation. She hoped it did. There was still no ranch staff to be found, but as Jessie had said, it was Sunday.

After eating a dinner of canned soup, she'd tackled the office, the one place that had been left fairly intact after the owner had moved out, hoping to find employment records that Milo had thought might be there—or any records that she understood—to help fill the evening hours. No luck. And then once night had fallen, she'd pulled the curtains and sat in one of the leather chairs and stared out across the room. The silence had almost hurt her ears. She'd tried reading on her phone; listening to music. Nothing helped with the thoughts jumbling on top of one another, so finally she'd resorted to pacing.

She preferred running—toward a goal if possible. And that was the problem. Until she had a goal, a written plan, she wouldn't be able to relax.

So instead she continued pacing, trying to order her thoughts.

Ellie didn't know what time she'd finally crawled into bed and fallen asleep, but she did know what time she woke: nine o'clock on the nose, when her phone rang. She rolled over in her unfamiliar bed to answer it.

"Hello, Ellie? How are you finding Montana?" her aunt inquired in her languid voice.

"So far, so good." Ellie lay back against the pillows and pushed her hair away from her forehead with one hand.

"Have you talked to your mother yet?" Which was code for, *Have you told her you're pregnant?*

"Not recently." Nothing new there. She'd traveled the globe without much contact with her mother, and vice versa. She was actually closer to her aunt, which was rather sad, considering the fact that Angela wasn't going to win any Mother of the Year awards herself. But she was slightly less self-centered than her sister.

"What do you think of the house?"

"It's…rustic," Ellie said, feeling it best not to mention that she'd found herself unable to imagine either her aunt or her uncle living there.

"I *know*," Angela said on a groan. "I have some work ahead of me. Sorry about the lack of furniture."

"There's enough for me," Ellie said. "By the way, I can't find the employment records."

"They should be there…somewhere," Angela said absently, telling Ellie exactly how important such things were to her.

"I can't find the employees, either."

"Really? Then who's running the ranch?"

"Good question." Ellie rubbed her fingertips over her forehead. "Do you have any idea what's involved in running a ranch?" She was curious whether Angela had any inkling at all, or if they were both equally clueless.

"No idea. This is Milo's baby." Angela spoke with tolerant affection and, indeed, she was devoted to her husband, who in return showed his love by giving her everything she wanted.

That said, Angela hadn't been all that broken up about her husband's retirement being delayed after he'd been named chief of staff three months ago, and Ellie understood why. Angela did not have a rural bone in her body. Milo, on the other hand, had appeared torn between accepting the job he'd always wanted and retiring to his ranch to take over operations. Ultimately, though, he chose the job he'd been striving for his entire career—and therein lay the rub.

There were a lot of unknowns about the Rocky

View Ranch that needed to be addressed. Such as could it be more profitable? Was it being run well? Her uncle had put off getting immediate answers to those questions, leaving the existing management in place after the purchase, thinking he'd be there within a year to observe operations and make decisions. But now things had changed, and that was where both Ellie and the consultant came in.

"Milo's baby is beautiful," she said to her aunt with a slight smile. "I'll find out what I can about operations, fill him in." This was not her field of expertise, but employees were employees and efficiency was efficiency. And until she figured out her next steps in life, she'd have plenty of opportunity to observe.

"Exactly what we wanted, dear. You really are doing us a favor."

Ha. They were doing her the favor. Ellie was about to say something to that effect when the back door rattled, startling her.

"There's someone at the door," Ellie said.

"Maybe one of your lost employees."

"Maybe," Ellie said. "I'll talk to you later." She set the phone on the table as she passed through the kitchen to the back door, which rattled again as the tall dark-headed kid who stood outside knocked.

"Jessie wanted me to bring you this," the boy said, holding out a box. Ellie automatically took it, noting that the bottom was warm just before the spicy pumpkin scent hit her nostrils full force and made her stomach roil. "It's a pie," he added helpfully.

"Thank you," Ellie said, looking around for a place to set the box out of olfactory range. "I'll, uh, just put it in the fridge."

"It's warm. Jessie says it'll do something funny if you put it in the fridge before it cools."

"Okay, then," Ellie said, setting the pie on the counter as she tried to gain control over her stomach. "I'm Ellison Hunter."

"Nice to meet you," the boy said as if by rote. Someone had taught him manners.

"And you are?"

"Oh. I'm Lonnie. I live one place over."

Well, that explained nothing. "Do you know where Mr. Feldman is?" she asked, noticing that the truck that had been parked next to the small house was now gone, although the long horse trailer was still there.

"No."

"How about Mr. Madison?"

"Ryan? He's probably gone." The kid kicked at the step, looking as if he wanted to escape.

Not yet. "Gone, as in…"

"He had a rodeo this weekend," the kid said as if that answered everything.

"How long does the rodeo last?"

"His part?" The boy screwed up his face. "Only a day usually, but it's a long drive home."

It was Monday. A workday in her book. Perhaps the employees worked flex time. Ellie had no way of knowing, since there appeared to be no records on the ranch other than a file folder with tax information.

"Great. Well—" she held out a hand "—it's good to meet you."

The kid grabbed her extended hand, pumped it once, hard, then released it. Ellie smiled briefly, waiting until the kid had started down the steps to the all-terrain vehicle parked near the front gate before rubbing her hands together to get the feeling back into the one he'd just crushed. The kid was almost to the bottom of the walk when he turned. "Hey, you might want to keep an eye out for Hiss."

"Hiss?"

"He catches mice. He's harmless."

"Hiss is a cat?" Ellie asked, wondering why she needed to keep an eye out for it.

"A snake," Lonnie called, then with a cheerful wave got on his ATV and started the motor.

"Great," Ellie muttered. "Thanks." Mr. Madison was at the rodeo, Mr. Feldman was nowhere to be found and she needed to watch out for Hiss the snake. She couldn't say she was overly impressed with Milo's ranch operations so far.

Ellie stepped back into the kitchen, then instantly turned toward fresh air as the pumpkin smell hit her. Taking a deep breath and holding it, she went inside, picked up the box with the pie and opened the sliding door off the dining room. She set the box on the back-patio picnic table, then quickly went back into the house. The smell lingered, not as strongly as before, but enough that Ellie knew she'd be spending some time at the other end of the house.

The baby suddenly seemed a bit more real.

CHAPTER THREE

"IT WAS BAD," Francisco said as he took the cup of coffee Lydia handed him. "Not as bad as right after he signed the sale papers, but I think he can't hold his alcohol as well as he used to."

"If he's going to do this every time someone from the family comes to the ranch... Well, that isn't going to work at all," Lydia said. "He's going to—" She abruptly closed her mouth as the bathroom door opened, and then slow footsteps came down the hall.

"Son of a bitch," Walt muttered as he walked into the kitchen, rubbing a hand over his forehead. "Where's the truck that hit me?"

"The truck had a big Budweiser logo emblazoned on the side," Lydia said as she folded a dish towel. "And you know better than to stand in the middle of the street in front of it. Sit down."

Walt sat. He was a small guy, with a thin, wiry frame that had caused a lot of people to misjudge his strength in his younger days. "Who rescued me?"

Francisco raised a hand.

"I owe you."

"Yeah, you do," Francisco said. "More than that, you owe Jessie. It was bath night."

"Sorry about that." He raised red-rimmed eyes toward Ryan. "You're quiet." Ryan shrugged. "Did you win?"

"Of course he won," Lydia snapped. "The question is, are you going to keep doing this?"

"What?" Walt blinked at her.

"What?" Lydia propped a hand on her aproned hip and waved her spatula at him. "Drinking yourself into oblivion whenever the Bradworths show up."

"That's not—"

"Bull. How do you want your eggs?"

"Scrambled."

"How about you?" she asked Ryan, eyeing him carefully.

She had her mother radar on full force, having sensed something was off the moment he'd walked in the door with Francisco, twenty minutes before. There was no way he was telling her he'd had contact with the Montoyas. As far as he was concerned, that episode was over and done—unless, of course, his father did something stupid.

"I've got to get to the vet clinic pretty soon," Ryan said.

"After you eat."

"Scrambled," he said. Another hard mother stare and then Lydia turned back to her eggs. Ryan scowled at Walt. "Francisco will take you home and then you'd better clean up—just in case this lady wants to talk to you."

"Just like last time," Walt muttered. When it'd taken Ryan a good day to calm him down after he'd discovered what Mrs. Bradworth had in mind for his ancestral home.

"I know what you're thinking," Walt said in a grim voice.

"Yeah?" Ryan bit.

"You're thinking that it's stupid of me to stay at the ranch when it hurts knowing someone else owns it." Walt placed his palms flat on the lace tablecloth. "Well, they might own the business, but I don't feel like they own the land. They don't know nothing about the land. That land is still mine."

Lydia's eyebrows went up from where she was stirring the eggs at the counter behind Walt.

"I'm part of it," Walt said. "I'm gonna die there."

Lydia gave her head a shake and poured the eggs into the pan.

Ryan tamped down the twinge of alarm that had started to rise. Walt had never talked of dying before. "If you're talking about taking yourself out—"

Walt's eyes flashed up. "I didn't say I was going to die *soon*. Or that I was going to take myself out. Just that I'm never leaving my property."

"In that case, play ball. Okay?"

"I'll do my best," Walt grumbled.

"See to it."

Fifteen minutes later Francisco escorted a muttering Walt to his pickup for the drive back to the ranch while Ryan hung around a few minutes to help his mother clean the kitchen. He figured, vet or no vet, it was the least he could do.

"I don't like this dying talk," Ryan muttered as he closed the dishwasher and set the controls.

"You aren't his keeper, son." Lydia brushed wisps of blond hair off her forehead. Despite the rather tumultuous life she'd led, his mother looked younger than her fifty years.

"Closest thing he's got," Ryan said, wiping his hands on a towel and then hanging it to dry.

Lydian touched his shoulder. "I heard about Matt Montoya."

Ryan sucked in a breath, wondering how his mom could mention Matt's name so casually. "Yeah."

"How you doing with that?"

Ryan met his mother's eyes, so like his own. "I don't quite know yet."

IT TOOK A good twenty minutes before Ellie could no longer smell pumpkin, nutmeg and cloves, even with the windows cracked open. The sad thing was that Ellie loved pumpkin pie—or rather, she had.

Finally she ventured into the kitchen and closed the windows, then took a cautious breath. All clear.

Relieved to have the kitchen back, she put the shiny new kettle on the burner to brew some of Angela's chamomile tea. She ripped open the packet, then quickly sniffed it to make sure the baby didn't object before dropping the tea bag in the mug.

Reality was definitely setting in. A reality she hadn't counted on and frankly didn't think she deserved. She'd planned her life so carefully, after all. Had dotted her *i*'s, crossed her *t*'s. Sacrificed. Stayed in and studied when other people went out during college. Worked overtime. Volunteered for assignments.

Sleeping with the handsome guy from Atlanta hadn't exactly been her usual modus operandi. Even flirting with him had been outside her usual code of conduct, since they were employed by the same company in different branches. But he'd been smooth and funny. Charming. Determined to get her to bed before she made her final consulting trip to Atlanta. And Ellie had enjoyed the journey.

He hadn't called after their hot night together. The pursuit had ended and Ellie had chalked it up to been-there-done-that. She'd indulged in a one-nighter and had enjoyed it…right up until the new regional manager, who would be overseeing her office from his Atlanta locale, was announced two weeks later. Nick Phillips.

That had been the first sucker punch. The second was when she'd discovered that Nick was now a newlywed. Ellie had been his last hurrah. Fine. He could have been more honest, but she hadn't been looking for a relationship.

And then she'd missed her period.

That was one too many punches. She could work for a man with whom she'd had a fling. The fact that he was now married made it easier. But she couldn't do that while carrying his child....

Ellie felt the familiar throb at the base of her skull at the thought. Anxiety and stress—a different kind of stress from the work-related kind that energized her.

She'd thrown up after reading her first pregnancy test, and not because of morning sickness. Another test, taken with hands that shook, gave the same result. And for the first time in her life, Ellie had no idea what to do or how to deal with the numb realization that her life would never be the same.

Denial seemed a viable option. Gallons of ice cream another.

Instead she had called Nick and told him the facts: she was pregnant and he was the father. He'd instantly offered her money, for medical costs, for support, for silence. The silence had been his utmost concern. Or perhaps she would consider a termination....

Ellie had made no promises, told him she'd think about the money, hung up the phone and then drafted her letter of resignation.

Never in her life had she reacted to a situation

with her emotions leading the charge, but never in her life had she encountered a situation such as this. Or dreamed she ever would. The reason planners planned was to avoid these kinds of situations.

Ellie took her tea to the dining room table, sat with a notebook and started doing what she should have done from day one: writing down her goals and the necessary steps to achieve them.

Goal— Her pen stilled. She briefly closed her eyes, then wrote *Have a healthy baby.*

There. No more denial. She was pregnant. In seven and a half months she would be a mother.

Steps to achievement. One: seek prenatal care. Two: research pregnancy.

Ellie's pen hovered for a moment before she wrote:

Goal—Use time at ranch constructively to prepare for personal future.

She had no idea what her steps were there, so she skipped a few lines and moved on to the next item.

Goal—Present Milo with understandable overview of ranch operations to enable him to make future ranch management decisions.

That was what he'd hired the consultant to do, but having another point of reference wouldn't hurt matters.

Steps to achievement. One: observe ranch operations on a daily basis.

She wasn't certain of what she would learn, since

she was starting from ground zero, but it seemed like the logical first step.

Two: informally evaluate employee performance, goals, strengths, weaknesses.

Now, that she could do.

Three: observe operations at other ranches and compare to Milo's operation.

Again logical.

Four: meet with consultant.

There. Two goals set out in a businesslike manner. Three if she counted the one with no steps, but she didn't because a nebulous goal was more like a wish.

Feeling slightly more in control, she pushed the notebook aside and sipped her tea. This was a start. A good start. She had direction. She reached for the pen again, hesitated, settled her left hand on her abdomen before she wrote, *Research OBs. Make baby appointment.*

Finally.

Ellie heard the truck approaching and pulled open the front room curtains to get a look at it, wrinkling her nose as dust wafted into the air. Whoever was cleaning this place needed a few lessons.

The red pickup pulled in between the small house and the barn, just as it had the night before, but this time she got a better look at the driver. Tallish, lean build, neatly dressed in jeans and a short jacket, ball cap over sandy hair.

He shot a quick look in Ellie's direction before he mounted the porch, and she instinctively stepped back even though he probably couldn't see her. As soon as he disappeared inside his house, Ellie slid her feet into her shoes and headed for the door, intent on intercepting him before he took off again.

The sun was out, but the air was crisp as she crossed the wide graveled area between the main house and barn. She hugged her arms around herself, wishing she'd grabbed a coat, but not wanting to turn back. She mounted the single porch step and crossed the creaking planks to the weathered six-paneled door, where she knocked once before rubbing her hands briskly over her upper arms. If this was what summer felt like in Montana, she didn't think she'd want to spend a winter here. She was about to knock again when she heard movement from inside the house, and then a second later the door opened and Ellie found herself face-to-face with a rather incredible pair of greenish-gray eyes in an angular, magazine-worthy face. No wonder Montana was so popular.

"Hi," the guy said with a frown that made Ellie realize she'd been staring. "Do you need help with something?"

"Are you Mr. Feldman?"

The frown cleared. "Madison. Ryan Madison."

Ellie extended her hand. "Ellison Hunter. I'm Angela and Milo's niece."

Ryan took her hand briefly, then released it, but not before she'd registered how very callused his palm was. "Nice to meet you," he said, sounding very much like Lonnie, the pie delivery boy. "I hope you enjoy your stay." And that had been Jessie's line.

"Yes, about that… It's more than just a stay." She sensed Ryan Madison taking a mental step back. After five years of working in human resources, she was pretty good at reading people, reading reactions. Most of the time anyway. She'd totally missed the boat with Nick and was now paying a very steep price. "I'm here to learn about the ranch."

"Learn what?" he asked.

"How it's run."

"Do the Bradworths have a problem with the way the place is run?"

"They don't know yet," Ellie said matter-of-factly. "That's why I'm here. I'm sure everything is fine, but you can see where my aunt and uncle need to be brought up to speed before moving onto the property."

"Of course," Ryan said. His hand was still on the door, as if he wanted to be able to close it as quickly as possible. "What can I do to help?"

"I'd like to meet with all the employees, discuss their duties. Get to know the operation and work from there."

Ryan nodded, but gave no answer.

"I'd like to start soon."

His eyebrows lifted. "How soon?"

"Well, as soon as it's convenient." She wanted something to do, something to focus on.

"Are you thinking today?"

"I was."

"Fine."

But she had a feeling it wasn't. "I need to get in touch with the other employees and don't have the means to do so. I can't find any records."

"There are three of us. Francisco Garcia, Walt and myself."

"Could you give me cell numbers?" she asked.

"I can for Francisco," he said. "Walt doesn't have a cell phone."

"Really?"

"Old school."

She didn't like the sound of that. Old school was not usually the best practice when it came to business, but then Angela had said the place was about fifty years behind the times.

"I'll have him get hold of you," Ryan said.

"That's what Mrs. Garcia said yesterday."

"Jessie's kind of busy with the kids right now. Maybe it slipped her mind. I'll have Walt down here by the end of the day."

"Thank you." She shifted her weight, wishing she wasn't feeling the urge to let her eyes travel slowly down his long body. "When would be a good time to meet with you?"

He looked over her head, out at the pastures, seemed to debate then said, "Whenever you want."

"Half an hour? At the house?"

Ryan shrugged. "Sure. Half an hour."

"See you then."

RYAN SLOWLY CLOSED the door. This woman was here to evaluate the ranch? Great timing.

He watched through the half-open curtains as she walked across the graveled drive toward the main house. Ellison Hunter wore jeans that hugged her legs, a long expensive-looking sweater and flat ballerina shoes. Her dark blond hair was twisted up into one of those French-roll things that made him want to pull out the pins and let it fall back down. Cool and elegant, she didn't look like any kind of ranch expert he'd ever seen, but looks could be deceiving. One of the best ropers he'd ever encountered was a sixty-five-year-old grandmother. And she wasn't half bad at flanking and throwing, either.

Ellison disappeared into the main house and Ryan stepped away from the window and headed back into the bedroom to find a decent shirt.

Damn. What was this about? It figured that the new owners were going to do something with the ranch, since it was, despite what Walt seemed to think, theirs. Walt had been hoping that the Bradworths would be like the new owners of the old Trail Creek Ranch and never set foot on the place, instead using it as some kind of a tax dodge, and, frankly, so had he. Not to be.

Twenty-five minutes later Ryan knocked on the main-house door. Ellison answered almost immediately and he noticed that she'd put on makeup. Nothing major—just brownish eyeliner that made her green eyes seem larger, and lip gloss. Her hair had been smoothed and she had changed out of the long sweater for a white blouse and black jacket that, despite the jeans, made her seem much more…official.

He didn't have a good feeling about official.

Or maybe it was just that he hated being in the dark. Until matters were settled with the family and Walt came to terms with whatever their plans were, things could be a bit dicey.

"Have a seat," Ellison said, waving him to one of a set of leather chairs near the tall windows looking out into the semitamed backyard. Walt had never been much for landscaping, but on Mrs. Bradworth's first visit she had made it clear that the lawn was to be mowed regularly and the bushes trimmed back. Flowers would be nice. Unfortunately, the deer and rabbits had thought flowers were nice, too, resulting in a lot of stems and not many flowers.

After Ryan sat, Ellison took the opposite chair with her back to the windows and settled a yellow legal pad on her knee. Then she smiled at him. A cool, professional, put-you-at-ease smile that only served to tense him up. He'd seen a similar smile once before—just before getting laid off from his last job during college.

"Just a bit about me," she said. "I work in the field of human resources, so I tend to focus on employees as…well, resources."

Cool. He was a resource. With her fake, distant smile, she looked like the type who saw employees as resources rather than people.

"Employees are the most valuable component of a smooth-running operation, as I'm sure you know."

The nasty feeling in the pit of Ryan's stomach intensified. "This place runs smoothly."

She smiled again, kind of, and clicked open her pen. "I'd like to talk to everyone employed here, find out what it is you do and how it contributes to the overall operation of the ranch."

"Is this a formal evaluation?"

"Not really. It's more of a get-to-know-the-operation evaluation." She cocked her head. "That's not a problem, is it?"

There was no way to answer that question honestly.

"It's just a surprise, you showing up to get to know the operation," Ryan said smoothly.

"My aunt told Mr. Feldman I was coming a week ago, so my visit is not really a surprise," she replied in a reasonable voice.

As he'd thought. And Walt hadn't said a thing until the very last minute when he'd phoned Jessie to send the keys and then gone off on his bender. Or perhaps he'd called midbender.

"The informal evaluation part," he said. "Did your aunt mention it to Walt?" Because he didn't believe Walt would have kept that secret. An evaluation was something they needed to prepare for—or at the very least, prepare Walt for.

"Actually, I'm not certain," Ellison replied.

None of this felt good, but good or bad, he had to deal with it. Ryan leaned back in his chair. "What do you want to know?"

Ellison squared up her notepad. "What is your job title?"

"Cowboy."

"No. Really."

He spread his palms in an I-don't-know-what-else-to-say gesture and she frowned as she realized he was serious. She wrote *cowboy* after his name.

"I guess you could call me a ranch hand, if it makes you feel better."

"No, I'm fine with cowboy. And your duties are?"

Ryan leaned his head back slightly as he debated where to begin. "What season?"

Ellison's eyebrows arched before she said with a faint note of challenge in her voice, "Spring."

"Calving, branding, fencing. First cutting of alfalfa. Evaluate the grazing."

Ellison made a note. "Summer?"

"Haying, fencing. Vaccinating. Moving cattle.

Irrigating." A movement outside the window caught his eye. A blue jay had landed on the flat box sitting on the picnic table. The bird turned his head to study the closed flaps through first one eye and then the other.

"Fall?" Ellison asked, and he turned his attention back to her.

"Getting the fields in shape for winter. Fall branding. Preg checking."

"'Preg checking'?" Strangely, her cheeks seemed to go a bit pink.

"Seeing which cows are pregnant, then deciding whether to keep or ship those who aren't."

"Ship?"

"Sell."

"Winter?"

His mouth curved into a sardonic smile. "In the winter we mend the harness, of course."

She gave him a cautious sideways glance. "Meaning?"

Did this woman have no sense of humor? "You can't do much in the winter here except for feed the livestock. In the old days, the ranchers and farmers would use the downtime to care for their equipment, which is what we do. Winter servicing. And feeding. And generally just trying to keep everything alive."

Outside the window the jay starting pecking at

the box. Ryan kind of wished he was outside with the bird.

Ellie pointed a finger at the legal pad. "These jobs you've mentioned, could you be more specific about what it is you do?"

"Like make a list or something?"

"If you made a résumé, what skills would you put on it?"

He simply blinked at her. "Am I writing a résumé? Or a job description that you might post somewhere in the future when you hire someone to replace me?" He didn't want to give her ideas, but he didn't want to make it easy to replace him, either.

Ms. Hunter blinked at him. "Neither. I want you to write the list so that the owners can be familiar with exactly what it is you do."

"Do you want bullet points?"

"Yes." There was no hint of humor in her voice.

Another jay landed on the picnic table, then two more. A squabble broke out, but the original jay held his position on top of the box.

"I'll do what I can," Ryan said. "I've been gone a couple days and I have a full schedule today. Maybe I can get something worked up tonight or tomorrow."

"I'd appreciate it."

Yeah. I bet you will. And I bet you'll be wearing that fake smile if you happen to announce you're letting us all go. If the worst happened, he could get another job, but Walt needed this position and

Ryan hated to think about what would happen if he had to move off the place—especially after his wild talk that morning.

"What else—"

Ellison sucked in a sudden breath, cutting him off, and jumped to her feet. It was obvious what had startled her. Birds. Lots of them.

The jays had managed to work open a flap of the box and now five of them were happily pecking at what looked like a pumpkin pie. Ryan rose to his feet and walked over to the window.

It was a pumpkin pie, and he instantly recognized what was left of the pastry leaf design on top.

"You put Jessie's pie out for the birds?" he asked as he turned toward Ellison, whose cheeks were flushed a deep pink.

"No." The word came out too fast.

"Then why is it out there?"

"I wanted it to cool so I could put it in the fridge."

"Last I heard fridges did a real good job of cooling."

Ellison pushed a few stray strands of hair back into place. "The boy who brought it—Lonnie—said I shouldn't put it in the fridge, so I put it outside."

"As opposed to leaving it on the counter in here?" Ellison went totally red. Good. Ryan cocked his head. "How much time have you spent in the country?"

"Some." She met his eyes with a touch of defiance.

Skiing, perhaps? "Don't put food outside. It brings in the animals. You're lucky that mob of birds isn't a bear."

Her lips started to form the word *bear* then tightened. "I didn't know," she said stiffly, giving Ryan the distinct impression that she did not like to be wrong.

"I really have to get to work," he said. *Not that this hasn't been fun and all.* But he needed to get out of there and regroup before he said anything that jeopardized his job, or Walt's. As it was, he was too damned close to pointing out that she wasn't qualified to evaluate a ranch or anything in a rural setting.

"I understand." Ellie walked to the window, close to where he stood—close enough that he caught the subtle scent of probably expensive perfume—to get a better look at the bird-infested pie. The biggest jay was now standing smack in the middle of it, orange pumpkin staining his underbelly. Ellison pursed her lips thoughtfully before looking up at him, her expression once again distant. Professional.

"Could we keep this between us?" she asked.

Afraid of owning up to your mistakes? The words teetered on Ryan's tongue, but instead he said, "The pie?"

"Yes."

"I'd hate to hurt Jessie's feelings, so yeah. I'll keep quiet."

For now. He'd make his final decision after he got a feel for how all of this was going to play out.

CHAPTER FOUR

THIS COULD GET ugly. Ryan made a supreme effort to relax his tight jaw muscles as he headed out of the house and across the lawn. He failed.

I view employees as resources.

Ryan agreed that employees were resources, but the way she'd said it had made it sound as if employees were interchangeable cogs. Things rather than people.

Maybe he was misjudging her intent, but he was certain that Ellison Hunter didn't know jack about ranch employees and she was in no position to judge them. She didn't understand the blood, sweat and tears that went into making a ranch run and prosper. The sacrifices made. The simple joys that compensated for giving up so much. She wouldn't understand that the characteristics that might appear undesirable on an employee evaluation—stubbornness, overt independence, speaking one's mind without regard to tact—were characteristics that helped a person to succeed in this business.

And how was she going to take his rodeo absences? Somehow he didn't think Ms. Hunter was going to be all that amenable to him disappearing for several days every week during the months of July and August. Tough. She wasn't there to take over management—at least not yet—so until he was told differently, he was going to continue as he had been doing, hiring Lonnie to cover for him and juggling his schedule. Francisco could watch Walt.

Instead of going into his house, Ryan shifted course and went to his truck. Lonnie had fed the livestock that wasn't on pasture that morning, and the rest of the day's work could wait.

Less than five minutes later Jessie had him seated at the kitchen table with a piece of warm coffee cake, while Jeff ran his cars back and forth over the opposite end of the long handmade table. Jessie was nervous. It showed in her jerky movements, the set of her lips.

"So Francisco has to make a résumé?" she asked. Ranch jobs were not easy to come by and even a hint that they would have to start looking was enough to chase the color from her face. Francisco would probably have no trouble getting a job as a mechanic, but getting another place to live with room for their livestock on a single salary would be rough.

"No. She wants a list of what I do and I'm sure she'll want the same from Francisco. And Walt."

Jessie gave her head a shake, her expression grim. "I don't like this."

"Neither do I," he muttered.

"More coffee?" She automatically reached for the pot, but Ryan stood before she got hold of it.

"No. I'm heading over to Walt's and I'll probably have more there." The way the day was going, he'd be lucky if he got to work by noon.

"I'll have Francisco stop by your place after he gets home."

"Sounds good."

Jessie bit the edge of her lip. "It was just so much better when Walt owned the place outright."

"The bank owned it, Jessie. And they were ready to take it."

"Maybe that would have been better," she muttered, bending to tie Bella's shoe. "Then the trauma would be over and we'd have other jobs."

"Maybe."

"By-eee," Bella called to Ryan, waving her chubby fist at him.

"Bye," he said with a half smile, taking the hint. He was supposed to leave.

WALT'S PLACE WAS dark. Ryan hesitated before he knocked. If the old man was sleeping off his rough night, he hated to disturb him, but if Ellison was going to talk to him today, he had to do some prep work. Walt had met with the owners before, but in those cases he'd gone on his bender after the talk, not before.

"Coming," Walt grumbled from the other side of

the door at Ryan's second knock. The door swung open and the old man blinked at the sun behind Ryan's back. "Yeah?"

"Can I come in?" Ryan asked.

"I guess." Walt stood back, allowing Ryan to walk past him before he shut the door, blocking the sun.

"Got something against light?" Ryan asked.

"Only when it burns a hole in my head."

Ryan looked his mentor over. He'd changed his clothes, so the bar smell wasn't clinging to him. Good.

"The lady wants to meet with you today."

"What are you? The go-between?" Walt asked, looking insulted.

"I'm the one who lives close. She came to see me and told me she wants to meet with all of us."

"I've met with these guys before. No big deal."

"Yeah, but this is a different kind of meeting."

"How so?"

"This lady is here to evaluate the ranch. She wants to know about our jobs. What we do and when." Ryan rubbed the side of his neck. "She's some kind of human-resources person."

"Human resources?" Walt scowled and Ryan could see that this was the first he'd heard of the evaluation, so the only thing he'd kept to himself was the fact that one of the family was coming for a visit.

"Okay, so I tell her what I do. Anything else?" He

gave Ryan a narrow-eyed look. "Shouldn't you be on the mountain looking for those four head by now?"

Ryan let out a breath. "I'm getting a late start. I had to go to town, you know. Pick someone up."

"No. You didn't. I would have made it back on my own this morning."

Walt never apologized for his benders. To him they were part of his stress-management program. He never drove drunk. More than once Francisco or Ryan had had to return to a bar to pick up the keys Walt had handed over to the bartender the night before.

Walt nodded. "I'll contact the lady and set up a meeting time. I can do it alone."

"I'm not trying to be your keeper or anything, Walt. I just wanted to warn you. This evaluation thing kind of blindsided me and I didn't want the same thing to happen to you."

"Thanks."

"And..." Ryan shoved his hands into his pockets. "You might want to write down a list of what you do around here."

"Justify my existence."

"Be prepared for the interview."

"All right. I will. Now go to work before I fire you."

Ryan walked to the door. Hopefully, Walt would have worked his way past his headache by the time he talked to the woman. Ryan would have given anything to be in on the meeting, run interference, but Walt was on his own. He was the manager, not Ryan. He just hoped Walt didn't do anything stupid, such as tell her he planned to die on the property.

EXACTLY THREE WEEKS had passed since quitting her job and Ellie had yet to acclimate to her new schedule. Having time on her hands made her feel antsy, almost guilty. Yes, she had a purpose here at the ranch, but it wasn't going to fill eight hours a day. The internet/satellite guy was supposed to show up tomorrow to work on the connection and hook up the television, and the fact that she was counting the hours until then bothered her. What kind of person was she that she *had* to have the internet and television?

The kind who'd been career driven and no longer had a career to fill her time. When was the last time she hadn't had a schedule so full that it was a challenge to simply make it through the day?

The day before she'd resigned.

Ryan had driven away shortly after she'd spoken to him—off to warn his boss, who had no cell phone, no doubt. Well, good. She wanted the staff to be prepared. It would save time…although right now saving time wasn't a concern. She needed something to fill time.

If she went now, she could familiarize herself with the layout of the ranch without wondering where

Ryan was and if he was watching her. There was something about him that she found unsettling.

Unmitigated hotness, perhaps?

She hadn't expected him to be so attractive. Hadn't expected to have to fight herself to keep from watching him walk across the living room to the door earlier that morning and wondering just what exactly he looked like without the worn denim jeans and white cotton shirt.

What the hell was she doing thinking thoughts like that? Nick had been hot, too. Hot, charming, dishonest. The dishonesty had been by omission, but dishonesty all the same. Ellie pressed her hand to her abdomen. She would not judge all men by Nick, but she wasn't going to allow herself to be taken in by general hotness anytime soon, either...although judging by the way Ryan Madison had responded to her during their first meetings, being tempted by hotness wasn't going to be an issue. She was the enemy, and he'd made little effort to hide his displeasure about her being there.

She slipped on her shoes and headed for the door just as the red truck drove past the house toward the barn. So much for him not being around. Ellie paused at the door. She couldn't spend her days cooped up in the house. The people who worked here were employees. She wasn't exactly the boss, but she was a representative of the boss. No different than anyplace else where she'd consulted.

Except that these people lived here.

Well, so did she and she was going to get to know her surroundings—although she'd really prefer to explore when no one was around. She was surrounded by the unfamiliar, and Ellie didn't like it when she wasn't in total control.

RYAN SADDLED SKIPPER and headed out to find the few head of cattle that had been reported on the mountain, wondering if he could possibly get back before Walt had his meeting with Ellison. Not that he could control any part of the meeting, but he wanted to know the outcome as soon as possible. It wasn't that he didn't trust Walt… No, it was that he didn't trust Walt.

He had just started across the pasture when he heard a sharp shriek. Skipper's head jerked up at the sound and Ryan reined the gelding around, various scenarios chasing through his brain. He pulled Skipper up at the gate, dismounted and then stood for a moment, wondering where the scream had come from.

The jays squawked from the trees near the house, probably wondering when the next pie was going to appear, but other than that the place was silent. Ryan looped the lead rope attached to Skipper's halter over the gatepost and then headed for the house, wondering what in hell the deal was.

He knocked on the door. A few seconds later it

opened and Ellison gave him a politely inquiring look that made him wonder if he had or had not heard a scream. No—he'd heard it. It'd been a woman's voice and since Jessie was a half mile away, Ellison had to be the screamer.

"Are you okay?" he asked. She looked okay. Not a blond hair out of place.

"Yes," she said simply.

Ryan waited a couple seconds and then, when it became clear that she was not going to expand on her answer, he said, "I thought I heard someone yell."

Color rose in Ellison's face but her expression remained controlled as she said, "I hadn't realized I was that loud."

"You were."

"Yes, well." She cleared her throat. "There was a snake on the steps. It startled me."

"That was probably—"

"Hiss. I know. The boy who brought the pie warned me, but I forgot."

Ryan regarded her for a moment, wondering how someone could belt out a shriek like that then appear so indifferent. Long practice? Ice water in the veins? He felt the urge to shake her up but, for the good of everyone involved, refrained. "Well, as long as everything is okay. Sorry to have disturbed you." He touched his hat, a gesture he'd picked up from Walt many years ago.

"It's not okay," she blurted as he turned to go. He turned back, surprised at the note of what had sounded a lot like desperation in her voice. She cleared her throat again, then said more calmly, "Something needs to be done about the snake."

"He's harmless," Ryan said. He didn't want her taking a shovel to poor old Hiss, who showed up every May and stayed until late July when he went off to who knew where.

"I don't think my aunt and uncle will welcome a snake this close to the house."

"I'll see if I can get Lonnie to catch him and move him…although he may come back. Snakes do that." And Hiss had. Every year.

"Then move him far away."

"Will do," Ryan said. "Now, if you'll excuse me, I have to go to work." He had a lot to get done before he left for the Wolf Point rodeo and he had to carve out some time to practice tonight.

"Of course," Ellison said. "Sorry to have delayed you."

"Not a problem."

ELLIE CLOSED THE door slowly and leaned back against it, then turned and watched through the leaded-glass panes as the cowboy returned to his horse. Her heart was still hammering from the snake encounter and it seemed to be hammering even harder after talking to Ryan Madison.

The snake had to have been six feet long, coiled up on the bottom stone step enjoying the sun. Ellie wasn't particularly squeamish about snakes, as long as they kept their distance, but she'd practically stepped on this one and if it hadn't seen her coming and slithered into action, she would have. But instead she'd seen the movement, recognized what it was and screamed.

Was there any way she could blame hormones? Ellie wasn't a screamer. She continued to watch as Ryan walked through the gate to the plain brown horse that waited on the other side, pulled the rope off the gatepost, coiled it and tied it to his saddle. Then he mounted, the movement quick and smooth and somehow very sexy, gathered his reins and urged the horse out across the field.

Yes. He was definitely a cowboy, as he'd stated during their interview.

One that came to the rescue of screaming women.

Ellie pressed her hands against her warm cheeks. Hormones or not, that wasn't going to happen again. The phone rang and Ellie followed the sound to the old-fashioned landline in the living room, answering it on the fifth ring.

"This is Walter Feldman," the man said stiffly. "I understand that you want to set up a meeting with me."

"I do." And she was going to keep an open mind about this guy that Milo said was hell to work with.

"When?"

"Anytime that's convenient to you."

"This afternoon work?"

Ellie glanced at the clock. It was close to eleven. "Yes. That would be fine. Say three o'clock?"

"I'll be there. Goodbye." The line went dead.

Ellie wrinkled her forehead as she put the receiver back in the cradle. *Open mind.* He'd said his piece, made his appointment and hung up. That at least smacked of efficiency. Ellie reached for her sweater. That gave her an hour or two to take her self-guided tour, maybe come up with some questions to ask about the ranch itself.

She paused at the top of the porch steps as she pulled the sweater up over her arms and checked for the snake. Nothing, thank goodness, but she still hurried down the steps. Realistically the snake had probably been as frightened as she'd been—but it probably wasn't as embarrassed.

It was no big deal, she told herself as she crossed the flagstones. She'd had a couple missteps with the local wildlife, but now she had more of an idea of what to do—watch out for snakes and keep the food in the house. And she might try thinking about the cowboy strictly as an employee, not as a rather fascinating man. It'd probably be better for her blood pressure.

WALTER FELDMAN WAS barely three inches taller than Ellie. His lined face was freshly shaved and he was dressed in a carefully pressed and starched white Western shirt and dark blue jeans. His boots were polished and he wore a string tie around his neck with a silver slide. Classic cowboy…who smelled vaguely of alcohol. It wasn't on his breath, but it was there.

"Have a seat," she said with a smile. He hesitated, then sat, his gaze traveling around the room that had once belonged to him. Maybe she should have arranged to meet at his place.

"I have my papers here," he said, shifting his attention back to her.

"Your papers?" Ellie asked with a lift of her eyebrows.

"Yeah. Ryan said that you'd want a rundown of what I do."

"Oh, yes. Of course. Thank you." She reached out for the papers, watching to see if his hands shook at all. Nope. Steady as a rock. He'd written out his job description on plain white computer paper in careful block letters—all caps. No sign of unsteadiness in his handwriting, either, and since he had to have written this today, after being warned by Ryan, she decided not to jump to any conclusions about him being an alcoholic.

But he had been drinking heavily recently. His redrimmed eyes, shining vividly blue in his lined face, gave testament to that. That and her hypersensitive sense of smell, thank you very much, progesterone.

"I, uh, put down everything I could think of, but might have left some stuff out because I didn't know what you wanted."

Ellie smiled, remembering her vow to keep an open mind. "Of course you didn't. I'd planned to let you know what I wanted when we met, but apparently Mr. Madison beat me to it."

"Ryan's efficient."

Ellie ignored the plug for Ryan and took a minute to read what the old man had written. He gave detailed information about cattle breeding and lineages he favored. He outlined the cattle-production schedule and had a section where he listed prizes and awards he'd won with his bulls.

"So your expertise is cattle breeding."

"It's what I do."

"And around the ranch, what are your management responsibilities?"

"Well, Ryan takes care of the pastures and grazing. Francisco does the mechanic-ing, keeps all the equipment running, maintains the buildings and roads and such. We're all on duty during calving."

"And you run the breeding program?"

"I do."

"Do you and Ryan and Francisco meet?" The old man wrinkled his forehead and Ellie said, "How do they know what to do and when?"

"Common sense is a big help."

"So you don't outline jobs for them?"

"If I see something that needs done, I mention it, but these guys are pretty much self-starters."

"Describe an average day for me." Another frown and Ellie explained, "I worked for a large software company until recently. I'm not familiar with ranching."

"Then why are you here?" he asked pointedly.

"To get familiar."

Walt took a deep breath, as if calming himself, then said, "On an average day I help feed the cattle. I might check fences. I might dig postholes. I might run the tractor or muck out the corrals. I might deal with irrigation." He gave a frustrated movement of his hands. "It all depends on the day and the season."

"I see." She decided to shift gears. "As the supervisor, are you satisfied with Mr. Madison's and Mr. Garcia's job performances?"

"They're still here, aren't they?"

She looked down at the paper Walt had given her, then back up at the old man. "My job is to collect information about how this ranch is run and organize it so that my aunt and uncle can see what present practices are in place and move forward. When the consultant arrives—"

"What consultant?" Walt snapped, his eyebrows coming together fiercely. "I've heard nothing about a consultant."

Probably because you aren't very good at com-

municating with your boss and are therefore skating on thin ice.

"Later this summer a ranch consultant will be evaluating practices at the Rocky View. I'll act as liaison between him and my aunt and uncle."

"Who is it?"

"The consultant? I don't know his name." Although that was on her list of things to talk to Milo about once she'd settled in and could get hold of him.

Walt shifted in his chair, his expression tight, threatened.

"When's he coming?"

"Later this summer and, before he comes, I want to be well familiar with the ranch. To do that, I need some idea of the hierarchy," she explained patiently. "How decisions are made. When they're made and by whom."

Walt let out an exasperated breath. For a second she thought he wasn't going to answer, then he said, "Ryan makes the decisions on the pastures and grazing. Francisco handles the maintenance and I handle the breeding program."

"That sounds like three separate entities rather than a team being managed by one person."

"Look, Miss…" He frowned as he fought to remember her name and then gave up. "This system works. Now, I'll admit to hitting some hard times, but after Ryan came on…things changed and we're making money again."

Some, according to Milo, but not a lot. "A business needs one manager," Ellie persisted. "Not three people working independently."

"It has one. Me."

Ellie sighed. He wasn't getting it and it looked, judging by the expression he wore, that he was thinking the exact same thought. They both jumped when a knock rattled the back door.

"That'd be Francisco," Walt muttered. "He has some business in town tonight and wanted to get this over with before he goes."

"Maybe we can talk some more later," Ellie said as Walt got to his feet. Obviously in his mind the interview was over.

"Yeah. I'll just tell Francisco to come on in." He was moving toward the door so fast that Ellie was surprised that she didn't get the Doppler effect.

Milo was correct—this guy needed work on his communication skills. And Ellie needed to keep an eye on him to see if his drinking was a problem.

"SHE'S BRINGING IN a ranch consultant," Walt repeated as he paced along the cedar rail fence behind the bunkhouse. He stopped to glare at Ryan. "You *know* what happened to the Vineyard Ranch when they brought in George Monroe to consult. That asshole."

"Nothing saying it's going to be George." But Ryan had a bad feeling it was. The Bradworths and the Kenyons, who'd bought the Vineyard a few years ago, were friends. The Kenyons were probably the reason the Bradworths had bought the Rocky View.

"It's George," Walt growled.

Ryan coiled his rope. There'd be no focusing until Walt got a grip. After the snake scare with Ellison, he'd spent a couple hours on the mountain looking for the cows, then he had come back to work on the broken irrigation head gate. He'd hoped to be finished in time to rope some calves, but had gotten back too late, so he'd had to settle for roping the dummy. Until Walt had shown up, livid.

Walt's scowl intensified. "Aren't you going to practice?"

"I'm good," Ryan said.

"I've never known you to be *good*."

"Good enough, then." Ryan rarely sloughed practice, but tonight he figured he needed to focus on Walt. Calm him down before he left tomorrow night. He had back-to-back rodeos three hundred miles apart, one of which had a rich purse he needed to win—a purse that his brother wouldn't be fighting him for. It still felt so damned strange.

"Having this woman around is very unsettling," Walt grumbled, resuming his pacing. "These people know nothing." He shot another fierce look at Ryan. "She *told* me she knows nothing. She's 'here to learn,'" he quipped, miming quotation marks.

"I know you hoped this would be like the Bar R and the Trail Creek," Ryan said, referring to two ranches that had sold to absentee owners solely interested in tax write-offs. "And it may still play out that way. Give it some time. Don't piss these guys off."

"If George has his way, then none of us will be here to piss anyone off," Walt muttered.

"You don't know that it's George."

"You don't know that it isn't," Walt growled.

Ryan came to stand in front of the old man, waiting for him to glare up at him before he said, "I'm not telling you what to do or anything—" although he really was "—but while I'm gone, kind of steer clear of Ms. Hunter, at least until you cool off. No sense burning any bridges just because she might be bringing in George Monroe."

"Afraid I'll muck things up for all of us?" Walt asked.

"Totally." The frustration of working with a person who knew nothing about ranching but was suddenly the boss was that there was a lot of explaining to do. Some people could take it, some couldn't. Walt was in the latter camp. He wasn't going to put up with micromanaging and questioning the wisdom of his decisions.

Walt considered, then gave a soft snort. "Maybe lying low is the best thing to do."

"For now," Ryan agreed, relieved. "No chance you want to come to the rodeo with me? Lonnie and Francisco could cover while we're gone."

"I have a lot to do rebuilding the calving barn,"

Walt said. "And hopefully I'll be here next spring to use it."

"Which is why you're going to lie low for now."

"Agreed," the old man muttered. "I'll be invisible. Or as invisible as I can be with power tools."

Walt got into his rig a few minutes later and took off for his house, or the Garcia's, depending on whether he went there to eat or not. Sometimes Walt liked being social and playing Grandpa to the kids, and sometimes he just needed to be left alone. Ryan and Francisco and Jessie understood that. Ellison probably wouldn't.

Once Walt was gone, Ryan threw a few more practice loops before deciding to call it a night. He'd asked Lonnie to handle the irrigating tomorrow while he took one last stab at finding Walt's missing cattle, and then it was simply a matter of showering and driving two hundred miles to the rodeo where he'd compete the following morning. It'd be a string of long days, but that was the way it was in the summers. Nothing he could do about it except deal with sleep deprivation.

"Excuse me?" Ellison's voice startled him. After Walt left for the day, Ryan was always alone.

Not anymore.

She stood at the corner of the bunkhouse wearing a long white shirt over slim dark jeans with those flimsy flat shoes, regarding him with those cool green eyes that he found more attractive than he wanted to admit. She started toward him when he didn't answer immediately and as she got closer he could see that her hair wasn't as perfect as usual. Instead it looked as if she'd been resting her head in her hands, loosening the strands around her face, giving her a softer look. "I was wondering if you were able to do anything about the snake?" she asked.

"I, uh, no," he confessed. He'd pushed the matter of Hiss to the back of his mind and left it there. "I haven't had time and I didn't see Lonnie today."

"Could you maybe call him?" Ellison asked with a polite edge to her voice.

So much for softness. "Sure."

"Tonight?"

"Tonight, but there's no guarantee that Lonnie's going to be able to catch him immediately."

"He can try."

"That he can." Ryan walked toward her, rope in hand. She cocked her head.

"Were you roping?"

"Yes." It seemed best to keep answers short and sweet, and then maybe she'd go back to her house.

"Like for exercise?"

A smile formed before he could stop it. "I guess."

She studied him for a moment, obviously trying to get a read. "Do you do a lot of roping on the ranch?"

"During branding, yeah." He stopped a few feet away from her, letting the rigid coils of the rope bounce on the side of his leg. "But that's not why I'm practicing. I rodeo during the summers."

"I've never met anyone who rodeos." She smiled that cool smile of hers. "I've never met anyone who uses the word *rodeo* as a verb."

"I guess that's because you're from the other side of the Mississippi." He bounced the rope off his leg again, the coils making a soft clacking sound, impatient to get back to his place, away from her. He debated about announcing that he'd be gone for the next couple days, but decided not to take a chance on her messing things up. She wasn't there to take over ranch operations. She was there to get a feel for how it was run. His absences were part of the package. "I didn't get a chance to write my bullet points yet."

"Let me know when you do." Spoken like a boss.

"I will. And I'll have Lonnie keep an eye out for Hiss. Now, if there's nothing else, I haven't eaten yet and I'd kind of like to."

"Of course," she said briskly as she took a step back. But there was something in her expression that he hadn't expected to see there. A touch of disappointment. A touch of...loneliness?

Welcome to rural life, lady.

CHAPTER FIVE

ELLIE WAS ALMOST at the house when a loud bellow made her jump. One of the cows out in the pasture was making a noise that she'd had no idea cows made until she'd arrived here. She went into the house, closing the door behind her, shutting out the cows, the night. Her closest neighbor who hadn't been able to get away from her quick enough.

It was understandable. These guys were concerned about their jobs with a new owner taking over. Since she spent her time advising people on hiring and firing issues, she was used to employees giving her a wide berth when possible, measuring words as they spoke to her, but she wasn't used to it happening in a situation where the employees were the only other human beings around for miles.

Damn it, she'd lived alone for years and being by herself shouldn't feel so overwhelming.

Except that now she was alone with a lot of time to think.

Ellie went to the kitchen and put on a pot of tea. She'd probably regret it later that night as she made her way to the john, but right now she needed something to help her relax and chamomile was her only option. While waiting for the water to boil, she opened her notebook, reviewed her goals. Tomorrow she would make progress on all of them. She'd research obstetricians, call Milo for more information on the ranch consultant and contact a few business associates. It wouldn't fill the day, but she'd be moving forward. She was going to be a mother—to a child who was offended by the smell of pumpkin—and she needed to get her act together.

A mother. Wow.

The thought still hit her hard. Ellie pressed her fingers against her abdomen, closed her eyes, tried to visualize. There was a baby in there. A little, tiny, totally vulnerable child. How long until she felt it move? Would she still be here at the ranch? Ellie dropped her hands, stared down at the notebook again. Funny how getting nauseous over the pie had made the baby seem real, made her realize that she no longer half hoped that nature would take care of matters. She wasn't ready for any of this, wished with all of her heart it hadn't happened, but it had and she was going to deal with it. All of it. Babies, jobs, ranches. She might not be able to follow her old path, have her old life back, but she could make a new life, a new path. She just wished that as she did it, she felt more like her old self. Confident. In control.

The kettle started to whistle and Ellie closed her

notebook. Instead of being confident and in control, she was afraid—afraid that she was never ever going to feel like her old self again. Afraid of being responsible for a child. Afraid of messing up.

And that was why she hated being alone right now. Too much time to think about just how afraid she was.

EARLY WEDNESDAY MORNING Ellie managed to get hold of Milo at the hospital before he started work and to ask for more information about the ranch consultant.

"I didn't get you that? I thought I forwarded the correspondence."

"Maybe it got lost in cyberspace," Ellie said.

"Or maybe I got busy and forgot," Milo said. "Sometimes I don't know what day it is.

"How's it going there?"

"I'm settling in. I've met the employees and taken a look at the property. Now I'm going to observe day-to-day operations." Although she'd yet to determine exactly how she was going to do that when the employees didn't want her around.

"Excellent," Milo said. "How's everything else?" Meaning, of course, her pregnancy.

"I'm researching obstetricians. I should have an appointment by this afternoon at the latest." It felt strange discussing OB appointments with her uncle, but Milo and Angela were the closest thing to grandparents as her child would probably have. Mavis would make the occasional appearance, but Ellie had no misconceptions about her taking a role in the child's life.

Although she had heard of people doing better with their grandchildren than with their own children. Maybe…?

Ellie refused to get her hopes up.

After talking to Milo, Ellie spent the morning reading reviews of obstetricians in surrounding cities and towns, noting the pros and cons of each: distance, insurances accepted, patient relations. It'd taken most of the morning for her to compile a list of acceptable doctors, only to call the top three and discover that they were booked full. They wouldn't be accepting patients for the next several months, although she could join the waiting list.

She didn't have several months, and the idea of joining a waiting list seemed ludicrous under the circumstances. Ellie felt the beginning of panic as she hung up for the third time. Apparently patients of her top candidates saw the doctors long before they actually got pregnant—as in they'd planned to get pregnant. Well, that'd been the way Ellie had thought it would happen to her, too. She'd meet a guy, date until she was certain she wanted to spend her life with him, they'd marry, wait two years and then get pregnant. They would, of course, have one boy and one girl. That had been the plan.

It was so thoroughly depressing that it wasn't working out that way for her. That she was going to have to scramble to find an obstetrician that met her standards.

Doctor number four was located in a smaller town close to the ranch, and when she called she was relieved to hear that they were taking new patients, but the soonest they could book a consultation would be in three weeks. Ellie took the appointment. She would have felt better, and more invisible, with a doctor in Bozeman or Butte, but people were going to find out she was pregnant sooner or later. She might even end up having the child here.

In a place where she'd alienated everyone in a ten-mile radius.

Maybe she needed to do something about that.

IF THERE WERE cows on that mountain, then they were doing a pretty damned good job of evading him. Ryan had spent almost ten hours in the saddle trying to find the strays, and he was beginning to wonder if someone had taken the animals. Whatever, he was late getting home and he still had to load PJ and drive two hundred miles tonight.

Ryan had just dismounted when he heard the door of the ranch house open and close. Great. The boss.

He continued to unsaddle the gelding as footsteps came across the flagstones, then crunched on gravel.

Ellison stopped several yards away from him and for a moment said nothing.

"I don't know if Lonnie took care of the snake," he said, answering the question he was pretty sure she was going to ask.

"He looked for it, but couldn't find it," Ellison said. "You were gone a long time today." She shifted slightly as he shot her a quick glance, wondering if the comment was a conversation starter, a criticism, or what. "I saw you ride away early this morning," she continued. "What do you do on a horse all day?"

Conversation starter. Maybe the boss was getting lonely. "Today I looked for missing cattle."

"How do cattle go missing?"

"Any number of ways. They can get through a hole in the fence. Gates get left open. Sometimes we don't find them all when we move them to different areas."

Ryan started brushing Skipper. "Walt says you're bringing in a consultant," he said without looking at Ellison.

"My uncle is."

"Do your aunt and uncle plan to take residence soon?"

"They'd originally planned to move to the ranch at the end of the summer, but my uncle recently took a promotion instead of retiring." Ellison's expression told him that she wasn't one bit surprised that her uncle had chosen work over retirement. "Now he's chief of staff at his hospital and the move has been pushed back."

"And you're here to hold down the fort."

"Milo wanted someone from the family here while the consultant did his evaluation."

"And you happened to be at loose ends."

"Yes," she said, meeting his eyes as if daring him to ask more. A nerve touched there.

Tempting as it was, he decided not to press matters. "Do you know anything about this consultant?"

"He comes highly recommended."

"By?"

"One of the neighboring ranchers." He cocked his head and she added, "The Kenyons."

"Is his name George Monroe?"

"You know him?" Ellison asked.

"I'm familiar," he said flatly.

"You don't seem too pleased."

Ryan turned toward her, keeping one hand on Skipper's damp back. "I don't know how to say this politely, so I'm just going to say it. The guy's a tool."

Her eyebrows lifted. "Why do you think that?"

"He fired a totally competent crew at the Vineyard and brought in another that was no better than the first. He shakes things up just because he can."

"That's your perception," Ellison replied calmly.

"Yes. That's my perception." Ryan tossed the brush into the bucket in the trailer tack room.

"One reason I'm here is to determine if I agree with his recommendations."

Was she trying to make him feel better? If so, it wasn't working. "By your own admission, you know nothing about ranching."

"I know about people and employee efficiency."

"But if you don't know this business, how can you judge its efficiency?"

Ellison's chin came up as he spoke, making it more than obvious that she didn't like being challenged any more than she liked being wrong.

"Efficiency is usually evident. Like, say, if someone leaves a gate open and then spends the entire day looking for the cattle that got out."

The first shot fired. *All right.* "They didn't get out through an open gate."

She settled a hand on her hip. "But if you mentioned the possibility, then I assume it has happened."

"Ranch gates are almost always left open by people who don't work on the ranch. Hikers. Hunters."

Her mouth made an O before she said, "Regardless, searching for lost animals doesn't seem the best use of time."

"*Seem* being the key word here, because, by your own admission, you don't know enough to make a judgment," Ryan pointed out reasonably, pulling his attention away from her lips.

"Then perhaps you could edify me."

"I'd be happy to," he said. "But not tonight." Even though it was only six o'clock, he had four hours of driving ahead of him.

"Plans?" she asked.

"Yeah." He didn't elaborate and after a few seconds Ellison nodded.

"I won't keep you," she said, her cool demeanor slipping back into place. She gave him a faint smile, then turned and walked back toward the house.

Ryan coiled Skipper's lead rope and then, despite his best intentions, glanced over the horse's broad back to watch Ellison retreat, feeling an unexpected twinge of regret. He could have made some inroads into her good graces, since it appeared that she'd come to the barn just to talk. But once George's name came up, everything had gone to hell, which was probably only a taste of what was going to happen once the consultant got there.

Ryan couldn't wait.

He heard the door to the main house close as he led Skipper toward the pasture. Ellison was back in her sanctuary, a place where he was fairly certain she was ready to climb the walls or she wouldn't be seeking out his company. She was lonely and because of that a few cracks seemed to be appearing in her walled-off facade.

He hated to admit it, but there was something about her touch-me-not quality that was drawing him in—no doubt the challenge of discovering if there was more to her than met the eye.

A challenge best not acted upon.

ELLIE GLANCED OUT the kitchen window and saw Ryan loading his black horse into the trailer. He disappeared into his house, then came out carrying a small gym bag and a cooler, stowed those in the front of his pickup and then drove away.

To where?

Did it matter? As long as he did his job, Ryan Madison was none of Ellie's concern…except that she was interested in where he was going so late with a horse and a cooler.

At least he had something to do. Tomorrow Ellie planned to touch base with some business acquaintances, let people know she'd be looking for a job soon, but at the moment she had nothing but TV to fill her time. Or she did until the wind suddenly rose around ten o'clock that night, howling through the trees and bending the birches in the front yard at an alarming angle. The lights flickered a couple times and then went out, leaving Ellie in the dark, staring in the direction of the blank TV screen and wondering how on earth she'd managed to get to this point in her life. It was then that she noticed that although the lights were off in the house, the yard light was still on. She was no expert, but that seemed wrong.

There were no lights on in Ryan's house, either,

but it wasn't until she was halfway across the gravel drive with her hair blowing wildly around her that she noted that the truck and trailer weren't in their usual spots. He hadn't come back.

She knocked anyway, just in case. No answer. He was well and truly gone and she well and truly had no electricity. She got into her car and drove the half mile to Walter's house, which was also well lit.

As she got out of the car, fighting to keep the door from blowing out of her hand, the old man opened the door and came out onto the porch.

"Hi," she called. "I don't have power."

"It's late," Walt said.

Ellie's chin lifted in surprise. "I know, but the yard light is on, so maybe it's just a fuse or something." He blinked at her as if to say, "And that's my problem because…?" Ellie pulled in a breath through her teeth. "I don't know where the fuse box is," she explained with more patience than she felt.

"Behind the pantry door."

"I don't know all that much about fuses."

"I'll be down in a few minutes." He turned and went back into his house without another word. Ellie watched the door close, then dived back into the safety of her car. She'd just started to turn around when Walter came out of the house and got into a truck and drove around her, leading the way back to the main house.

He got out and waited for her to park, then followed her up to the house, a big flashlight in one hand.

"Sorry to bother you," she said in a stab at making peace once the door was shut against the wind. "I tried to get Ryan, but he isn't home."

"Nope," Walt said, and he walked through the darkened house to the pantry, where he fiddled around behind the door. After a few muttered curses, the metal fuse-box door slammed shut and then Walt headed through the kitchen and out the back door. Ellie followed as far as the door, where she waited. A few minutes later Walter was back.

"Branch fell on the line. I'll have to call the power guys."

"So it's going to remain dark."

"I don't see it getting light all of a sudden," he said.

"I wonder if there are some candles around here?" Ellie couldn't imagine why there would be. Angela wasn't a big one for emergency planning.

Walt simply shrugged. "I wouldn't know."

"Do you have an extra flashlight I might borrow?"

"You don't have a flashlight?" He shook his head, then grudgingly held out his. When Ellie hesitated, more because of his attitude than because she didn't want to deprive him of his light, he said, "Take it."

Ellie took it, and because she was trained to be professional, which meant being polite even when she didn't want to be, she said, "Thanks." She even meant it, but she really hated being beholden to this surly man.

After Walt left, it didn't take long to search the house for emergency lighting. After ten minutes Ellie gave up and crawled into bed, since there wasn't much else she could do. She couldn't read on her phone because she didn't want to waste the battery, and she didn't want to use the flashlight any more than she had to because it was already growing dim.

"This isn't how I pictured ranch life in Montana," she muttered, nestling farther down under the blankets. But it still beat being at her job, working with that liar Nick.

THE NEXT MORNING broke clear and still, with the exception of the birds, which once again woke Ellie up way too early. She walked out onto the porch, hugging her sweater around her. Ryan still wasn't back. Walt was at the barn, doing whatever he did with the cattle, and Lonnie, who as far as she knew wasn't on the payroll, had driven a tractor out into the fields a few minutes earlier. But Ryan was nowhere to be seen.

Ellie walked to the barn and followed the noise of cattle to the far side where she watched as Walter and his two dogs shifted some cattle from one pen to another, the big animals moving grudgingly in front of him. Every now and then one would shake its head at one of the dogs, who would then crouch and stare, as if just daring the cow to do something. The cows always moved on.

"Hello," she called once he closed the gate. About twenty eyes turned her way, bovine, canine and human.

"Good morning," Walter said gruffly.

"I was wondering if you had a chance to call the power company."

"I left a message. Probably hear back once the office opens."

"Surely they have an emergency number."

"I think that's for emergencies," he said.

Ellie instantly started to ask just what he considered to be an emergency, but stopped herself before displaying what Walt would no doubt interpret as weakness. Montana mornings were cold, even in July, and she would have loved to have turned on some heat to take the chill off the house. She wouldn't have minded being able to make some tea and to microwave some oatmeal. But neither of those was possible without power.

"Is there anything else?" he asked, indicating with a movement of his head that he had work to do.

"Yes. Who's on the tractor?" Ellie asked, even though she knew.

"Lonnie. He's a neighbor kid."

"He works for the ranch?"

"Sometimes. When we need him."

"Why—"

Ellie's words were cut off by a commotion in the corrals and Walt instantly started off, calling, "Hey now!" at his dogs, who were facing off, growling. One lunged at the other. He separated the battling animals. "Would it be all right if we talked later?" he asked on a note of supreme exasperation as he held a dog by the collar in each hand. "I've got work to do." Then he abruptly let go of the dogs, turned and started off across the corral without waiting for a reply. The dogs followed side by side, casting each other dark glances.

"You know," Ellie called, "it wouldn't kill you to be civil."

Walt stopped and slowly turned back to face her. "I am being civil. I just don't have time to wipe your nose whenever you need it." A tool clattered to the ground from where Francisco was working inside the barn as the last words came out of the old man's mouth.

At that moment all Ellie could think was that her mother had trained her well. Even though she felt as if she'd been smacked, she managed to raise an eyebrow, as if to say "Really?" and hold the man's challenging gaze until he finally gave a small harrumph and started back across the corral, a dog on either side of him.

Dismissed again. This guy was doing himself no

favors and Ellie wondered if he even cared. Wipe her nose, indeed!

She hadn't gotten close enough to smell whether or not he'd been drinking, but from the surly way he was behaving, she had no problem believing he was battling a hangover.

Milo and Angela would never put up with this type of behavior, no matter how talented this guy was in the ranching arena—and she didn't yet know if he even had any talents. George Monroe was supposed to supply that information, and right now she couldn't wait for him to get there.

RYAN LOOSELY ROLLED his bedroll and stowed it on the shelf formed by the nose of the gooseneck trailer. He was up in the first round of ropers, and after his run he'd push on to Shelby. He'd gotten to Wolf Point in a decent amount of time last night, but hadn't been able to sleep for the life of him. He was worried about Walt. The old man had made it through the week that the Bradworths had stayed shortly after buying the place because he'd been in a numb haze. Grateful to have sold and gotten out from the pile of debt that threatened to put the place on the block for lack of payment of taxes, sickened that he'd lost the family heritage, even if he had no one to pass it on to. But now that the stress of constant debt was gone, he was more sickened than grateful. Ryan understood. Walt felt powerless on the place he'd lived for his entire life. And he felt rebellious. That was the part that concerned Ryan.

Things will be fine. There was no reason they shouldn't be.

He stepped out of the trailer, fed PJ, who was standing, one leg cocked, in the small travel corral, and then went to fill a bucket of water. After the horse was taken care of, he checked in with the rodeo office and then walked over to the concession area to buy a breakfast burrito.

"Hey, Madison." Tommy Walking Dog came to stand behind him in line. "What's the good word?"

"Hopefully that I'll drive home richer than when I drove in."

"Should be a little easier without Montoya in the lineup, but you still have me to contend with."

Ryan just smiled and turned toward the window as the guy in front of him collected his change and coffee. It would be easier without Matt there. Ryan wasn't all that familiar with easy, though. Very little in life had come easily, and he appreciated things more because of it. He hadn't always thought that way, but his mom had finally managed to hammer that message home by repeating it over and over again—what comes easy is taken for granted.

So had Matt taken what he'd had for granted? Ryan had learned via the high school rodeo grapevine that Charles had simply handed him the keys to the big fancy rigs he'd driven and financed the expensive horses he rode. Ryan had hated being jealous, but the truth was that he'd been jealous as hell. Had Matt been appreciative of what had come easily?

Did any of that matter now that Matt's leg had been crushed and his career was over? Ryan felt the oddest urge to seek him out and ask, but what purpose would that serve?

Maybe he could get to know his brother?

His gut told him it was too late for that.

"Breakfast burrito," he said to the perky little girl behind the counter. "And coffee. I'll get the guy behind me, too."

"Hey, thanks," Tommy said with a wide smile. "But I'm still going to beat you."

"You can try," Ryan said as the girl set the coffee on the counter. "But I won't make it easy."

ELLIE HAD EXPERIENCED power blackouts before, but usually for a matter of a few hours. The storms that had ravaged the East Coast over the past few years had knocked out power for days at a time in places, but she'd been lucky and the power in her area had always come back on within hours of going out.

She didn't trust Walt, so had called the power company herself shortly after their discussion at the corrals that morning, only to discover that they were dealing with wind damage all over the place and would get to her as soon as they could. Soon had ended up being seven hours after her call, when a big truck rolled in, a guy in a blue hard hat jumped out and half an hour later her fridge started humming and all the lights flickered back on.

Ellie had thanked him, then celebrated the perks of civilization by turning up the electric heat, making tea and toast and then stripping down for a hot shower. For a long time she simply stood in the gloriously warm water, letting it take the chill out of her bones, then reached for the shampoo. Being without power wasn't that bad, if one was prepared. Next time she would be prepared. Flashlights. Candles. Kindling. Firewood for the fireplace. If she were properly set up, she could handle eating cold food and not having a computer.

But what she couldn't handle was having the shower slow to a trickle just after she'd lathered her hair…as it was doing right now. Ellie desperately tried to work the suds out of her hair as the last of the water dripped out of the spigot. She was not successful.

Cursing under her breath, she opened the shower door and reached for a towel. Suds dripped down her neck.

What now? Was this someone trying to tell her that running away from her problems was not going to work? That she would encounter problems wherever she went?

"I get the message," she muttered. In the mean-time, suds, hair. Problem.

Knowing it was futile, she twisted on the kitchen faucet. Not a drop. Where had the water gone? And what was she supposed to do now? Towel the suds out of her hair?

The pond.

There was water there. Maybe not the best water, but if she boiled it or strained it or whatever was nec-essary, then she could use it. Anything was prefer-able to letting soap harden in her hair. So with the towel wrapped around her head, Ellie headed out the door with a large pan. There were probably buck-ets in the barn, but the pan would do. Watching for the snake, she trod down the flagstone walk, then walked past the barn and Ryan's house to where the path led through the tall grass to the pond. Ducks lifted off the water as she approached. Great. She was about to rinse her hair with duck water. But when she got closer to the pond, she heard the sound of running water and changed course.

A small stream flowed over colorful rocks on its way to the pond, the water crystal clear. Ellie bent and tilted the pan under the flow, collecting as much water as she could. It wasn't enough to do the job and she wasn't going to traipse back and forth to the house. She could go get another pan or… She pulled off the towel, leaned forward to protect her clothing and poured the water over her head. Every pore on her head went into shock as the icy water hit it. Damn. Was there an iceberg farther upstream?

Gritting her teeth, Ellie collected another partial pan and repeated the process. This time it didn't hurt as much. A third time and she called it good, wrapping the towel around her throbbing scalp. A shiver ran through her body, but she bent again and collected as much water as she could before heading back to the house. Who knew when she might have water again, the way Walt took care of the place?

Marching back to the house carrying the pan with two hands, the towel bobbing and slipping lower over one eye with each step, she rounded the corner of the barn and came face-to-face with Lonnie.

Both took a step back.

"Are you…all right?" Lonnie asked as the towel fell farther forward. She couldn't do anything about it without putting down the pan, and she wasn't doing that. All she wanted to do was to get back to the house. Water dripped down the back of her neck.

"I have no water in the house," she said.

"You want me to tell Walt on my way home?" the boy asked.

"*Would* you?" Ellie asked with exaggerated politeness.

"Sure thing," Lonnie answered earnestly.

"Have you found the snake yet?"

"No. I've looked, but so far…" He spread his hands.

"Keep trying," Ellie said before she continued

on to the house. The towel fell off her head just as she kicked the door shut behind her. She set down the pan and pushed the sodden hair out of her eyes.

Really? Was this how her life was going to be from now on? Was her stint as golden girl over forever? Ellie pressed her palm against her forehead. She'd liked being the golden girl. It made up for a lot of missed childhood.

TOMMY WALKING DOG had beat him. Twice. The Wolf Point rodeo had gone okay. He'd placed second behind Tommy, which at least gave him some earnings. The second rodeo, the one he'd hoped to win… He didn't want to think about. All those miles, all that gas, for nothing. As the announcer had said, even good cowboys had bad days, but Ryan couldn't afford bad days, literally or figuratively.

Too much on his mind. But, as he'd argued with himself more than once on the long drive home, he'd always been able to focus, to shove trouble out of his brain and catch the damn calf.

Maybe he was just getting old.

It was going on midnight when he approached Glennan, but he turned off the highway and drove down the narrow street to his mother's house, as he always did after a rodeo. She expected it. There was no curb, so he was able to pull the truck and trailer well off the road. His mother's lights were on and so was the porch light as soon as he got out of the truck.

"I won't be long," he said to PJ, who shifted restlessly in the trailer.

"I got some supper for you," his mother called out the door before he'd taken more than two steps up the walk. "You want me to pack it to go, or eat it here?"

"Both." He hadn't eaten after his run and he was starving.

"Sorry to hear about your times," Lydia said, holding the door open.

"Yeah," he said, pulling his ball cap off as he walked past her into the house. "One of those weekends." The house smelled of pot roast and potpourri. They hadn't had a lot of money while he was growing up, but Lydia had always made the house seem like home, doing what she could with what she had. Pretty much that meant good food and a lot of what she'd called shabby chic.

"I can't stay long," he said as he picked up the plate waiting beside the Crock-Pot and started dishing up.

"I know. Work tomorrow."

A long day tomorrow. He was going to have to abandon his search for the missing cattle for the time being and focus on other projects.

"How're things at the ranch?" Lydia asked casually as she packed the remaining meat and vegetables into a container.

"Not that great." Ryan reached for the horseradish. "The owner's niece is there learning what she can before George Monroe shows up to evaluate the operation."

"George?" Lydia snorted. "Well, he's competent enough, if he could just get past his need to bully people."

And that was the problem—George was a bully. He'd grown up on a ranch, worked on a ranch, but had always seen himself as a bit better than everyone else. As soon as the Montana land rush had started, he'd set himself up as a ranch consultant, helping the rich new ranch owners evaluate and operate their new properties. His love of shaking things up and firing people he'd grown up with just because he could made *bully* the perfect word for George.

"I'm worried about Walt."

"No doubt," Lydia said, scraping out the last of the gravy. "Is this niece of theirs a reasonable sort? Can you kind of explain Walt to her? And George?"

"I'm going to try." Although given their last conversations, he didn't feel all that optimistic about it. "The problem is she knows nothing about ranching, so it's going to be hard to convince her Walt's essential when I'm pretty damned certain George will do his best to persuade her otherwise."

"It might be time for you to move on anyway," Lydia said gently. "I know you're staying out of consideration for Walt, but sometimes there's nothing we can do to fix the problems of others."

Ryan smiled wryly. "You're a fine one to talk."

"I don't stick my nose in other people's business."

He said nothing and she glanced down at the table. "Not unless they're too stubborn to ask for help."

"Kind of like Walt?" Ryan asked.

"Walt doesn't even know he needs help."

Lydia took a seat across the table from Ryan, who could see by her expression that she had something on her mind besides Walt and the Rocky View.... Something she wasn't comfortable broaching. He waited, wondering if his father had anything to do with whatever she was about to say.

His question was answered a split second later.

"Has Charles been in contact with you?" she asked suddenly.

"No." He'd been in contact with Charles, but that hadn't been the question. "Why?"

"I just wondered."

"Again, why?"

Lydia simply shook her head.

"Damn it, Mom—"

She held up a hand, cutting him off. "Cindy said something that made me curious. That's all."

The mother voice. Which he would heed for now. Until he got a little more information as to what was going on...from somewhere.

"All right." Ryan picked up his empty plate, stacked the flatware on top and headed to the sink.

Lydia put her hand on his as he reached for the

faucet handle. "I'll do them. You need to get home. Get some sleep. Think of a way to keep Walt from shooting himself in the foot job-wise."

"Thanks, Mom."

Lydia walked him to the door, then said, "Wait. I almost forgot Walt's scraps." She went to the kitchen and came back with a plastic container with an aluminum foil–wrapped package on top. "The bottom one is for Walt. The top is for the dogs. Make sure he doesn't get them mixed up."

"Will do," Ryan said, reaching out to hug his mom with his free arm. "Talk to you soon." And in the meantime, he might just have to contact Cindy to ask her to let him know if she ever heard of Charles contacting Lydia.

ELLIE WAS WIDE-AWAKE when the truck and trailer drove past the house. She got out of bed and headed for the door. A blast of chilly air hit her and she went back into the bedroom, grabbed her coat and draped it around her shoulders before stalking back through the house.

Walt had yet to contact her about the water situation, and she'd found that life without water was worse than life without electricity. She didn't know why she had no water, but she was damned certain Walt did and he was making her suffer for some unfathomable reason. Didn't he know that his professional future was in her hands? Didn't he care?

The trailer was parked directly beneath the yard light, so Ellie didn't bother with the porch light. She let herself out of the house and marched toward the trailer. She had no idea where Ryan had been for the past two full *work*days, but her life would have been a hell of a lot better if he'd been there, and they were going to discuss this matter here and now.

CHAPTER SIX

RYAN PARKED IN front of the pasture gate to unload
PJ, rolling his stiff shoulders as he walked to the
back of the trailer. It'd been a hell of a long day.

"Do you work here?"

Ryan swung around at the sound of a taut female
voice. Ellison stood a few feet away from him, a coat
draped over her shoulders and a take-no-prisoners
expression on her face.

"Yes," he responded, his hand still on the trailer
latch. Inside, PJ shifted, anxious to get out of the
trailer and into his pasture.

"When?" she asked coldly.

He was way too tired for this. "The ranch gets all
the hours it pays me for," he said, answering what
he assumed was the big question.

"It doesn't seem like it."

"Not to be disrespectful, but you haven't been
here long enough to see how many hours anyone
works."

"I've been here for six days and you've been gone
for three of them."

"It's my time off."

"You were also gone the day I arrived."

"That was my time off, too."

She hugged the coat more tightly around her as wind gusted over them. "You seem to have an awful lot of time off."

"What's this all about?" Ryan asked, figuring if he was going to get any sleep, he may as well cut to the chase—set up a meeting to talk or whatever it was she had on her mind.

"There's no water in the house," she said abruptly.

Not even close to what he expected. "Have you told Walt?"

"Lonnie was supposed to tell him about it, and either he forgot or Walt didn't care enough to come down here and do something about it."

"So you've been sitting here stewing about it instead of contacting Walt?"

"I haven't had a lot of luck talking to Walt," she replied in a clipped voice. "The power went out earlier due to the wind storm."

"Nothing Walt could have done about that."

"I know," she said from between her teeth. "But when I tried to discuss calling the power company's emergency number…" She let out a breath that told Ryan more than if she'd described the interchange she'd had with Walt. "Never mind about that. The power company eventually came, the power came back on and then the water stopped running. Lonnie was supposed to tell Walt. When Walt didn't show up, I tried to call Francisco."

"On Friday evenings he goes to Mass and then visits his family in town. Sometimes they spend the night."

"And *you* were nowhere to be found."

"I'm here now," he said. "And I'll fix the water."

"Tonight?"

"As soon as I take care of my horse and park the trailer."

"You know what the problem is?"

"I have a good idea."

"Which is?"

Damn, lady. Let me unload my horse. "You used up all the water in the storage tank and the pump isn't on."

"But the power came back on and there's still no water."

"When there's a power bump, sometimes the pump has to be reset."

"It would have been nice if *someone* had done that."

"There's a good chance that Walt didn't think about resetting the pump after the power came on."

"Oh, I think it occurred to him. I think he totally resents having me here and is taking every opportunity to make me uncomfortable."

She was probably right. Ryan rubbed a hand over the back of his aching neck, more to buy time while he thought than to ease the stiffness there. PJ stomped a front foot, rattling the trailer. "Look, I need to take care of my horse—"

"Fine. Just take care of the water, too. Okay?"

"I'll do that."

Ellison turned without another word and started toward the house, stopping when she reached the flagstones. "I'd like to set a time to talk about a few things."

"Tomorrow?"

"If you're here," she said pointedly.

"How about at seven? Before I go to work?" That way he could get the damned meeting over with and concentrate on work.

Her mouth opened and he had a feeling she'd been about to say no, when instead she said, "Fine. Seven."

ELLIE STALKED DOWN the hall to her bedroom, snapping off the light as she walked into the room so that Ryan couldn't see her through the curtainless window. Outside, the truck headlights cast odd shadows across the yard, but it wasn't the shadows that caught her attention. Ryan had just led his horse into the pasture and pulled the halter off, but the animal didn't walk away. Instead he turned to face Ryan, lowering his head as Ryan reached out to rub his ears. Ellie was about to turn away, feeling as though she were spying, but she stopped when

Ryan took the horse's face between his hands and lightly rested his forehead against the horse's. Ellie turned away from the window, but the image stuck. Man and horse in silent communication, as if drawing strength from one another. Or maybe Ryan was so tired he'd fallen asleep leaning against the horse.

Ellie wondered how he was going to look after four whole hours of sleep, but the bigger question was whether or not he could get the water running. After he parked the truck and the headlights went out, Ellie had no idea where he went. To bed, if he was anything like Walt, but a few seconds later she was startled by a cough from the kitchen faucet that she'd left on. Another cough and as she walked into the kitchen, water started to sputter out. Soon a thin stream formed, gaining volume with each passing second. When the pressure was at full bore, Ellie turned off the faucet and headed to the bathroom for a late-night shower.

All right, cowboy, she thought as she pulled the shirt over her head while she walked, *I'll give you the benefit of the doubt. But your alleged boss, the ranch manager...not so much.*

IT WAS A good thing that his mother never once let Ryan sleep in after he'd rolled in late from a night of partying back in his younger days, because getting out of bed after a grand total of three hours of sleep seemed almost easy when he didn't have a hangover. He found Walt graining his calves, muttering to the animals as they pushed at each other.

"Morning, sunshine," he said as Ryan walked up. "How'd you do?"

"Lost twice to Tommy Walking Dog. How'd you do?"

"What do you mean?"

"You didn't reset the pump after the power came back on and I heard about it when I pulled in last night."

Walt put his hand on top of his head. "I forgot."

"Did Lonnie tell you?"

"Left a note on the door, but I got back after dark, got busy with the dogs—Betsy needs her medication and it's hell getting it down her throat—and I guess it just slipped my mind."

Right. "You can't do stuff like this."

"I forgot," Walt repeated stubbornly. "It didn't kill her to go a few hours without water—although I imagine she doesn't think that way. Did you reset the pump?"

"Is she out here yammering at us?"

Walt glanced toward the house. "Good point."

Ryan let out a breath and it was cold enough that it showed, but by late afternoon, he'd probably be taking his shirt off. "I've got to meet with her and I'm going to do what I can to convince her that you had a good reason not to do as she'd asked, but, Walt… honestly…while the family is here, you've gotta play ball. Convince them that you're the competent manager they can't live without." He wasn't quite ready to tell him about George coming in as a consultant, because Walt was going to blow a gasket once he knew his worst fears had come true.

"Shouldn't I be the one meeting with her?"

Probably. "I think she wants to talk about me being gone for three of the six days she's been here."

"That's none of her business."

Except that she was a representative of the owner. "Yeah. I'll talk to you later," Ryan said.

"Good luck," Walt muttered.

Ryan had a suspicion that Ellison was not an early riser. She'd agreed to 7:00 a.m., yet he'd knocked twice and there was no sign of life on the other side of the heavy wood door. He raised his hand to knock again, then heard the sounds of movement inside.

Ellison pulled the door open, a serene expression on her face, which made Ryan believe that she was unaware that her blouse was buttoned crookedly or that the lace of her pale blue bra showed through the gap.

"Good morning," she said, stepping back to allow him to come inside. He pulled off his ball cap as he crossed the threshold. "I was just making some tea," she said as she started for the kitchen. Ryan followed. The kettle was indeed on, so perhaps he'd been wrong in thinking that she'd been in bed when he'd knocked and had hastily thrown on her clothes.

"I hope I'm not too early," he said as she busied herself getting two mugs out of the cupboard. Walt had kept a hodgepodge of cups and mugs, some dating back to the 1940s, in that same cupboard, which now held four generic white cups.

"Not at all." She looked over her shoulder. "Do you like tea? I don't have any coffee."

"I, uh, really don't need anything."

"Suit yourself." She dropped a bag in the mug, then came to sit at the table, waving him into the chair opposite. And then she smiled a little, a smile Ryan couldn't read. "I want to apologize for ambushing you last night. I was a little…stressed. I also want to thank you for the water."

"No problem," he said automatically, surprised at the unexpected apology and wondering if he should tell her about her blouse, which was gaping even more now that she was seated. "I talked to Walt. There's no excuse, but he honestly did get caught up in some stuff and simply forgot." He wasn't about to say that Walt was old and it was understandable if he occasionally forgot.

"Let's talk about Walt," Ellison said, taking the opening Ryan had purposely given her.

"All right," Ryan said, hoping he could do Walt some good.

"He's not very friendly."

"What Walt lacks in social skills, he makes up for in ranching knowledge."

"My aunt and uncle are big on social skills," she said simply. "I don't know how Walt survived their first visit here, but I'm actually kind of surprised."

Did he tell her the truth here? That Walt had still been in a depressed funk and that Ryan had pretty much seen him through all the meetings under the guise of being foreman?

"You need to understand where Walt is coming from. His family owned this ranch for three generations. His great-grandfather homesteaded it and he was the one who lost it. You can see where, at his age, that's a sore point."

"Then after selling the ranch, he should have moved on." Her response was matter-of-fact. Cold. And it pissed him off.

"Where to?" Ryan asked.

"Surely he got enough—"

"To pay back his creditors. Once that was done and he paid back the private loans he'd taken out trying to keep the place afloat, well, he probably could have bought a small parcel, but he couldn't have kept his cows." Ryan made a small circle on the table-top with the tips of his fingers, debating before he met Ellison's eyes. She was watching him intently. "It would be hard for him to leave this place." *He plans to die here.*

"Even if it belongs to someone else."

"I don't know if he can go yet. And you shouldn't let him go. Yes, he's behaving badly, but he has a knowledge of this place that only someone who grew up here could have."

"Yet he lost it."

"I don't think you understand the economics here. Lots of people lost their places. The ranch suffered drought followed by wildfire. On top of that, he was advised poorly in financial matters by someone he trusted and took a fall because of it. Frankly you guys are lucky that he wants to stay on."

"Expertise means nothing if he's too surly to communicate with."

"I'll help him out there."

"Surely you have other things to do than to manage the manager."

Maybe it was because she'd hit the nail on the head that Ryan felt his back go up. "Yes," he said shortly. "I have a lot to do, and in a few minutes I really should be getting at it."

"If you have so much to do, why are you taking so many days off?"

"Like I told you, I participate in rodeo," he said. "I'm a roper. The busy part of the Montana Circuit is July and August, so during those months, I hire Lonnie to take over my duties on the days I have to be gone. He can only do certain things, so I make up for what he can't do during the days I'm here. The ranch loses nothing. I make sure of it." He spoke with conviction, because what he said was true, but he didn't think Ellison was buying it.

"Shouldn't your job take precedence over your hobby?" she asked, her eyes narrowing thoughtfully.

"It's a little more than a hobby."

"How so?"

"I make pretty good money."

"How good?" she asked suspiciously.

"I paid cash for my truck."

She seemed reasonably impressed, to the point that it took her a thoughtful moment to say, "You're not dependent on the ranch for your income."

"I didn't say that. It costs a lot to do what I do. Especially during the early season when I fly to the rodeos. Right now it's a decent second income, but it won't last forever. Shoulders and knees wear out." *Horses fall on you. Things like that.* "The ranch is my first priority."

Ellison shook her head and leaned back in her chair. The gap in her blouse closed with the movement…not that he was looking. "I have to admit that circumstances here are different from those I'm used to working with. Not that there's any excuse for Walt's behavior."

"Circumstances have to be different, because this is the type of job that entwines intimately with people's lives. They don't work here and go home. They live here."

Just as Ellison was living here….

One corner of Ryan's mouth twisted slightly as

the thought struck him. Maybe it was time for *her* life to become intimately entwined with the ranch.

SOMEHOW ELLIE WASN'T surprised to hear that Ryan made good money roping. He had an air of competence about him, the assuredness that comes from knowing you do something well. This explained it. He made another circle with just the tips of his long fingers, the palm of his hand staying planted, his expression thoughtful. "How will you know if the ranch consultant is blowing smoke or making decent recommendations?"

The out-of-the-blue question surprised her. "Like I said before, he comes highly recommended."

His fingers stopped moving. "How can you judge what you don't understand?"

"Meaning?"

"You should learn about operations."

"That's why I'm here," she said on a note of confusion. She'd thought she'd made that clear.

"I mean really learn. As in, instead of holing up in the house, come out with us and work."

The kettle went off and Ellie instantly got to her feet, glad for the interruption. "I have my own work."

"Judging us from a distance?"

Ellie lifted the kettle off the burner. "I can evaluate performance without going shoulder to shoulder with you," she said without turning to look at him.

"Afraid of getting your hands dirty?" he asked on a note of quiet challenge. "Because I promise you will."

Ellie hated backing down from a challenge. Especially since it was fairly obvious that he didn't think she would do it—spend the day with him.

"I suppose you'd take me along for your most obnoxious chores," she asked, dunking the tea bag with a bit too much vigor and splashing water on the counter.

"Nope. Just a week of regular days."

"A week?" She looked over her shoulder at him. His intensity made her breath catch, and because of that her voice was more acidic than she intended when she said, "Will you be here for a whole week?"

"Okay. Four days. And maybe a couple more once I get back from the next rodeo. Then you'll be in a better position to judge."

"Evaluate," she corrected, wondering why he was making such a point of keeping his eyes on her face, never looking away, as if he was trying to stare her down.

"Whatever. A few days with me, a few with Francisco."

"And Walt?"

"Maybe an hour or two with Walt."

Ellie sucked in a breath, prepared to argue, and she then realized that all of her arguments were based on her being out of her comfort zone. She hated not knowing what she was doing, and if she went to work in this foreign environment, she would truly be out of her element.

No, make that further out of her element. She put her hand on her stomach, a movement that was becoming habitual when stressed, then casually let it fall to her side.

"When do we start?" she asked calmly.

His expression didn't change when he said, "Today?"

"I, uh—" she saw a hint of victory light his gray eyes and shifted course "—can be ready in about fifteen minutes, after I grab some breakfast. Will that be all right?"

"That would be fine. I'll meet you at the barn. And don't worry about lunch. I'll bring enough for two." He got to his feet, his gaze finally dropping lower, toward her chest, almost as if he couldn't help himself, then he put on his hat and said goodbye.

Ellie stayed where she was, waiting until the door had closed behind him before she looked down to see what had caught his eye. A lot had caught his eye. Ellie could almost put her entire hand in the gap at the front of her shirt.

Damn it all. That's what she got for throwing on clothes, trying to look as if she'd been up for ages after he'd knocked and caught her in bed. What else could she have done after so snottily insisting on a meeting?

She unbuttoned the shirt as she walked down the hall and then took it off. She'd wear a T-shirt and hoodie for "work." And jeans instead of the khakis she'd thrown on after he'd knocked. Thankfully she hadn't left the fly open.

She shook out the denims she'd bought just before the trip and grimaced. Too bad she didn't have jeans with her that cost less than a hundred bucks, because she had a feeling from the look on Ryan's face as he'd issued his challenge that these jeans were going to suffer. Despite what he'd said, Ellie assumed that she was going to spend a few days watching him do the worst jobs on the ranch. But he'd said *she'd* get dirty. Doing what? Except for tending the garden at boarding school as part of the science curriculum, and cleaning house, Ellie hadn't partaken in a lot of manual labor. And she was pregnant. She hesitated for a moment, then continued dressing, sitting on the bed to pull on her new hiking boots.

She didn't have to do anything she didn't want to do. Everything she'd read had said that if a pregnancy was healthy, it would continue regardless, but if she felt she was doing anything that would hurt her kid, well, Ryan and Walt could simply have to consider her too good to get her hands dirty. She wasn't going to endanger the baby.

"How'd it go?" Walt asked as he screwed on the gas cap of the four-wheeler. His dogs, Betsy and Clive, were already on back, tongues lolling as they waited to begin the day's work.

"She's coming to work with me today."

Walt frowned ferociously. "What the hell for?"

"Think about it," Ryan said. "The more she knows, the more likely she might not blindly buy what George tells her."

"I don't think it'll do any good."

"Can't hurt."

"So what will you and the princess do today?"

"We're going to reset some fence posts."

"Sounds like a good day."

"Yeah. I gotta go put some lunch together." Ryan headed off to his house, where he slapped together four peanut-butter sandwiches and set them in a cooler along with apples, granola bars, a bag of M&M's and a bag of jerky. Figuring that should be enough to feed them for the day, he filled up two water jugs and set everything in the bed of the old Chevy ranch truck.

Ellison came out of the main house just as he was loading the tools in the back. Her chin was set high enough to indicate discomfort, but her expression was all business. She was wearing brand-new jeans, a hooded sweatshirt and boots so new he was surprised they didn't squeak. Her hair was, of course, neatly twisted up and pinned to the back of her head.

"Ready?" he asked.

"Ready," she replied, walking around to the passenger side of the truck. "My shirt's buttoned and everything." She opened the stubborn Chevy door with a hard yank then drilled a look into him. "Why didn't you tell me?"

"I didn't know how to broach the subject," he said truthfully, getting into the truck.

"Plain speaking is the best way. 'Hey, your bra is showing.'"

"I'll keep that in mind."

Ellison frowned at the dusty interior before gingerly climbing into the cab. "You can't go wrong with honesty," she added as she twisted around, apparently looking for the seat belt that had been stuffed into the cracks between the seats for at least a decade.

"Oh, yes, you can."

Ellison shot him another look. "All right, you can, but *I* want honesty."

"All right," he said, hoping she never asked him if her butt looked big. It didn't, but all the same.... "You're not going to find a seat belt," he said, dragging his thoughts away from her butt.

"Oh." Ellison gave up the search, clasping her hands loosely in her lap and turning her profile to him. She looked jumpy as hell.

"You don't need to be nervous, you know."

"I'm not nervous," she said in a scoffing tone.

Ryan shook his head and put the truck into gear.

So much for honesty. "Hang on," he said, putting the vehicle into gear.

"It's going to be a bumpy ride?" she asked, her gaze still fixed straight ahead.

He cut her a quick sideways glance. "Yeah. I have a feeling it could be."

WALT APPEARED FROM the direction of the barn as they approached the pasture. He opened the gate and they drove through. He made no eye contact with either her or Ryan, focusing instead on something in the distance. Ellie braced a hand on either side of her seat as they bounced along a rutted road that crossed an expanse of tall pasture grass.

Ryan stopped at the gate that led out of one pasture and into another and for a moment they sat facing it until he said, "The passenger opens the gates."

"Oh. Of course." Somehow she'd figured the guy that knew what he was doing opened the gate. It only took a few seconds to figure out the weird spring latch, and then Ellie swung the gate open. They drove on through a belt of trees and into yet another pasture. She got out and opened and closed gates, figuring out the chains and latches as Ryan waited patiently in the beat-up truck. After the last gate, number three, they drove to the far side of the pasture where Ryan parked and then started pulling out tools from the back of the truck.

"What's on the agenda?" Ellie asked, looking around blankly.

"We're pulling fence posts." He took a pair of leather gloves out of one of the buckets and handed them to her. "These are for you." Ellie took the gloves and pulled them on. Her hands swam in them. "You might want to pick up a pair of your own when you go to town," he added.

"I'll do that."

He picked up one of the buckets and gestured for her to grab the other. It was empty except for an odd pair of pliers lying in the bottom. They crossed the short distance to the fence line and then Ryan set down his bucket.

"See how some of the posts are leaning?"

"Yes." It would have been hard to miss.

"We're going to jack those out of the ground and set new ones."

Jack them out of the ground? "What happened to them?"

"The soil. They're old and they weren't treated properly, so they rotted off."

"Do you have to do this often?"

"On a place like this, we're always working on the fences. They sag in the winter and have to be tightened in the spring. Wildlife walk through them, wires snap. Sometimes cows jump and don't quite make it."

"Cows jump fences." Right.

Something in her expression made him smile. "I'm being straight with you, Ellison. You asked for honesty."

"Call me Ellie," she said automatically. "And I believe you." *Kind of.*

She was still getting her bearings with this guy. He was different from the other men she'd worked with. Evaluated. Found herself attracted to at a gut level.

She wasn't going to lie to herself and say there wasn't a lot about Ryan Madison to notice, because there was. Hard body. Fascinating face. Kate would love him. She'd always gone for the outdoor types, while Ellie preferred business professionals with jobs and hobbies she understood. Like Nick. She'd understood his life—she just hadn't known everything about it.

She cleared her throat. "As you've probably guessed, I've never done anything like this before."

"Fencing?"

She gave him a withering look. Of course she'd never fixed a fence. "Or much of anything involving tools. So I'd very much appreciate it if you didn't laugh at me."

"What makes you think I'd laugh at you?"

She snorted. "Gee. I wonder. City girl learning to do ranch stuff. Sounds like sitcom material to me."

"Yeah," he agreed as he took hold of a post and moved it back and forth, testing its give. "It does."

"Is that why you asked me out here? To get me out of my comfort zone and thus gain a position of advantage?"

He smiled at her. A breathtaking smile that faded too soon, leaving her wanting more. "Pretty much, yes. But I also want you to understand what we do. I figured you could ask questions as you think of them and get an appreciation for the job."

"I could probably do that sitting in the truck and watching you work."

"But then you wouldn't really *appreciate* what we do."

"Touché," she said. Although she thought she could work up some appreciation as she watched him, but it wouldn't be for ranch work. "What am I going to do?"

"We have to drop the wires, so you'll take out staples. Like this." Ryan shoved the pointed part of the tool beneath the staple that held the barbed wire to the post and pried the staple until it popped out of the wood. He leaned down, picked it up and dropped it into the bucket. "Don't want the animals driving these into their feet."

"I'll be careful. Where should I start?"

"The first post after the gate. Bottom wire first," he said. "I'll start at the far end and we'll work toward each other."

Ellie walked over to the post, took her pliers and worked the pointed part under the edge of a staple.

She could do this. How hard could it be, popping staples out of rotting wood?

Really hard when the wood wasn't rotten and she couldn't get good leverage with the tool.

"Put a rock under the head of the pliers," Ryan called from where he was watching a few yards away.

"What?" Ellie asked, dropping the hand carrying the heavy tool to her side.

"Like this." He searched the ground until he came up with a flattish rock, which he carried over to her. "Put it under the head of the pliers as a fulcrum."

Ellie did as he said and the staple eased out of the wood with a sharp metallic squeal. Ryan gave a nod as she dropped the staple—the first of many— into her bucket and then headed off to his end of the fence.

And Ellie, heaven help her, watched him go.

You're pregnant.

But you're not dead.

CHAPTER SEVEN

RYAN LEFT ELLISON—no, make that Ellie—awkwardly prying out staples, thinking it was good to put some distance between them and let her work out her own method for removing metal from wood. He just hoped she didn't hurt herself doing it. At first she pulled one staple to his three or four, but she kept at it, getting faster. After a while, he noticed that she kept glancing over at him, as if judging his speed, and then it hit him that she was trying to pull staples as fast—or faster—than he was. He slowed down a little, but if anything she worked even faster. Finally, he stopped for a short break. Ellie kept right on working. So the Ice Queen was a competitor. He wasn't surprised.

"Want something to drink?" he asked.

"Not yet." Her hair was falling out of the twist on the back of her head and as he opened the water bottle, she dropped the pliers, yanked the clasp out of her hair and shoved it into her pocket. Her hair tumbled down past her shoulders in loose waves and Ryan watched over the top of the bottle as she shook it back and gathered it into a ponytail, fastening it with an elastic band she slid off her wrist. Then, sensing he was watching, she turned toward him.

"What?" she demanded.

"Nothing." Slowly he tilted the bottle up, holding her eyes as he drank, just because.

Her gaze didn't falter. "Maybe I will have some water," she said, picking up the fencing pliers and putting them on top of a post before walking to where he sat on the tailgate. He pulled the other water bottle out of the cooler and held it out to her, feeling a ripple of awareness as she took it from him.

"What happens after we pull out the staples?" she asked before removing the cap and drinking. Water dribbled down her chin and spotted the front of her T-shirt. It was sexy as hell.

"We jack the posts out of the ground." Ryan tore his eyes away from her shirt and put his bottle back in the cooler. He held the lid open and Ellie did the same. Without another word they went to their respective ends of the fence and continued to release the wire from posts until meeting close to the middle. Ryan pulled the last staple, then stepped back, wiping his arm over his forehead before returning to the truck where he lifted the handyman jack out of the brackets. He grabbed the chain and, after shouldering the heavy jack, walked back to where Ellie stood next to the first post. Her arms were crossed over her midsection, her expression cautious as she waited to see what was going to happen next.

"I'll handle this part," he said, wrapping the chain around the post in a loop and then placing the other end of the loop over the nose of the jack. Steadying the jack with one hand, he started slowly pumping the handle. The chain tightened and the post inched upward until it started to topple. At that point Ryan released the jack, letting the chain go limp, and laid it on the ground.

"And this will be your job next time," he said, taking the post in a bear hug and wrestling it out of the ground.

"Why don't *I* do the jacking part?" Ellie asked drily as he let the post fall with a heavy thunk. In reply he held up his crooked left thumb. "A jacking accident?"

"The ratchet slipped and the handle smashed my hand. Hurt like a son of a bitch." Thankfully it hadn't been his roping hand. "Walt broke a tooth once."

Ellie eyed the jack with new respect. "Fine. You can handle the jack and I think we both know who's going to take the post out of the ground."

Ryan smiled as he hefted the handyman and walked on to the next post.

Ellie followed, saying, "I had no idea that a jack could be dangerous."

"They're not if you're paying attention. I was seventeen, stuck in a bog, worried about getting the truck back to the ranch in one piece—" worried about Walt taking a strip off him "—I got distracted."

Just as he was getting distracted now. By her.

Ryan pulled out the last post just as the sun hit the tops of the steep mountains to the west. He eyed the long line of posts lying on the ground next to the holes they had come from, then turned to Ellie. "Can you drive a stick?" he asked, fairly certain of the reply.

"Of course," she replied offhandedly, having no idea how glad he was to hear her unexpected answer. The rest of his workday had just gotten a whole lot easier.

"Great. You drive, I'll load."

"All right," Ellie said in businesslike way. She opened the driver's-side door and got inside, moving carefully as if afraid of stirring up dust. It was a valid concern. It took her a few seconds to shift the stubborn seat forward, and then she adjusted the mirror, making him smile. Yeah. A lot of traffic coming up from the rear out here.

She started the truck, tested the gearshift then swung the rig smoothly past him in a circle and came to a stop next to the first post. Ryan followed, hefted the wooden post into the bed with a loud clatter, then waved for Ellie to move on to the next one as he walked behind.

Once the truck was loaded, he went around to the passenger seat and got in. Ellie shot him a quick glance, then put the truck back in gear and started driving down the rutted road leading back to the ranch. When she stopped at the first gate, Ryan got out and opened it, and from her expression as she drove through, he got the feeling that she rather liked being the driver. Or maybe she just liked being the boss. The one in control. Ellie parked the truck behind the barn and pulled out the key.

"Just leave it in the ignition," Ryan said.

Ellie shrugged and put the key back before gathering up her borrowed gloves from the seat beside her. "This was an interesting day," she said, reaching for the door handle. "And you didn't make a case for Walt once. I kind of thought you would."

"I will. When the time comes."

"You'd best be eloquent in your argument," she said as she pushed the door open.

Ryan got out on his side and walked around to meet her at the back of the truck. She held out the gloves, but he shook his head since she'd need those tomorrow. "What if the consultant recommends Walt be kept on?" he asked. As if George would recommend keeping Walt. But maybe if someone threatened him…

"He'd still have to develop a better style of communication." Ellie took hold of the gloves with both hands, working the leather with her fingers. "Whether he likes it or not, he's employed by Milo and Angela now. They'll never put up with the kind of behavior he's shown me. They're kind of used to special treatment."

"How about you?" he asked.

"Am I used to special treatment?" Her eyebrows lifted in a way that told him she was patently insulted. "Why? Do you think I'm spoiled or something?"

Ryan sucked in a breath and went for damage control. "Not spoiled so much as I don't think you've had to rough it a lot."

"Maybe you don't know as much as you think you do," she said abruptly.

"How so?" Ryan asked, more interested in her reply than he wanted to be.

Ellie simply shook her head. "Same time tomorrow?" she asked in the reserved voice she used when her guard was up.

"Same time," he said. She started toward the house without another word, and he watched her go before heading for the barn to feed the calves. If she ever asked him about her butt, he wouldn't have to lie to her. He pulled the door open and waited a moment for his eyes to adjust to the dim light.

The day had gone better than he'd expected—much better. He'd thought there'd be more questions and complaints. More prima-donna attitude. Oh, Ellie had attitude, but he was beginning to suspect it was a means of protection, not a manifestation of privilege, and her last statement about roughing it had reinforced that. More to Ellie and her life than he had first supposed.

So why was she so guarded? And why was she here on the ranch, where she seemed uncomfortable? And lonely. Was she here because she was between jobs as she had indicated, or was there more to the situation?

And was it really any of his business?

Nope, but he was interested all the same.

Once in his house, he pulled off his dusty work boots before checking his phone. One missed call, one voice message. Automatically he clicked the voice mail icon and brought the phone up to his ear to hear, "Mr. Madison, this is the office of Benson, Harding and Myers calling to discuss of a matter of some importance. Please contact us at your earliest convenience…"

Instantly, Ryan's stomach knotted. Why in the hell would lawyers be contacting him? Ignoring the fact that he was going to be late for roping practice, he turned on his computer and plugged the names into a search engine. A law firm in Billings. That made no sense at all, since he knew no one in Billings, and if the caller hadn't mentioned him by name, he would have thought it was a wrong number.

And now he was late. He jammed his feet into his cowboy boots and grabbed his hat as he headed out the door to load his practice horse. He wouldn't be able to get cell service in the pasture tomorrow, so that meant he either had to go out late or come in early—neither great options while trying to demonstrate to Ellie that he wasn't cheating the ranch out of hours.

ELLIE HADN'T THOUGHT she was out of shape. Before coming to Montana, she'd done her fair share of gym time, but apparently working out hadn't prepared her for one day of standing in the sun, prying staples out of fence posts. Her face was sunburned and her body ached from using muscles that were not involved in treadmill running or biceps curls. She absently rubbed her upper arms as she headed for the shower.

Her mother would have died had she seen her daughter wielding fencing pliers.

Her mother, whom she needed to call.

She wasn't certain what kept her from picking up the phone now that she'd eased out of the land of denial and accepted that she was pregnant. It wouldn't be a pleasant conversation, but Ellie wasn't afraid of Mavis or her judgments. Heaven knew she'd had practice enough deflecting them.

Resentment, maybe? Ellie was going to be a mother in a matter of months, and she had no idea how to do that. Instinct was good, but modeled behavior from her mother would have been nice, too.

Ellie cranked on the shower and water obligingly flowed out of the spigot—something she'd never take for granted again. She stepped under the spray, letting the water beat on her tight muscles until she decided they were never going to loosen up and turned it back off again. After twisting her hair up into a towel and slipping on a robe, she headed into the kitchen, where she poured a bowl of cereal and sliced a banana on top. A movement outside the kitchen window caught her eye and she glanced over in time to see Ryan's truck and trailer drive past.

Really? She was ready to collapse and Ryan was heading out with his horse?

Okay, so he had more stamina than she did. Big deal. He wasn't pregnant.

Secretly pregnant.

Ellie set her spoon back into the bowl. The time for secrets and avoiding her mother were over. Before she could talk herself out of it, she picked up her cell phone and punched in her mother's number. The call went straight to voice mail and Ellie ended the call, realizing as she set the phone down with a shaky hand that her heart was racing. She was afraid to tell Mavis…or maybe she didn't want to hear that her mother wasn't all that interested.

Yeah, that was what was twisting her stomach into a hard knot. A knee-jerk reaction with its roots in her childhood; the recurring reminders that she really didn't matter that much.

Ellie settled back in front of her cereal bowl, her hands folded in her lap as she regarded the banana slices and cornflakes floating in milk. She was thirty and still hadn't come to terms with her mother issues—no matter how many times she convinced herself that she had. The child in her still hurt.

Her child wasn't going to hurt like this.

Ellie let out a breath and reached for the phone again, this time dialing Kate's number.

Kate picked up on the second ring. "Ellie!"

"Don't make it sound like you never thought you'd hear from me again," Ellie said, wishing she'd come clean with her friend days, or maybe even weeks, ago. She could have used the support and Kate didn't judge. At least she hoped she didn't judge.

"How are you?" Kate asked, her voice edged with concern. "*Where* are you?"

"Still in Montana, and to be honest…I'm not sure how I am." Ellie hesitated for the briefest of moments before confessing, "I'm pregnant."

"I thought so."

"You did not!"

"Yeah, I did. Along with about twenty other possible reasons for you to quit your job and disappear. It's someone at work, isn't it?"

"Yes," Ellie said as she sank into the leather chair and curled her feet up under her. She told Kate the story of how she'd indulged herself with a hot guy and then how her world had pretty much fallen apart when she—one, got pregnant; two, found out he was newly married; and three, he got promoted to district manager.

"The lying asshole," Kate muttered.

"I could have dealt with the lying," Ellie said, leaning her head back against the leather. "I would have been pissed, but I could have worked with him."

"But you got pregnant."

"Yeah," Ellie said, her voice growing husky as she thought of how he'd tried to buy her off—pay for either an abortion or silence. "I don't want him anywhere near me or my baby." She felt the phone pressing into her cheek as she said, "I can't believe he's the father."

"He's out of the picture, El."

"And I'm out of a job."

"Now I understand why you went to Montana."

"I needed a place that was cheap to stay where I could think. Plot. Plan."

"So the story about helping your uncle was bogus?"

"No. I'm actually helping him out." She rubbed her fingertips between her eyebrows, soothing the frown that had formed there. "It gives me something to focus on."

"Seems to me you have a lot to focus on."

"Something else," Ellie amended. "I need something to occupy my brain so I don't spend all my time worrying about the future."

"I've never known you not to have a carved-in-stone plan," Kate said, and again Ellie could hear the concern in her voice.

"Amen," she said softly. Everything in her life had fallen into place because she'd always had a plan. "I can't stay here forever."

"Of course not," Kate said.

"I'll have to find a job, a new place to live until my sublet contract expires."

"You can move in with me."

"I'd like to be able to pay my part of the rent," she said drily.

"You'll be able to get a job."

"I'm pregnant."

"You can't be refused employment because of that."

"Not officially," Ellie said. She knew of people who had landed jobs while pregnant, but in a tight job market it wasn't exactly a point in her favor. She could keep it secret if she interviewed before she ballooned up, but that was no way to start a positive working relationship with a new employer. "I have a lot to figure out, but I'm feeling better about it than I was only a week ago. Plus I'm getting a lot of fresh air. How are you doing?"

"Well, after that bombshell, the stuff in my life seems pretty mundane…." Kate sighed. "I just wish you were closer so I could help you out." There was real warmth in her voice and not for the first time, Ellie counted the one blessing that was the direct result of being dumped at boarding school. Having a real mother would have been cool, but a friend like Kate was the next best thing.

ELLIE BARELY SLEPT after she'd confessed her pregnancy—probably because now that she'd told her best friend, she had to tell her mother. Finally, around 4:00 a.m., she picked up her phone from the nightstand, knowing that with the time difference on the east coast Mavis would be out of bed.

"Ellie," Mavis said upon answering, "why on earth are you calling at 6:00 a.m.? You know this is my yoga time."

"I'm calling because I knew I could catch you now," Ellie said. And because the thought of making this call was eating a hole in her stomach.

"Is there a problem?"

"There's news," Ellie said. "I'm pregnant."

The long silence she'd anticipated followed her blunt announcement. Ellie heard the sound of her own breathing as she waited for a reaction.

"Well," Mavis finally said. "That is news."

"There's more. I have no relationship with the father and don't intend on having one. He wants nothing to do with the baby."

She heard her mother inhale deeply before proclaiming, "This is not what I expected of you, Ellie, but it's your life."

"I made a mistake, Mom."

"Obviously."

Ellie waited, but when Mavis said nothing more, she added, "I quit my job and I'm staying on Angela and Milo's Montana property." She realized then that she was trying to push her mother's buttons with this recitation of blunt facts, trying to get some kind of a reaction. An explosion. An indication that she was concerned. *Something,* for Pete's sake.

"I see."

Ellie could almost see her mother staring off into the distance, brushing her hair back with one hand as she did when she was anxious to get on with her own affairs. "Don't you even want to know how far along I am? When the baby will be born?"

"How far along are you, Ellie? When will the baby be born?"

Tears stung Ellie's eyes. This was useless. "The baby will be born in February."

"February." Mavis cleared her throat and for a moment Ellie thought she was going to say something important. Instead she said, "That should give you time to get a new job. I'm sure you'll do fine in that regard, but if you need any financial help, I'll be happy to assist."

"Thank you, Mom," Ellie said, wishing she could reach out and shake her mother a few times, get her full attention.

"I take it Angela has known for some time?"

Ellie sucked in a breath and then confessed, "She was easier to call than you."

"Of course she was," Mavis said briskly. "Well, if you need anything, please call."

"I will."

"Goodbye, Ellison."

"Goodbye."

Ellie leaned back against the pillows, still holding the phone loosely in one hand. The conversation had gone exactly as she'd thought it would, so it shouldn't have hurt.

Shouldn't have, but it did.

RYAN COULDN'T REMEMBER the last time he'd had such a rotten practice. Yes, he was dealing with out-of-the-blue complicated shit he didn't need right now, but he'd always been able to push issues aside and focus on his craft. He thought he'd been doing that last night, but his times had sucked.

It was on the drive home that he'd realized roping felt different now that his brother was no longer in the picture. He'd lost his past two rodeos, and while it bothered him, it didn't eat at him the way losing had when Matt was competing. He didn't feel like a failure. For as long as he could remember, he'd competed against Matt. It was what he did. He beat his brother…or his brother beat him. And now the game had changed. So was it just the shock of discovering how fast things could change that made things feel off? Or had his only motivation been beating his brother, which seemed pretty damned shallow?

It was something to think about…something besides the freaking lawyer's mystery call.

Ellie wasn't waiting at the truck the next morning as promised when Ryan came out of his house, so he tried the law offices, once again getting the voice mail giving their hours. What happened to the eighty-hour attorney workweeks he'd heard about? He did not want to spend the day wondering why these guys wanted to speak to him, but it looked as if he had no choice.

As he pocketed his phone, Ellie came out of the house wearing close-fitting jeans and the same hooded sweatshirt as the day before. She shoved her hands into the pockets as she walked across the flagstones, head down. She looked exhausted. Her gaze came up as she stepped onto the gravel, meeting his as if she'd been well aware he'd been studying her.

"Sorry I'm late," she said. "I overslept."

"Me, too."

"What's that for you? Four a.m.?" she asked grumpily.

"Five," he said as she came to a stop in front of him, hands still deep in her sweatshirt pockets.

"What are we doing today?"

"Putting new posts into the holes we took the old posts out of yesterday." He motioned to the truck with his head. "You can drive, I'll load."

A few minutes later Ellie pulled the truck up to

the post pile and sat in it while he loaded thirty posts. She acknowledged him with a look when he got back inside, then put the truck in gear and headed for the pasture gate.

"Something wrong?" he finally asked. She shook her head without looking at him, which told him, yeah, something was wrong.

"Why?"

"You seem preoccupied," he explained.

"I'm fine." She made an obvious effort to speak lightly. "Just tired after being in the sun all day yesterday."

"I didn't think you were going to show this morning."

Her gaze jerked toward him. "Why not?"

She sounded so insulted that he felt like smiling. Wisely, he did not. "You made your point yesterday. You did a day's work."

"The deal was for a week."

"We never shook on it," he said.

Ellie took her right hand off the wheel and shoved it toward him, meeting his eyes dead-on as she did so. "Fine. Let's shake."

ELLIE'S HAND HOVERED and she was starting to feel foolish, but she wasn't going to have him thinking that her word was no good. After a second's pause, Ryan took her hand, closing his warm, callused fingers around hers, causing unexpected heat to unfurl deep inside her. She had the sudden urge to pull her hand back while she still could, but it was overpowered by an even stronger urge to leave her fingers right where they were. What would the pleasantly rough fingers feel like on her body?

"Deal?" she asked, glad that her voice sounded so steady.

"Deal."

"I don't shirk my commitments," she muttered, putting her hand back on the wheel, still feeling the warmth of his touch. "I'm not that spoiled."

"I shouldn't have said that," Ryan acknowledged. "And I apologize. Spoiled women don't spend the day in the sun fencing. And they don't staple race."

"What?" Ellie pulled to a stop in front of the gate. "Staple race?"

"You were trying to pull staples faster than me yesterday."

"I was not." He met her eyes, a wanna-bet gleam in his. Ellie tried to keep from blushing, but felt color creeping into her cheeks despite her best efforts. Damn fair skin. "What if I was?"

"Nothing." Ryan got out of the truck.

"It kept me from getting bored," she said as soon as she'd driven through the gate and he'd gotten back inside. "How do *you* keep from getting bored?"

"I don't know. I guess I just get into the zone. Sometimes I visualize."

"Visualize what?"

"Roping. I go through everything in my head over and over and over." He shrugged. "It seems to work."

"I looked you up on the internet," she said. It had been something to do last night when she was having trouble going to sleep after calling Kate. "Quite an impressive career. I have no idea what the stats mean, but apparently you're doing something right."

"Does that mean I can have my days off this week?"

She knew he wasn't really asking—that he would take them anyway—so she said, "As long as you're covered."

"I'm covered. You can even go out with Lonnie, if you want…but he'd probably be a fumbling tongue-tied mess. Maybe you'd better wait until I come back."

He smiled at her and Ellie felt herself smile back. Warmth flowed through her and she told herself it was gratitude. He had no idea how glad she was that he was keeping her talking, which in turn kept her from thinking about her fun-filled early-morning hours.

Ellie had developed a whopper of a headache from replaying the conversation with her mother. And even after the headache had faded, she kept going back to Mavis's comment about it being her life.

Yes, it was. Her life. Emphasis on *her*. All by herself. It'd been like that for almost as long as she could remember.

"Ellie?"

Ellie glanced over at Ryan, wondering from the way he was looking at her if he'd had to say her name more than once. "Yes?"

"I'm going to have you drive along the fence line and I'll drop off posts. Just go slow."

"Sure."

Ryan climbed into the back and she put the truck in gear, focusing on slow. Slow was good. Fast had gotten her into trouble.

For once in her life she'd wanted to do something without planning, to be impulsive…and she'd gotten burned in a big way. Which wasn't fair because Kate had escaped unscathed more times than she could count.

Well, you're not Kate.

But if she had been Kate, she would have at least had a supportive family. While at boarding school Kate had been a townie—she'd gone home for the weekends. Eventually she'd gotten permission to take Ellie with her. Ellie loved Kate's family.

"I might be all you have," she muttered to her midsection as Ryan threw off the first post and it landed with a hollow thud. "But I will be there for you."

Even if her maternal instinct never kicked in, as Mavis's never had, she would fake it. She'd win an award faking it.

Another post hit the ground. Ellie looked into her

rearview mirror to see Ryan's long, strong legs as he balanced himself near the tailgate. "Hey!" she heard him yell, and realized the truck was drifting.

"Sorry," she called back. She held a steady course down the rest of the fence line, slowing to a stop after Ryan had pushed off the last post. She turned off the engine and pushed open the door, looking at the long line of posts.

"There's a lot," she said.

"We'll do half today."

"And then?"

"I have to check a couple stock ponds." He pulled a bucket out of the back of the truck and then handed Ellie a strange two-handled contraption as if he expected her to know what to do with it. "It'll be an easy way to end the day."

Ellie put a hand on each of the wooden handles and moved them back and forth, opening and closing the two-part metal cylinder on the end. "To clean out the holes?" She was guessing.

"Yep," he said. "That's your job."

"These do not have a history of injuring people?" she asked.

"They'll blister your hands if you don't wear gloves."

Ellie smiled at him as the wind blew little wisps of hair across her face. She was growing to like this guy, but even as the thought struck her, she tamped it back down.

As the morning wore on, Ellie realized that she was engaging different unused muscles than the ones she'd used the day before, and that she was going to be sore again tonight. But she wasn't sitting alone in the ranch house thinking, and if she spent time out like this, she'd be in a better position to understand the ranch-consultant recommendations. A week working in the field wasn't much, but it was better than no experience at all, and she had to admit that Ryan had had a good idea when he'd suggested this—although she was fairly certain his objective had been to make her uncomfortable. He had no idea how much she'd needed to get out of that house.

"Tell me about what part of your job you like best," Ellie said after Ryan got done tamping earth around their fourth post. He sent her a where-did-that-come-from look and she said, "That's one of the standard questions I use in the course of my job."

"What exactly is your job?"

"I evaluate employees and workforces." Ellie felt heat building in her face as she lied by omission. She no longer did that. "I help to decide who to hire and fire, although we didn't use those particular terms." She stabbed the diggers into the next hole, brought up some loose dirt, deposited it at the edge of the hole and then stabbed them in again. Before she pulled them out, she tilted her head at Ryan. "You have amazing patience."

"How so?"

"I can see how badly you want to take these away from me and do this more quickly and efficiently."

"You're doing fine."

"I know I am." She hauled more dirt out of the hole, peered down inside then stepped back. "But I've also seen impatient males wanting to take over."

"Have you, now?" he asked as he dumped the post into the hole and held it vertical with one hand while he shoved dirt down the hole with his boot.

"Yes. And I just ignore them."

"Somehow I don't find that hard to believe."

Ellie considered his answer for a moment, trying to decide whether or not she'd been insulted. Did it matter? Oddly, she decided it did. "Meaning?" she asked.

He flashed her a quick look. "Are you fishing for a compliment?"

"No." The word dropped like a stone. She most certainly had not been.

"All I meant was that a person like you has probably had a lot of practice ignoring impatient males... which was exactly what I said."

"I don't believe we were speaking in the same context."

"No kidding," he said drily before kicking more dirt into the half-filled hole. When she didn't respond, he moved on to more mundane matters. "You asked about what I like about my job."

"Yes," she agreed, glad they were moving back to steadier ground.

"I like managing the grazing land. Over the past couple years, I've developed a system that allows for more re-growth and therefore more forage on some of our poorer pastures. We get more animal-unit days."

"Which are…?"

"AUs are basically the amount of forage needed to support an animal for a day."

"Sounds very scientific."

"Ranching is all about science in one way or another."

"Not my best subject in school."

Ryan leaned on the bar he used to tamp the earth. "I bet you got As."

"Why?" Ellie pushed her hair back again.

"Did you?"

She smiled wryly. "Yes."

"As I thought." Ryan started tamping again. "I studied a lot of science in college. It *was* my best subject."

Ellie watched him work, filing away information as he continued to talk about grazing and pasture management while they set the next six or seven posts. Ellie lost count. He spoke with simple eloquence about a subject she'd never much thought about—okay, she'd *never* thought about—managing ranchland. "Technically your job title isn't cowboy, is it?"

Ryan grinned at her and Ellie swore her heart stuttered a little. "Range manager might be more appropriate, but I always think of myself as a cowboy."

As did she.

Ryan stabbed the bar into the earth, focusing on what he was doing as he said, "I have to admit that Walt wasn't the best grazing manager—a lot of guys of his generation weren't—and then when the drought hit, followed by the wildfire...too much to recover from. He hired me right out of college, but we couldn't turn things around fast enough."

"He was in pretty deep debt, I gather."

"Oh, yeah. He did everything but sell organs to hang on to this place. And I hate to think what would have happened had he thought of that." Ryan leaned on the bar for a moment. "Does your uncle know anything about ranching?"

"He'll be dependent on his manager," Ellie said tactfully. "Which is why that manager needs to have communication skills and not bite people's heads off because he's angry that he lost his property."

"Walt will come around."

"He's not showing signs yet."

"He's still acclimating to the idea."

"It's been over a year."

"He's grieving."

"He needs to get over it," Ellie said. "If he doesn't…" She didn't need to finish the sentence. She could see that Ryan got her drift…and that he didn't like it. Well, reality was reality. Milo was already of the opinion that Walt was a difficult employee and so far Ellie hadn't seen anything that would allow her to go to bat for the man.

RYAN AND ELLIE parted company at the gate. He was kind of sorry to see her go, even if they didn't see eye to eye about Walt. He parked the truck behind the barn then headed straight to his house, where he dialed the lawyer's number, something he'd both been looking forward to and dreading all day. There was an immediate answer and one associate put him through to another.

"Mr. Madison, I'd like to arrange a meeting."

"Am I being sued?" Ryan demanded.

"No," the associate said in a placating tone. "But this is a sensitive matter that we'd prefer to address in a private meeting."

"Look," Ryan said. "I'm not big on mystery."

"And we don't want this to be a mystery, but as I said, this is a sensitive matter."

"I'm going to hang up."

"I represent Mr. Charles Montoya."

What the hell? Why was his father siccing a Billings law firm on him? "He'd like to meet with me?"

"As his representatives, he'd like *us* to meet with you."

Somehow Ryan wasn't surprised. "When?"

"We'd like to arrange something next week. In Billings."

"No. If you want to meet, we meet in Glennan. I think Mr. Montoya can afford to pay you for your travel time."

The associate cleared his throat. "I'll have to confer with Mr. Montoya."

"You do that," Ryan said. "I can meet with you next Tuesday or Wednesday. You can set the time."

"I don't know—"

"And I don't care." With that, he hung up.

For a few seconds Ryan sat staring across the room. What in the hell could his father want badly enough to set up a meeting? It had to have something to do with whatever had upset his mom, and if push came to shove, Ryan would go to Billings to meet with the attorneys and find out what the deal was.

But he didn't want Charles to think that he was calling all the shots here.

CHAPTER EIGHT

FOR ONCE ELLIE was up near sunrise. There was an avian symphony outside the bathroom window and even though she'd slept soundly, once she woke, she couldn't roll over and go back to sleep as usual. Partly because the birds were making so much noise, but mostly because she'd felt a jolt of pleasant anticipation at seeing Ryan again. Inappropriate, she told herself as she flopped over and tried to go back to sleep.

It wasn't inappropriate if he didn't know.

And why should he?

She was barely willing to acknowledge it to herself—it wasn't as though she was going to announce it to him.

"Hormones," she muttered as she got out of bed. Coupled with a little too much alone time.

Maybe that was it. She just needed to be with people. Yesterday she hadn't obsessed over the frustrating conversation/confession with her mother or thought about being pregnant more than a couple dozen times—as opposed to the several hundred times a day that had become the norm of late. For almost the entire time she'd been with Ryan she'd felt normal. Like her old self.

You can't be your old self.

No doubt. Her old self wouldn't have put on these filthy, scuffed-up hiking boots. Ellie wrinkled her nose, then shoved her foot inside. She didn't want to be late for work.

Walt was opening the barn door when she left the house, a thermos of herbal tea in one hand, a jug of water in the other. He looked at her, started inside then stopped and turned back around.

"Good morning," he said stiffly.

"Good morning," she answered, thinking he sounded very much as if someone was twisting his arm to make him speak.

"If you have any questions about operations, you can ask me anytime. And if you'd like to know more about the cows and the breeding program, I can carve out some time."

"I'd like to learn about the cows," she said, stopping a few feet away from him. The invitation sounded anything but sincere, but he'd made it and she was going to take him up on it—even if it killed both of them.

He grunted in reply and then headed off into the barn, leaving Ellie staring after him.

"Problem?"

Ellie turned to see Ryan approaching from his house.

"Walt just invited me to a sit-down to learn about his cows."

"You take him up on it?"

"I did, but we didn't set a date."

"Maybe I can be there, too."

"To referee?"

"Possibly." He started toward the pickup. Ellie smiled a little. She was fairly certain that Ryan was responsible for Walt's grumbling invitation. It touched her that he was so loyal to the old man, but it was going to take more than a cow talk to turn Walt into the kind of manager Milo was looking for.

RYAN FOUGHT A yawn as he waited for Ellie to open the gate. Practice had gone okay, but he'd been unable to sleep afterward as he'd replayed the conversation with the attorney a few million times in his head. When Walt had showed up he'd helped him grain the calves, and then suggested that he make a few overtures of friendliness toward Ellie.

Trust Walt to consider the invitation to hear about his cows an appropriate gesture.

When she got back into the truck, Ellie gave him a quick once-over. "Are you all right?"

He was surprised at the question, which smacked of personal interest. "Long night. I got in late from practice."

"From what I've read, guys who hold down full-time jobs have a hard time competing in professional rodeo."

"Which is why it's good that I have an employer who allows me to work flex time."

Ellie took hold of the armrest as the truck lurched forward over the worst of the ruts. "I was thinking more about the amount of time it takes to both practice and compete."

"That's probably why I don't have a girlfriend."

Ellie flashed him a quick look, then directed her eyes straight ahead. "I'm surprised at that. You do seem like a catch," she said matter-of-factly.

"I own my truck."

"You're a bit of a local celebrity." Ryan snorted. "No, really," she said.

"How much research have you done?"

"Enough," she said lightly.

Ryan rolled his eyes and started to drive, realizing that just having Ellie there helped stop the vicious cycle of his thoughts, which had been bouncing from Charles to the mystery of the meeting and back to Charles again. And there was something to be said for that.

A WEEK AGO Ellie wouldn't have believed that she'd be something of an expert on fence-post setting, but after twenty-five posts, she'd say she qualified.

"Why are all of these posts wood," she asked as

Ryan pulled up to the last gate, "while those are skinny and metal?"

"Those are T-posts. Walt wanted to use wood on the property boundary, because that was what was there before."

"He's not big on change, is he?"

"He's a traditionalist," Ryan replied.

Ellie let the remark pass, seeing no sense in arguing a case with Ryan that Walt essentially needed to win himself. Besides, she wasn't in the mood for arguing. She wanted to get outside, enjoy the sun. Watch Ryan work under the guise of professional interest, and damned if she was going to feel guilty about that. She had enough to worry about without adding guilt to the plate.

When they got to the fence line, they started on the first post without speaking, following the process they'd worked out the previous day. Ryan put his hand on the finished post, testing it.

"I think we set a record on this one."

"Have I been slowing you down?" Ellie asked, brushing the hair back from her forehead with the back of her wrist.

"Even if you were, it wouldn't matter."

"Why?" she asked, realizing that she cared about his reply more than she probably should.

"It's nice having some company out here. Usually I work alone." He held out his hand and Ellie gave him the post-hole diggers instead of insisting on doing it herself. He stabbed them into the hole, pulling out about double the amount of dirt she usually removed. "I don't mind being alone, but not all the time. You know?"

She knew.

Ryan tipped the post into the hole and they both started scraping in dirt with their boots, working on opposite sides while Ryan held the post vertical with one hand. "Can I ask a personal question?"

"Okay…" Ellie said even as alarms went off inside her.

"How is it that you're able to be here?"

"I don't understand."

"Are you independently wealthy? On vacation? Sabbatical?"

Maybe it was because he was so matter-of-fact and down-to-earth and didn't seem to have a thing to hide himself that Ellie was able to answer with as much truth as she felt comfortable telling. "I'm out of work."

He stopped pushing dirt. "Unexpected?"

"About as unexpected as you can imagine."

He frowned before reaching for the tamping bar. "That bites." He appeared to mean it.

"It's good to see the other side of the coin," she said philosophically. "I've been responsible for layoffs and now I know what it's like."

"Do you really mean that?"

She smirked at him. "It's the most positive spin I can put on it."

He smiled at her, seeming to like the candidness of her reply. "You're different than you first come off, Ellie."

"Yeah?" she asked, again feeling warmth curling inside her.

"I think you know that."

"All right. I do." She paused thoughtfully, then added, "In my line of work, it doesn't pay to become too attached to those you work with. So I don't."

"Makes sense." He tamped dirt around the post, his muscles flexing under his light cotton shirt in a rather spectacular way. "In my line of work, the rodeo line, I do make friends. I have to beat them, of course, but I still like them."

"How about Matt Montoya?"

Ryan's head came up, and there was something about his expression that told Ellie to tread lightly. "What about him?" he asked slowly.

"I read a few articles where you talked some major smack about him."

"That doesn't mean I don't like him," Ryan said as he walked to the next post.

"If that's how you talk about people you like, then I don't want to think about what you say about people you don't like."

"All part of the game."

"Rough game," she murmured.

"Rodeo ain't for sissies."

No doubt. But Ryan's demeanor had changed when she'd brought up Montoya, which made her believe that the smack talk hadn't entirely been fun and games.

"This'll be our last post for today," Ryan said. "Want to save some fun for tomorrow." He started dropping tools into the bucket.

It was early, but Ellie couldn't say she was sorry to stop fencing. She absently rubbed one of her shoulders as they walked back to the truck. "What now?"

"I thought we could drive up onto the mountain. I can show you the grazing area we use in the spring and see if we can spot those four lost cows."

"How many man hours have been tied up in those four cows?"

Ryan dropped the bucket on the tailgate, making the tools inside rattle. "More than should have been. However, considering the market value of the animals, not enough to make it a waste of money."

Ellie had no idea what the market value of the four cows was and she wasn't going to ask. She'd look it up. "Just checking," she said.

"We kind of know what we're doing," Ryan replied as he lifted the tool bucket into the back of the truck.

"And I'm kind of here to learn." The quiet camaraderie that had been growing between them as they worked had started to fade, and Ellie felt a stab of disappointment as they slipped back into their roles. She was there to evaluate on behalf of her uncle; Ryan was there to try to sway her thinking. They weren't friends.

As they drove onto the mountain, Ryan tossed out grazing facts and figures while maneuvering the truck up the narrow dirt road, negotiating switchbacks and easing around deep ruts.

When they finally cleared the tree line, he parked and got out of the truck. Ellie did the same, coming to stand next to him near the front of the truck as he pointed out fence lines and boundaries. When he was done, Ellie simply drank in the incredible vista for a moment—the forested mountains surrounding lush valley meadows. In the distance she could see a town—Glennan, no doubt, where she'd soon be going for her first baby appointment. And for once the thought didn't seize her up. Her pregnancy was a fact of life and she would deal with it.

She took in a breath and lifted her chin so that the crisp breeze blew the escaped wisps of hair back from her forehead. What would it be like to live and work in an environment like this every day of your professional life? She'd read about the land shaping the men that worked it, but had never really thought about what it meant. But she knew without a doubt that Ryan was shaped by this land, as was Walt, most probably. These guys dealt with issues totally foreign to her, foreign to Milo and Angela.

Which was where the ranch consultant came into the picture. An expert in the field. Milo and Angela weren't the first people in the area to buy a retirement/investment ranch, and they'd learn.

She glanced over at Ryan, who continued to stare off into the distance, deep in thought. "Looking for your cows?" Ellie asked.

"Always," he said, smiling a little as he turned toward her. "We should probably get back."

"I assume you're practicing tonight?" While she, no doubt, would be soaking her sore muscles in a hot tub.

"Actually, I'm going to Jessie and Francisco's for posole."

"What's 'posole'?" Ellie asked as they started for the truck, walking side by side, neither in a great hurry to leave.

"You're kidding, right?"

Ellie shook her head. "Sounds like a card game."

Ryan laughed as he opened the truck door. "It's pork-and-hominy soup. Amazing stuff when Jessie makes it."

"Ah," Ellie said politely. She'd never had hominy, either. Her education, it seemed, was lacking in certain foodstuffs.

Ryan started the truck and put it in Reverse, Ellie automatically steadying herself with a hand on the seat as the vehicle lurched backward over a rut. The movement had become second nature and that realization gave Ellie a vague sense of satisfaction. She was adapting, feeling more comfortable in her environment. More comfortable with the people she was essentially living with. She glanced sideways at Ryan. No, *comfortable* wasn't the word. In some ways comfortable was the opposite of what she felt around Ryan. *Edgy* was a better description.

Ellie was slowly becoming a fan of edgy.

AFTER OPENING THE last gate to allow Ryan to drive through, Ellie walked across the drive to the main house. She was inside by the time Ryan had parked the truck and walked around the barn. He stood for a moment, debating, then went into his own house to shower before dinner.

It hadn't been a half-bad day despite the matter of his father's lawyers continually shoving itself into his thoughts. Ellie wasn't afraid to put in a day's work and when she let herself relax, she was actually kind of fun and easy to talk to. He smiled to himself as he opened his door, recalling how she'd thought posole sounded like a card game. How could anyone not know what posole was?

But something else she'd said had stuck with him—that bit about not letting herself get too close to the people she worked with because of what she might have to do later. But she was allowing herself get to know him. Hell, she'd researched him on the internet. He still wasn't quite sure how to take that, but it showed interest in him as a person and she'd even consented to answer what had to be a difficult personal question: why she was able to be there. Being out of work had to be rough on Ellie, whom he suspected judged herself by professional success, but she'd confessed. That showed a level of trust. Now he just needed to give Ellie the opportunity to get to know the rest of the crew under pleasant circumstances…. Ellie, who'd never had posole.

He picked up the phone and called Jessie. "Hey," he said when she answered, "is it all right if I bring Ellie to dinner with me?" Jessie always made enough dinner to feed a crew and then froze whatever was left over for Walt to eat later.

"Ellie?"

"The boss."

"I know who you mean," Jessie said with a touch of exasperation. "I'm just wondering why."

"The more familiar she is with us before George comes, the better for all of us."

There was a brief silence before Jessie said grudgingly, "Sure. She can come…but I still think she's going to fire us all."

"Thanks, Jessie. And try to keep an open mind, okay?"

"Yeah, yeah." A squeal sounded in the background. "Emmie! No! I gotta go." She hung up without a goodbye.

Well, that part was done. Now to see if Ellie was tired of spending her nights alone.

She didn't answer the door immediately, and when she did, she was wearing a robe and her hair was down, falling in soft waves around her shoulders, making him wish she'd stop pulling it back.

"Hi," she said uncertainly as if wondering why he was there after the workday had officially ended.

"Hi," he replied before diving in. "I called Jessie, and if you'd like to come to dinner, you're invited."

She looked startled. "Why would you do that?"

"I thought you might be tired of spending all your nights alone. You don't have to come."

"It wouldn't look too good if I didn't go now."

"You could have a previous engagement."

"But I don't." One corner of her mouth tilted up wryly. "And I appreciate the invitation. Give me a few minutes to dress and I'll be right with you."

Ryan waited for Ellie in the truck wondering how much she really did appreciate the invite, since something akin to alarm had crossed her face when he'd made it. Her hair was pinned up again when she let herself out of the house, but she was wearing white jeans and a pale blue sweatshirt, which was a change from the expensively casual clothing she'd worn the first few days she'd been on the ranch. But he wondered how familiar she was with both posole and kids if she was wearing white to a family dinner....

The kids charged him as soon as he opened the door and almost instantly he had a twin in each arm happily chattering at him while Jeff jumped up and down in front of him. "Good to see you guys, too," he said on a laugh. He turned toward Ellie, who'd taken a step back at the charge and was now eyeing the kids in a way that confirmed his suspicion that she hadn't spent much time around young children.

"Ellie, this is Emmie and Bella—" he nodded to the twins in turn "—and this kangaroo in front of me is Jeff."

"Hi," Ellie said cautiously.

Emmie drew back against him, clutching his collar with one chubby fist as she stared at Ellie, but Bella reached out to Ellie. She looked startled as the twin leaned toward her, then awkwardly reached out to take the girl in her arms before she toppled.

"Oh, you're heavy," Ellie said with a self-conscious laugh as she hefted the little girl higher in her arms and then awkwardly balanced her on her hip.

"They're growing fast," Jessie said, wiping her hands on the dish towel tucked in the waistband of her jeans as she walked into the room. "If my mom didn't sew, I'd have a hard time keeping them dressed."

"They're adorable," Ellie said, moving closer to Jessie as Bella reached for her mother. "And handsome," she added, nodding at Jeff.

"Just like his daddy," Jessie said with a smile as

she took Bella from Ellie. "Who should be here any minute," she said to Ryan, before setting Bella down, ignoring the girl's upstretched arms. "Your feet will be fine on the floor while Mama cooks," Jessie said firmly. "Come on into the kitchen. You can stir for me." Bella brightened and Emmie immediately struggled to get out of Ryan's arms to join her sister.

"Come on in and talk while I finish up," Jessie called to Ellie as she followed the giggling twins into the kitchen.

Ryan had to give Jessie credit for doing her best to treat Ellie like just another casual guest instead of the boss or enemy, which was how he knew she thought of her.

"Thanks," Ellie said, following the girls into the kitchen, leaving Ryan to entertain Jeff, who was now digging through his pile of toys to show him his new car. She cast him an uneasy look, almost as if seeking reassurance, before disappearing through the kitchen door. Ellie was as nervous as she'd been the first time they'd worked together. Maybe more so…. And in a way, that made Ryan like her better.

"Dad!" Jeff shouted as the front door rattled. He dropped the car and headed for the door.

"Hey-a, big guy," Francisco said, swinging his son up into his arms. "Were you good today?"

"I was, but Emmie wasn't."

"I'll let Mama tell me about that," Francisco said

before meeting Ryan's eyes. "So you survived another day with the boss?"

"Who's with Jessie right now," Ryan said, jerking his head toward the kitchen. The change in Francisco's demeanor was almost comical. "I thought she might like to get to know us all a little better before George gets here."

"Ah. Not a bad idea."

But he still looked as though he'd just tasted something nasty.

"She's not that bad," Ryan said.

"You should know." The girls stampeded out of the kitchen then for their hello hugs. Francisco swept them up laughing as they kissed his cheeks and simultaneously told him the many events of the day. While his friend was busy with his offspring, Ryan ambled into the kitchen, where Ellie sat at the table as Jessie stirred a pot on the stove.

"Damn, that smells good," Ryan said. "Too bad Walt's not here."

"I invited him, but you know he won't miss that poker game for anything," Jessie said.

"Thursday-night poker at the Crescent Bar," Ryan said to Ellie. "Walt never misses." Then, in case she thought Walt had a nasty gambling habit on top of his other faults, he added, "Penny poker."

"I think he has a lady friend," Jessie said absently.

Francisco came in carrying the girls. Jessie smiled

and offered her cheek. He took her lips instead, making the girls giggle.

"Down you go," he said to the girls.

"Could you get them their juice?" Jessie asked her husband as she started taking bowls down from the cupboard. Ryan automatically took them from her and started setting the table.

"Let me do that," Ellie said, getting to her feet. Ryan was about to say he was used to it when he caught her expression. She was trying to be part of this, just as he'd wanted, so he handed her the bowls and went to take silverware out of the drawer as she set the four adult bowls and three children's bowls at the table.

"Mine goes here," Jeff announced, moving the bowl to an empty place.

"How about the others?" Ellie asked.

"I'll do it," Jeff said importantly.

"Thank you," Ellie said, taking her seat again. Bella toddled over to her and situated herself between Ellie's legs before she absently tilted her cup and orange juice poured out, soaking Ellie's thigh.

Ellie gasped and instantly righted the cup, but it was too late.

"Oh, no!" Bella said dramatically, patting the orange juice into Ellie's white jeans with her small hand. "Oh, no."

"I'm so sorry," Jessie said, rushing to the rescue,

giving Ellie a towel and handing Bella off to Francisco. "The lid must be on crooked."

"No problem," Ellie said, grimacing a little as she pressed the towel onto her leg.

"Do you want to go home and change?" Ryan asked.

Ellie looked up in surprise. "No. I'm fine. Things like this happen."

"Oh, yeah," Jessie scoffed. "I suppose you get a lot of orange juice poured on you," She reached out to stop Emmie, who was toddling toward Ellie, tilted cup in hand.

"Don't worry," Ellie said with a smile, holding out her hands to Emmie. "A little orange juice is no big deal."

"Well, I admit that I wear a lot of the stuff," Jessie confessed as she let Emmie go, and Ellie laughed as both girls rushed her. After that, the atmosphere changed. Jessie set a steaming pot of soup on the table and then showed Ellie how to load it up with fried tortilla strips, green onions and cheese. Ellie took a sip of the broth, closed her eyes and let out a heartfelt sigh.

"This is good," she said.

"I'm glad you like it," Jessie said. "It's Francisco's mother's recipe."

"She never made it this well," he said, sitting after maneuvering each of the girls into a high chair.

Jessie smirked. "My husband is a wise man."

Ryan gave a cough at the comment and when he caught Ellie's eyes a second later, he saw laughter there, and smiled at her. She immediately glanced back down at her soup, fighting an answering smile, and damned if it didn't look as if her color was rising. Had to be steam coming off the posole.

But she didn't look back at him, turning instead to speak to Jessie. Ryan watched the two women talk, saw that Jessie was starting to relax a touch and recognized that Ellie was making an effort to connect with her.

And somehow, now that she was here, with orange juice on her pants and making a sincere effort to fit in, Ryan allowed himself to acknowledge what his hornier self had been shouting out for the past two days. Ellison Hunter was sexy.

CHAPTER NINE

AFTER THEY SET the last fence post, a post Ellie was very glad to see vertical, they ate lunch sitting side by side on the tailgate of the truck, enjoying the sun while Ellie tried to see the deer Ryan pointed out in the shadows of the trees. His shoulder would occasionally press against hers as he pointed, setting every nerve in her body on alert.

"To the left," he said, leaning close when she'd failed to see the third one in a row. It wasn't that she hadn't seen deer before—every morning they grazed in the field with the cattle—it was that she wanted to see these deer that appeared to be invisible to her. Or was she just so very aware of the man next to her that her other senses were shutting down? Her awareness of Ryan had intensified since going to dinner at the Garcias' two days ago, but thankfully, it appeared to be one-sided. Ryan was warm and friendly, but no more so than he'd been prior to the dinner, making Ellie fairly certain that even if he felt equally drawn toward her, he wasn't going to acknowledge it. For which she was grateful. Not acknowledging meant not having to deal with it. It might be wrong, but she enjoyed the pull of secret attraction and didn't want to ruin the one positive that managed to distract her from the reality of her life. Distracted her, entertained her…frustrated her. Frustration, she'd decided, was a small price to pay.

"You're hopeless," Ryan said on a wry note.

"Guess I'll have to cross 'big-game hunter' off my list of job prospects."

"I would," he said, sliding off the tailgate to his feet.

Ellie followed him, wishing that they could have sat in the sun and watched invisible deer for another hour or two.

"I have to check a pond," he said after packing up the lunch, "and then we'll head home. I have a few things to do on the main ranch."

"What do you check for?"

"The water level, mainly, and the flow of the source."

Ah. Flow of the source. Of course. Ellie smiled a little as she got into the truck. She was enjoying learning all this stuff. Or maybe she was just enjoying her teacher.

The pond was close—only a half mile from where they'd been working. Ryan drove to the top of a small hill, and on the opposite side was a pool of lovely, still water. There were reeds growing at one end and a large bird floating on the other.

"Is that a goose?" Ellie asked.

"Appears to be," Ryan said as he started down the hill. Ellie followed and as they approached the water she realized the bird wasn't swimming. In fact, it appeared to be tethered in place. As they got closer, the bird became alarmed, letting out a warning honk as it struggled, spreading its wings, flapping and going nowhere.

"She's stuck," Ellie said.

"Yeah."

"We have to rescue her."

Ryan gave her a frowning look. "She's going to beat the shit out of me with her wings if I try to rescue her."

"Fine. I'll do it." She started for the pond, but Ryan took hold of her arm before she took more than a couple steps.

"*What* are you going to do?"

"I don't know. I thought I'd get closer and assess."

"I'll come with you."

The goose again struggled wildly as they approached, flapping her wings and trying to lift off. When that failed, she stilled, keeping her wings out, the tips dipped into the water, and let out a long evil hiss as she eyed them balefully.

"She's not happy," Ryan muttered.

"Would you be, stuck in the mud like that?"

"She's not stuck…she's tangled up in the branch there."

Ellie followed Ryan closer, mirroring his slow

movements so as not to distress the goose any more than she already was. "How?"

"Fishing line, probably."

"We're going to untangle her. Right?"

Ryan gave his head a weary shake. "Right." He took off his shirt and Ellie made a concerted effort not to stare. She was not entirely successful. "We're going to get wet, you know."

"I'm familiar with the effects of water," she said.

"Just checking." He dug a knife out of his pocket and handed it to her. After Ellie flipped the knife open, then closed it again, he turned to face the goose. "Here goes."

"Good luck."

"You'd better be right behind me." Rolling his shoulders in an exaggerated manner, Ryan started toward the hissing goose. When he was close he stopped for a few seconds and gauged the best line of attack to avoid her snaking head, then made a dive for the goose, dropping the shirt over her. The goose went ballistic, her head popping out of the chambray fabric, biting and stabbing at any part of Ryan she could reach.

"Son of a bitch," he muttered, fighting to get the head back under the shirt. Finally he got her body jammed under his arm and the head under the shirt. A low, angry hiss emanated from the quivering bundle. Ellie moved to join him then, kneeling in the mud beside him to open the knife, and cut the fishing line tangled around the goose's leg free from the branch. Ryan kept hold of the bird, wading the few feet toward shore after the bird was free, so that Ellie could work on the line still wound around the bird's leg.

"It's tight," she said, hurting for the poor animal. She took her time, trying to figure out the direction of the wraps. Every now and then the goose gave a mighty squirm, trying to snake her head free of the shirt, but Ryan maintained his hold.

"I don't think she's been tangled for that long," he said. "The line's not cutting her leg yet."

"Not much anyway," Ellie said.

It took a good five minutes before Ellie unwrapped the last bit of line. She met Ryan's eyes as she closed the knife. "Is this the part where she beats the shit out you with her wings?"

"I guess we'll see. You might want to stand back." He waited for her to move away before he set the shirt-covered goose on the ground and took a few quick steps back. The goose poked her head out from under the cloth, then waddled back toward the water, dragging the shirt behind her.

"Well that was anticlimactic," Ryan said, wiping mud off his arm.

Ellie bit her lip, trying to keep from smiling. "You sound like you wanted her to attack."

"Maybe I wanted to show off my goose-fighting skills. She's definitely not as tough as my mom's old goose. That bird used to tree me on a daily basis."

"Really? You got treed by a goose?"

"You have no idea how terrifying an angry goose can be. They come at you hissing and beating those wings…" He gave an exaggerated shudder and Ellie laughed. It sounded low and sensual, even to her ears. She wondered if Ryan noticed, or if she was being overly sensitive.

Oh, yes. He'd noticed. Their eyes connected and, for one long electric moment, held.

He wanted to touch her. She could sense it. And worse yet, she felt the same, as if a wall had fallen away and she'd realized it was possible to touch.

Dear heaven, how she wanted to. She wanted to step closer, take his face in her hands and kiss him. Softly the first time, hard and deep the second time. To find out what all those lean muscles felt like under her fingers. She wanted to wrap herself around him, experience what this cowboy had to offer, and for one brief moment just feel and not think.

But it wasn't possible. That was what had gotten her into this situation, and she'd been stupid to let herself meander along this path. She was pregnant. She was leaving. She couldn't toy around with this guy—it wasn't fair to either one of them.

Ellie stepped back.

SOMETHING MAJOR HAD just shifted between him and Ellie as they stood at the edge of the pond, the goose peacefully swimming at the far end as if nothing had happened to it.

Shifted, and then abruptly shifted back again as Ellie tore her gaze away from his and took a step back, looking out over the pond. There was no sign of anything approaching mutual awareness now and all traces of laughter were gone from her eyes when she turned back to him.

"I'll get your shirt," she said, wading out into the pond where it was floating free. Ryan made no move to stop her or to say that he could get it himself. She wanted to go because she wanted to put distance between them.

Ellie came back with his shirt, doing her best to wring it out. She gave it a shake and handed it to him. "We'd better get going," she said.

"Yeah," Ryan agreed as Ellie started toward the truck. Ryan followed, trying to sort out what had just happened, struggling to put on his wet shirt as he walked. It felt like hell, but given what had just happened, he thought it best that he cover up.

What *had* just happened?

Lightning followed by a dousing rain.

They drove back to the ranch in stony silence, the tension between them growing by the minute, and he continued to replay what had just happened. One minute he'd had the feeling she was ready to lock lips with him and the next she was ten miles away.

Was she married or engaged or something? She

wore no ring, but that didn't mean she wasn't committed. And if she was, well, that he could understand. But he didn't like it.

When they stopped at the last gate, Ellie half turned in her seat and said, "I don't think I'm going to come out with you tomorrow."

"That's your choice," he replied evenly.

"I'm not trying to be unfriendly," Ellie said.

"Yeah?" He left it at that.

She reached for the door handle, seemed to think better of it and turned back. "I agreed to spend time with you in order to get a feel for day-to-day ranching operations." Spoken in that professional tone he hadn't heard in a couple days.

"And you feel like you have enough of a feel to make informed decisions?"

"More than if I hadn't come out."

"And what happened back there has nothing to do with it?"

She blinked at him and her lips parted a moment before she spoke. "What do you mean?"

"Really?" he asked flatly before letting out a frustrated breath. "You're going to play dumb?" He wasn't. "Are you involved with someone?"

Ellie gave her head a slow shake, her eyes holding his, as if surprised he'd been so candid.

"So it's a simple matter of not getting too friendly with the help?" he said, taking a guess based on her comment the day before.

"There are boundaries in the employer-employee relationship," she said coolly. "There have to be."

For a moment Ryan studied her, trying to wrap his mind around what exactly was happening. This morning he'd driven to the pasture with a warm, appealing woman. Now there was a professional corporate gunslinger sitting beside him. Ellie's gaze did not waver. If anything, it became more stubborn. "Noted," he finally replied. "Shall I get the gate, being the employee?"

"No," she said. "I'll do it." She got out of the truck and opened the gate. Ryan drove through, stopping on the other side. She waved him on, so Ryan jammed the truck into gear.

There was no reason to be angry, except that he hated it when people weren't straight.

Ellie was not being straight with him.

ELLIE WOKE UP the next morning to the sound of the old ranch truck rumbling to life. She wanted to go. She didn't want to stay in the house all day. Researching. Biding time. Contacting people who were friendly enough, but didn't seem overly enthused in helping her land new employment. When had her network become so static?

She got out of bed and walked to the window, edging back the curtains in time to see Ryan drive by with a large metal tank in the back of the old truck. What was he doing with that?

Ellie stepped back from the window. Chances were she'd never know...yet she was curious. She sank down on the bed again. Closed her eyes. Yesterday she'd helped rescue a goose with a truly attractive guy she wanted to get to know better, even if deep down she'd known that growing closer was a bad idea. She'd wanted to kiss him there at the pond during that moment of perfect connection, and he knew it. He'd called her on it.

The truth as to why she'd backed off had stuck in her throat. Why? If she'd told him she was pregnant, he would have understood and she could be out with him right now learning about the ranch instead of kicking around the house waiting for George the ranch consultant to show up...someday.

Ellie gave up trying to go back to sleep, showered, dressed and headed out to her Land Rover. She needed to get out and if she couldn't go with Ryan, then she was going to buy groceries. She locked the house and started across the porch, stopping in her tracks when she caught sight of the snake. Hiss, sensing danger, slowly slithered into a large crack between two of the stones.

Ellie pressed her hand to her chest to slow her heart as she watched the end of his tail disappear. Ryan had assured her the snake wasn't dangerous, but even so, she walked to the other end of the porch and descended the steps there.

On her way down the drive, she passed Ryan coming in the opposite direction, the tank now missing from the truck. He nodded curtly as she passed and that was that—if Ellie could just shove him out of her mind and focus on more pressing issues. Getting enough food in the house to eat for two was a good place to start.

LATER THAT AFTERNOON, as she was putting away groceries, Ellie was startled by a knock on the door. She shoved cornflakes into the cupboard, and then walked into the living room where she could see Ryan through the leaded-glass windows. Aware of a ridiculous increase in her heart rate, she went to open the door. Without a word, Ryan held out a folded paper, which Ellie automatically took from him.

"What's this?"

He shifted his weight. "I made a calendar for the rest of rodeo season showing when I'm here—when I'm gone, the hours I'm working, the hours I pay Lonnie for. That way you'll know what's going on."

And that the ranch is getting its hours. He didn't say the last, but Ellie could practically hear him thinking it. The Ryan Madison standing there in front of her was so different than the guy she'd driven to work with yesterday. He was simply an employee talking to his boss, because that was what she insisted he be.

Make peace with him.

She pushed the thought aside and took a quick glance at the calendar. "I appreciate being kept in the loop."

He touched his hat, just as he'd done after coming to the rescue when she'd first encountered Hiss, turned and left without another word. Ellie watched him go, feeling equal parts regret and relief. He was angry at her and she couldn't really blame him. He'd felt the same thing she had and had acted on it. She'd slapped him down. It wasn't his fault she had reasons not to get involved.

It's better this way. You know it is.

But she didn't have to like it.

THAT EVENING AT dusk Ryan pulled out of the driveway with his horse trailer in tow. Off to a rodeo in Miles City according to the calendar, back in a day and a half. Tomorrow Lonnie would show up to fill his shoes. Lonnie, who Ryan had assured her would become all thumbs if she tried to tag along with him.

Instead Ellie explored the barns, leaned through the fence to try to pet the calves. She read several articles on pregnancy and tried to make herself do a bit more networking. She read Walt's "papers" and used those as a starting point to learn something about cattle breeding. She printed out a diagram of an Angus bull with perfect conformation and walked down to the corrals to compare it to the bull there. Everything seemed to be in the right places and the proper proportions. Walt came up behind her, startling her.

"Oh," she said, feeling an urge to hide the picture behind her back. "I was just comparing this picture of an Angus bull to your bull to see how they compare."

"Not well, I hope," Walt said testily.

"Why's that?"

"Because that's a black Gelbveih."

"Really?" Ellie asked, refusing to be intimidated by his off-putting tone. Walt had apparently forgotten his invitation to discuss cattle with her. "Guess I need to print a new picture."

"Guess so," Walt said as he continued on into the barn.

"How do you spell Gelbveih?" she called after his retreating back. Walt didn't even slow down. As she walked back to the house she half wondered if she should just fire him now and save everyone the trouble of trying to rehabilitate. Why was Ryan so damned attached to this man?

And why was he still so heavy on her mind?

Milo called later that day, breaking the monotony, to tell her the consultant would possibly be there sooner than expected. He'd give her the exact date as soon as he had it. Ellie took the opportunity to broach the matter of the crew.

"I've heard rumor that your consultant tends to be a new broom sweeping clean."

"He has a reputation for identifying problems and doing what's necessary. The Kenyons were quite satisfied with his recommendations," Milo said. "He's a specialist in his field."

Milo did love specialists. Ellie sucked in a fortifying breath. "I'm also a specialist," she reminded him.

"Of course you are. You know the kind of people Angie and I can work with."

Indeed. Angela was hell on help at times, so it was more of a question of who could work with *her*. Could Jessie?

"So if he wants to fire the whole crew, like he did at the Kenyons', and I see reason to keep one or two…"

"We'll discuss it. The three of us."

The words were right, the tone was not. It was just a little too placating, making her think that perhaps, while Milo valued her opinion, she was going to play second fiddle to the ranch expert in the area of personnel management. Ellie pushed a hand through her hair.

"It's your ranch, Milo. Your decisions. But I hope you will take advantage of what I'm learning. I think the crew interacts with me in a way they probably won't with a consultant who'll only be here for a few weeks."

"True, and I think that's a benefit. You understand efficiency. Mr. Monroe understands ranching. Together you'll make an excellent team."

The consultant understands ranching. That could be the rub if it came down to her opinion against his. "I'm sure you're right," she said. "I'm looking forward to seeing you, showing you operations."

"Me, too, Ellie. See you soon."

CLOUDS HUNG LOW over the mountains the next day and it'd been raining for several hours by the time the sound of Ryan's diesel truck brought Ellie's head up. Ellie, who'd spent too much time thinking and now wanted to set a few things straight. She wasn't going to spend her time at the ranch dodging the man because of a few uncomfortable moments. No. They wouldn't be friends, because she knew instinctively that her unsettling awareness of Ryan was not the stuff of which friendships were made. It was the stuff of which hot sex was made, and her recent sojourn into the land of hot no-strings sex had not ended well. She would not repeat the journey. But she wouldn't hide out, either. They would make a peace. Of sorts.

Ryan pulled the truck to a stop next to the barn and Ellie walked across the drive to intercept him. "Why don't you park under the port at the front of the barn?" she asked from under the hood of her jacket.

"Because your aunt doesn't want vehicles parked in view." He walked around to the trailer and opened the door. PJ, who had not been tethered, stepped out into the rain, and Ryan caught his halter in one hand.

"She's not here," Ellie said impatiently.

"But you are," he said over his shoulder as he led the horse away.

Ellie let out a frustrated growl but stayed where she was, knowing he'd be back, since all of his gear was still stowed in the backseat. But Ryan didn't come back to the truck. Instead, he headed for the barn and she moved to intercept him.

"I don't care where you park," Ellie snapped as she met him at the door. "And I didn't mean to come across as having an elitist attitude the other day."

"It's a matter of employer-employee protocol. I got it." He opened the door and she stubbornly followed him inside even though she knew she should just retreat to her house.

Ryan started shoveling grain into two large buckets.

"Why didn't Walt grain the calves?" she asked.

"We worked out a deal before I left. He's the manager."

Ryan hefted the buckets and headed out the door. Ellie followed, stopping when he opened the gate and stepped into the mucky corral to empty the grain. The calves converged on the grain as Ryan stepped back, his boots making suction noises in the mud.

"I think there're some things we need to clear

up," she said. "But I don't want to talk in the rain. Or in the barn."

"Well, then, let's pencil in a meeting."

Ellie bit back the retort that rose to her lips and instead said, "You want me on your side when this consultant comes."

"Is that a threat?" he asked mildly.

"No. I'm just saying that what happened between us shouldn't play into it. I have some say—" *I hope* "—and I'm going to do my best for the crew."

"*All* of the crew?" he asked.

"Most of the crew," she replied honestly. No matter what, she didn't think Walt would make the cut.

"Well, I'm glad to hear that for Francisco's sake."

"What about yours?"

"Walt goes, I go," he said simply.

"That's a little shortsighted, don't you think?"

"Here's what I think," he said, facing her over the gate, rain dripping off his hat onto his boots. "This ranch will change. Your aunt and uncle will not understand how things have been done for generations, so they will hire alleged experts and, despite you 'being on our side,' will eventually fire all of us when that expert tells them to—and he will, because that's the way this particular expert does things."

"Maybe it doesn't have to be that way."

"I'll tell you what else I think," he said as if she hadn't spoken. "I'm not buying this employer-employee excuse of yours."

Ellie opened her mouth to protest, then decided it'd be wiser to hear him out rather than defend a lie.

Ryan came out of the pen, closing the gate and latching it with a quick shove of his hand before he turned back to her. "Believe it or not, I understand the words *not interested*. You didn't need to come up with bullshit excuses." He brushed past her and went back into the barn where he picked up his cooler and then started for his house, head bowed against the rain.

"Have a good evening," he said before disappearing around the corner.

"Sure thing," she muttered back as she crossed the wet gravel. "I hope you lost your event."

CHAPTER TEN

ELLIE WENT BACK into the house and peeled out of her wet coat, hanging it on a hook near the door where it could drip harmlessly onto the tiled floor. She headed down the hall to the bathroom, planning to take a nice, long, hot bath…except that would mean time to think, and she was so damned tired of thinking. Instead she cranked on the shower, letting it warm as she paced back and forth.

Okay, so she'd done a less-than-stellar job of hiding her attraction to Ryan and now he was totally pissed at her. She'd screwed up, but despite what Ryan thought, her excuse for stepping back was valid—employers and employees had to have boundaries. Ellie snorted as she stepped in under the blessedly hot spray and tilted her head back, letting the water run through her hair. Too bad Ryan didn't seem to see it that way. Too bad he knew a bullshit excuse when he saw one.

After a shower that did nothing to ease her tense muscles, Ellie blow-dried her hair, paced through the house a few times, started to dial Kate's number and then hung up.

Slowly she sank onto a leather chair. She liked Ryan. She hated burning this bridge, but it had happened and she didn't feel right about mending it. Yet she didn't feel right about not mending it, which left her in limbo. How could she explain her actions?

With a deep sigh she reached over to turn off the single lamp that lit the room, then used the light of her phone to walk through the dark house to her bedroom. Her very lonely bedroom.

Get used to it, baby.

She'd barely gotten between the sheets before she passed out, only to wake with a start.

Ellie had no idea if she'd been out for minutes or hours or what had woken her. She lay still, heart thumping against her ribs, and then she heard the heavy tread of footsteps just outside her window, and her throat went dry. Who would be walking around her house at this time of night? And more important, had she locked the door?

Ellie forced herself to breathe. Slowly she raised her head just enough to see that she was alone in the room, and then she gingerly got out of bed and moved to the window. Blood pounded in her ears as she looked out to see a half-grown calf walk past her window. Upon closer inspection, Ellie saw that there were at least twenty calves milling around.

Snapping on the light, she scooped up her phone, only to remember that she didn't have Ryan's cell number. He'd never given it to her, just as he'd never given her his bullet-point list of responsibilities.

Well, someone had to do something about these calves. She couldn't leave them running around until daylight when Walt got here. Ellie pulled on her jeans, jammed her feet into her flats, then thought better of it and instead put on her boots. It was damned wet and muddy out there. Tucking in her oversize sleeping T-shirt as she walked, she found her coat and headed for the door. It wasn't until she stepped outside—and the calves, startled at the noise and the possibility of a predator, scattered wildly— that she realized she might have made a mistake.

Damn Ryan for not giving her his number. Figuring she couldn't do much more damage than she already had, she marched toward his house as fast as she could in her untied boots. Another calf spooked as she approached, smacking the door of the ranch truck as it lunged sideways, blindly trying to escape in the dark.

A light came on in Ryan's house a split second after the collision and Ellie stopped in her tracks. He came out onto the porch a moment later, wearing only jeans, holding a flashlight in one hand, a sweatshirt in the other. The light traveled over the calves, and then he started across the porch, coming to an abrupt halt when he saw Ellie.

"I was coming to tell you that your calves were out," she said before he could ask.

"Can you get the gate at the front entrance?" he asked, pulling the sweatshirt on over his head. "I'll get the one at the back."

Ellie turned without a word and started jogging toward the front gate, which was a lot farther away than she remembered. When she got close, she saw a small group of calves hanging close to it and she slowed her steps, stopping when they looked at her.

"Shoo," she said softly. The calves looked at each other, as if making a plan, then started walking toward the open gate. "No!" Ellie raced forward, trying to head them off when her toe caught on something solid and she went down. Hard. The breath left her lungs and it took a moment before she was able to push herself up. As she did so, the calves trotted past her single file, disappearing into the darkness on the other side of the gate.

Ellie got to her feet and closed the gate, figuring it was better to have a few calves out than the entire lot. She rubbed the mud off the side of her face as she walked back to the house, grimacing as she did so. Damn. It'd been a long time since she'd fallen and it hurt a lot more than she remembered. But at least she'd landed on her side so hopefully the baby was fine. No. It *had* to be fine.

"What happened?" Ryan demanded, appearing out of the dark.

"I fell," Ellie said, not slowing her steps. She wanted to get back to her house, out of her wet, cold, muddy clothing. Her calf duty was done. Ryan could deal with the damned things.

"Fell?"

"Tripped. A few of the calves got out. I couldn't stop them, but I closed the gate." Ryan put his hand on her forearm and she stopped walking, raising her chin to meet his eyes as a chill ran through her, making her shiver.

"Come on," he said gruffly, jerking his head toward his house, his grip on her arm tightening.

"Where?" she said, automatically holding back.

"I'm going to make you something hot to drink."

"I'm fine. I just want to wash the mud off."

"Then we'll go to your house."

"There's no need. Take care of your calves."

"They're contained and I can't do much until morning when Walt gets here with his dogs."

She didn't know why he was persisting, but she was tired and dirty and she could practically feel the warmth of his body. It was so tempting to just lean closer, but she didn't. Not after the way they had parted earlier.

She started walking again and he fell into step beside her when all she wanted was for him to go back to his house. Remove temptation. Let her be. But she couldn't find the words to tell him to go. He'd walk her to her door for duty's sake, and then he'd leave and she'd deal with wet muddy clothes and tempting thoughts.

When they stopped at the front door, Ellie hesitated before reaching for the knob, dropping her gaze toward the porch planks, trying to come up with the words to set things straight between them.

"Ellie?"

She looked up, still frowning, half-afraid to meet his eyes. It was a justifiable fear. Her breath caught at the intensity of his expression. How fair was it that he was looking at her like that? In a way that made her want to do something about it. At a time when she couldn't.

"I was out of line earlier," he said in a low voice. "I apologize."

"You're just grateful over the calves," she said softly, wishing she'd never met his eyes.

A corner of his mouth turned up as he gently touched her chin and Ellie drew in a breath. *He was going to kiss her...and she couldn't let that happen.*

"Do it and you're fired," she murmured.

"Yeah?"

So much for threats. Ellie swallowed, knowing she needed to stop him, because his mouth was about to settle on hers and she very much wanted to meet him halfway. She eased back even though she wanted more than anything to get even closer to him.

"I can't do this."

"Ellie..."

"And it's not because I'm your boss," she said,

thinking it was time to put an end to things once and for all. "It's because I'm pregnant."

Ryan stepped back so quickly she was surprised he didn't trip.

"Pregnancy, not leprosy," Ellie muttered.

He folded his arms in front of him, as if he couldn't think of anything else to do with them. "I had a pregnant woman digging fence-post holes?"

"I'm not that pregnant," she said.

He started to speak, stopped, then finally said, "Well…a few things now make more sense than they did."

"Like me being impervious to your charm?" Except that she wasn't. She wondered if that had been as obvious to him as it was to her.

"Well, there's that. And you being here, instead of out conquering the business world."

"I needed some time." She hugged her arms around herself and started for her house, her sanctuary. "Milo needed another set of eyes. It seemed a good solution."

"The father?" he asked softly.

"Not in the picture," she replied, waiting for the judgment. She couldn't tell if she got one.

"You need to get inside," he said as a deep shiver ran through her. "If you need help…or anything… just yell."

"Will do." But she knew she wouldn't. "I have to go," she said, reaching for the door handle.

"Ellie."

Don't...

But she did. She looked back at him.

"How alone are you in this?" he asked.

"How alone can you be?" she replied.

His expression shifted, concern and—empathy?—playing over his handsome features as he reached out to carefully push the damp strands of hair away from her cheeks.

Ellie took in a breath at his gentle touch, and a heartbeat later he cupped her face in his hands, holding it for a moment before he lowered his head to kiss her.

Fire ignited inside her, but Ellie forced herself to stay still. The kiss was hot, intense. Something she wasn't prepared for. Yet Ellie met his tongue and the heat flared before Ellie abruptly stepped back.

Craziness.

Once she'd put a good foot and a half of space between them, Ellie met Ryan's eyes, trying to read him, but the analytical part of her brain was frozen. Useless. She started to speak, even though she had no idea what she was going to say, but he touched his fingertips to her lips, silencing her.

Again their eyes held and Ellie knew she had to escape. If he kissed her like that, knowing she was pregnant—

"It won't happen again," Ryan said softly.

Ellie nodded before she silently turned and walked

into the house, closing the door after her. She could still taste him.

After turning the lock, she stood at the window, watching Ryan cross the distance to his own house. He'd barely shut the door when a calf walked across the flagstones in front of her and disappeared into the darkness.

Damned calves.

Ellie headed toward the bathroom then for her second shower in less than six hours, mud crumbling off her sweatshirt as she pulled it over her head. And for once she wasn't going to think. She was going to do her damnedest to get some sleep. She had a feeling that tomorrow she was going to need some strength.

HE WAS HOT for a pregnant woman. Ryan didn't know what to make of that…or of the fact that Ellie *was* pregnant and hiding out at the ranch. It wasn't his business, but he couldn't seem to shake the question that kept shooting into his head.

Where was the father?

Had he abandoned Ellie? Had she abandoned him? Had it been a one-night stand?

It disturbed him that he had so many questions about her private affairs, and it didn't take a rocket scientist to see the connection to his own life. Kind of a sore spot with him, fathers not taking responsibility for their kids.

He'd finally fallen asleep well after midnight, only to be woken by Walt hammering on his door very early in the morning with the news that the calves were out.

"Are you sure she wasn't the one who didn't latch the gate?" Walt asked twenty minutes later after Clive and Betsy had rounded up the calves and put them back in the pen with a minimum of fuss.

"I'm the one," Ryan said. He remembered shoving it shut while he and Ellie had been having it out and not double-checking to see if it latched.

"Rookie move."

"Yeah." The lawn and the gardens, such as they were, were a mess and there'd be hell to pay if they weren't back into shape by the time the Bradworths came. Walt got on his four-wheeler, Clive and Betsy jumped on the back and the three of them drove away down the muddy drive, leaving Ryan to start his day's work—loading mineral to leave out in the pastures.

He'd just closed the tailgate when his phone rang. The Billings number. He frowned as he answered and found himself talking to an associate who made it clear that his only function was to schedule an appointment. Would next Tuesday at 11:00 a.m. work for Mr. Madison?

Mr. Madison assured the man that it would and was then informed that they would meet in a conference room in the tiny Glennan city hall building.

Ryan hung up and leaned back against the truck, studying the ground at his feet. It appeared he was about to meet his own fatherhood issues dead-on.

THE NEXT MORNING Ellie woke up to find Ryan in her backyard, surveying calf damage. Figuring she had to face him sometime, she pulled on her robe, ignored the fact that she had bed head and let herself out the back door. The flower beds were pretty much denuded and the calves had generously fertilized the lawn, as well as the graveled areas leading around the house.

She wrapped her robe closer around herself as she studied the mayhem, feeling Ryan watching her and also feeling utterly self-conscious. Was that because of the kiss? Or him knowing she was pregnant?

"I'll make this right," he said, but she had a strong feeling that making the gardens right wasn't the foremost thing on his mind.

"Actually, I'd like to do it," Ellie said, glad to have something superficial to talk about. He looked so good standing there in his worn jeans and faded black T-shirt, and last night he'd felt so good. Facts she couldn't deny, but had to deal with realistically.

Ryan looked around. "Are you sure?"

"Yes. Besides, if I hadn't been arguing with you, maybe you would have latched the gate."

"I doubt it," he said straight-faced. "I suck at gates."

A smile fought its way out. "Regardless, I'll handle the backyard."

"Let me know if you need help."

His gaze drifted down toward her abdomen, and Ellie answered his unspoken question. "Two and half months."

He flushed. "I wasn't…" He closed his mouth and shook his head. "Sorry." His voice was low, sincere. Sexy.

"No apology necessary." She glanced at the house, knowing she needed to get away from him, regroup. "I, uh, left the teakettle on."

"And I left the tractor running."

She could hear it running in the distance. He, at least, hadn't lied about his excuse to escape as she had. Ellie smiled a little before turning and retreating to the safety of the house.

The guy still made her palms sweat.

HE SHOULDN'T HAVE kissed her last night. The woman was dealing with issues, and judging from her skittish behavior this morning, he'd added to them. That hadn't been his intention. What he'd thought would be a comforting I'll-be-your-friend kiss had exploded into something intense within seconds of their lips meeting. So intense he felt himself growing hard at the memory, which pissed him off.

He crossed the yard to the idling tractor and climbed into the seat, raising the bucket before putting it in gear. He wanted to get the barn and corrals mucked out before his next rodeo and he had to get to the feed store to pick up the grain delivery. Lots of time alone to think, to wonder about the friggin lawyer, Ellie, Walt's future…and roping.

What had once been the center of his existence during the competitive season suddenly didn't seem all that important, which wasn't the attitude to have if he was going to make it to Nationals. He didn't know if his sudden ambivalence was related to his brother, or if it was merely a coincidence that about the time his top competition disappeared he was no longer as interested in dominating the field as he'd once been.

It'll pass. He'd get his competitive drive back.

The tractor bounced as he pulled it forward and started toward the pen the calves had occupied until last night. Walt had put the calves in a pen on the opposite side of the barn—one with a loop safety latch in addition to the regular latch. Ryan didn't know whether he should be insulted or amused.

He'd just parked the tractor after a good hour of mucking the empty corrals when he heard the door of the main house shut. Through the open barn door he watched as Ellie cautiously approached the flagstone steps where Hiss liked to sun, then after ascertaining that it was all clear, walking briskly to her Land Rover. Was she as alone as she'd indicated?

He hated the thought. Yes, she had a place to live, but did she have anyone to lean on?

You're not that someone.

No doubt, but it still bothered him to think of her facing her situation alone.

It HAD SEEMED as if she'd had to wait forever for her OB appointment, but now that Ellie was there, in the office, she felt totally out of place—just as she'd felt on the ranch during the first few days. She didn't belong here. This hadn't been in the plan.

There were four other women waiting with her, two with small children, all on the same journey as she, but they seemed more relaxed, as if they'd clued in to whatever secret there was to raising children and felt confident in their future.

Ellie felt anything but.

"You're new in town?" the nurse said as she directed Ellie to the scale.

"Brand-new."

"Have you seen a doctor previously?"

"No. I spent some time in denial and then I moved here and couldn't get an appointment for a few weeks."

The nurse's eyebrows went up at her candid denial, but all she said was, "How far along do you think you are?"

"I know exactly how far along I am because there's only one time I could have gotten pregnant."

Ellie told her the date and the nurse jotted it down.

"Hmm. Ten weeks on the nose. That's right when we first want to see you."

"Why so late?" Ellie asked.

"If the pregnancy isn't viable, nature generally takes care of it during the first eight weeks." The nurse removed the blood pressure cuff, seemingly satisfied with the reading. "In some larger practices, it's hard to get an appointment during the first trimester unless you're already a patient." She took a paper cup off the top of a stack, wrote Ellie's name on it with marker and then handed it to her. "The restroom is on the right, the instructions for collection are on the door."

Almost an hour later Ellie walked out of the office into the clear Montana morning reassured that the fall she'd taken while chasing the calves had done no damage. She had another appointment scheduled in four weeks' time, a plastic bag of reference materials and a due date.

Very sobering.

She had six and a half months to prepare to be a mom. It'd taken her longer than that to decorate her last apartment.

As soon as she got home, Ellie was going to seriously start applying for jobs. She'd had her grieving time and her adjustment time. Now she needed to set about making a life for her and her kid.

A life where?

Wherever she could find a job and afford to live as a single mother. She was facing an awesome responsibility here and it was time to get off her ass and make things work.

Ellie bought groceries and several flats of flowers at the hardware store next door, then drove back to the ranch ticking items off a mental list—people to call, areas to explore. She rounded the last corner before the ranch house, then slowed almost to a stop when she spotted a shiny black truck with a lot of chrome parked in front of the house.

She'd lived for too long in the city to feel comfortable with this situation and was seriously considering swinging the Rover around and driving back to the Garcias' place when a man got out of the truck, smiling broadly as he raised a hand.

He was dressed very much as Walt had been the first and only time she'd met with him to discuss his position—white starched shirt, dark jeans, shiny boots. His gray hat was immaculate, as were his teeth. A large silver buckle covered a good portion of his flat abdomen. He looked like a highly successful rancher—or ranch consultant. Was this George?

CHAPTER ELEVEN

ELLIE DROVE THROUGH the gate and parked, but kept the engine running as she cracked the window down a few inches.

"Are you Ellison Hunter?" the man asked in a congenial voice.

"I am." Wavy dark hair showed from under the edge of his hat and there was a smile in the man's hazel eyes. He was really good-looking.

"George Monroe."

"I had a feeling," she said, turning off the ignition. "My uncle said you might be early, but I don't think he thought it would be this early."

"It's not, but I was in the area and decided to stop by. Introduce myself." He straightened, placing his hands on his hips as he surveyed his surroundings with a practiced eye. "I can't wait to get to work."

Ellie wasn't certain what that meant, but after talking to Ryan, she had an idea that it didn't bode well for Walt.

"If you have a minute to spare," Ellie said after getting out of the Rover, "would you like something to drink and we can discuss your plans?"

"Sounds excellent," he said.

George stayed for thirty minutes. Ellie had started to usher him out to the back patio with the iced tea, then remembered the mayhem the calves had caused. She stopped in the middle of the living room, smiled at George and said, "Why don't we sit inside?"

He shrugged and followed her to the kitchen.

"What I like to do," he said, "is to take part in the daily ranch activities. Get a feel for who does what and how." He paused as if expecting her to be impressed by his hands-on approach. Ellie gave an encouraging smile and he went on. "Having grown up on a ranch, and worked on a ranch, I know the qualities that make a competent ranch hand and ranch manager."

"Good to know," she said politely. How many of those qualities would Walt have? Two? Three?

"I also do a complete financial evaluation, going over the records for the past several years, make recommendations based on those. I have a background in agriculture, range management and beef husbandry. I'll evaluate the breeding program, the forage, the wildlife management practices."

There didn't seem to be much George couldn't do. He flew his own plane, brewed his own beer and sometimes he sang with a trio at the cowboy poetry gatherings that had become popular in the West over the past few decades.

After he finished telling her how he operated and

that he'd be in contact soon with a definite arrival date, Ellie walked him to the porch and then watched as he drove away.

Charming guy. Seemed to know his stuff. Highly recommended.

Ellie ticked through the reasons she should welcome George Monroe to the ranch. But there was something about him that kept Ellie from fully embracing his presence there. Maybe Ryan had prejudiced her toward him, but she was going to hold off on her judgment of Mr. Monroe. See what *he* did, how *he* operated. She was also going to tell Milo that he'd stopped by and firmed up his arrival date. She waited until the late afternoon to call, but as she'd half expected, her uncle was still at the hospital, so she gave Angela the news.

"Milo will be glad to hear that," Angela said.

"Shouldn't he be home by now?"

"He's never home because we're going on vacation and he wants to make certain all the loose ends are tied up before he goes."

"Is that possible in his job?" Ellie asked.

"Of course not, but that doesn't keep him from trying."

"Where are you going on vacation?" Ellie asked, because it didn't sound as if they were coming to the ranch and she'd thought that was the plan.

"Two weeks in Belize, followed by a few days at home so that Milo can put his staff back in order and then we fly to Montana for two weeks at the ranch. I can't wait to see you. How are you feeling?" Angela asked, plowing right into the next topic.

"Good," Ellie answered. "I saw a doctor and I guess everything is progressing as it should."

"I heard from Mavis."

"And…?"

"Your life is your own."

"That's what she told me," Ellie said, feeling a twinge of disappointment that her mother hadn't at least said that she was looking forward to a grandchild. Of course she wasn't, but Ellie still had allowed herself to fantasize in the odd moment.

"So do you have any idea when you might get here?" she asked, needing to change the subject. "I'd like to have some food in the house, have the bedroom ready."

"Isn't there someone to do that?" Angela asked. "The woman that does the payroll?"

"I'll do it," Ellie answered.

"Beginning to get that nesting instinct?"

"It gives me something to do."

"Feel free to buy anything you need to make the place more comfortable. We'll reimburse."

"Careful, Auntie. I haven't been shopping in a while."

"Then go for it, dear. Carte blanche. On me."

Ellie hung up the phone and leaned her head back into the leather chair cushion. It wouldn't matter how much she spent, this place was never going to be comfortable for Angela. Maybe if it was closer to a larger city, with a golf course, shopping and four-star restaurants…but it wasn't. It was close to a small town with no golf course, two small restaurants and a seasonal drive-in. Angela was moving here for Milo and she was convinced that she could do it. After living here for a couple weeks, Ellie thought otherwise.

She set the phone on the side table and slipped on her shoes. Surely, once reality set in, Milo and Angela would work out a schedule where they stayed at the ranch only part of the year. Angela might survive that. Maybe Ellie could even come and visit them. Show her child some cows and horses.

See a hot cowboy when her life was more settled.

But why? It wasn't as if it would go anywhere.

Hiss was on the steps when she opened the front door and stepped out onto the porch. Sucking in a breath, she skirted around him. He sensed the movement and slithered off the step and into the grass, coming to a stop a few feet away, lying perfectly still as Ellie walked past. Lonnie was at the shop— she'd seen him go by a few minutes before calling Angela—and now would be a perfect time for him to catch the snake.

She crossed the gravel drive to the shop and walked through the open door, stopping just inside to allow her eyes to adjust.

"You need something?" Walt barked.

Startled, Ellie turned toward the direction of his voice to find him standing next to a workbench. "I was looking for Lonnie."

"He's out in the field."

"Hiss is out and I thought maybe Lonnie could catch him and move him."

Walt scrunched up his face into a disgusted expression and went back to digging through the tool chest in front of him.

"If someone doesn't move him, then Angela will probably call in an exterminator." Ellie was not exaggerating.

"What in the hell are people like that doing buying a ranch?" Walt muttered just loud enough for her to hear over the clattering of tools.

"Saving your ass, from what I gather," Ellie retorted, turning to leave before things got ugly and running smack into Ryan. His hands automatically caught her shoulders, steadying her. She glanced up at him, gave a small snort to cover the instant reaction of her body to his touch and walked on out of the shop.

"What just happened?" she heard him ask Walt before she got out of earshot. She was barely to the flagstones when she heard the crunch of boots on gravel behind her. She turned around before Ryan reached her.

"You don't need to act as peacemaker between me and Walt," she said before he could open his mouth.

A corner of his mouth tightened as if he was stopping himself from arguing the point. "Where's the snake?"

"In the grass by the stone steps." Ryan immediately started across the flagstones and she followed. "He *was* there," she said, pointing at the grass where she'd last seen the snake.

"Must be under the porch," Ryan said.

"Comforting thought," Ellie muttered, although truthfully she was no longer all that disturbed by the snake, which seemed to want as little to do with her as she did with it. She brushed the hair away from the side of her face as a cool gust of wind swept over them. "George stopped by."

Ryan stilled. "What did you think?"

"He seems very accomplished."

"How white were his teeth?"

"Pretty white," she said. There hadn't been much about him that hadn't been polished and perfect, from his impeccably styled hair to his lizard-skin boots.

"He was a few years ahead of me in school and kind of notorious for being nuts about his teeth."

"Being nuts about your teeth doesn't mean you don't know what you're doing."

"I never said George didn't know what he was

doing. I said that he liked to fire people because he can."

"If that's indeed the way he operates, then I'm aware and can make sure he's fair in his recommendations."

"Even with Walt?"

"Walt is his own worst enemy."

"I've heard that before."

"I'm probably the one that said it."

"I think you were." Ryan regarded her for a moment, a half smile on his face, but she could see that his thoughts were traveling along serious lines. "When's George showing up?"

"Early next week."

"I'll warn Walt," he said.

Ellie nodded, thinking *good luck,* but seeing no reason to say it out loud. They both knew what Ryan was dealing with.

"By the way," he continued, "I have a business appointment tomorrow, so I'll be gone for a couple hours. I'll make them up—"

"When you get back from the rodeo the following day?" Ellie smiled a little, trying to keep her attitude friendly yet businesslike. "Don't worry about it. I figure you put in more hours than we pay you for anyway."

"Thanks," he said.

"No problem," she replied. Because that wasn't the problem. Still being attracted to him was.

ABOUT THIRTY SECONDS into the lawyer meeting, Ryan understood perfectly why his father had used an attorney from Billings, many miles away. While lawyers could not break confidentiality, Charles was obviously not comfortable having a local guy knowing him for what he was. A man who refused responsibility for his son.

Ryan sat stiffly, hardly able to believe he was hearing what was being laid out in front of him. Charles wanted him to sign a confidentiality agreement saying he would never claim kinship, never challenge his estate after his death, in return for a lump-sum settlement now.

"Do you understand the agreement?"

"Pretty hard not to. My father wants to buy my silence."

The lawyer's expression didn't change. Apparently he was used to such things. Well, Ryan wasn't. "Is he offering the same agreement to my mother?"

"I can't discuss that."

"I can find out, you know."

"I can't discuss anything that doesn't pertain to the matter at hand."

Ryan leaned back in his chair, wanting very much to tell the dapper fellow across the table to tell his father to shove the deal up his ass. However, as satisfying as that would be, there was more than just himself to consider here. The sum Charles offered was generous, although not as generous as a third of the Montoya Ranch.

"Mr. Montoya did request that you discuss this matter with your mother prior to making a decision to act in *any* regard." The lawyer emphasized the last words in a way that made them sound like a subtle threat.

"Meaning to talk to her before I announce to the world what he's offered?"

"I believe that's exactly what he means."

Charles was taking a chance, but he'd lived for years wondering if Lydia or Ryan would break their silence, and apparently after their last encounter at the rodeo that had taken Matt out, Charles wanted some kind of a guarantee. "I want a copy of these papers."

"I can forward them to your lawyer for review."

"And if I don't have a lawyer?"

"I would think with a matter such as this, you may want to retain services. Have him contact me here." The lawyer pushed a card across the table to Ryan, who tucked it into his shirt pocket without looking at it.

"Mr. Madison?" Ryan met the lawyer's eyes then, saw a touch of empathy. "Seek legal counsel."

"Yeah." He'd already figured that this was nothing he wanted to deal with alone and, surprisingly, he felt very much like his father—he didn't want to do this through a local attorney. Of course, he could just say take a flying leap, walk out of this office and make Charles suffer.

He kind of liked that idea…except that it wouldn't be that easy. If he did things to Charles, it was quite possible that Charles would retaliate against his mother. An ugly can of worms. One he'd had no part in creating but now had to deal with.

"I'll be in contact," he said, getting to his feet. He didn't know if the attorney was done, but he was.

Ryan drove straight to his mom's beauty shop, only to find that she was elbow deep in foils, coloring Kadie Larson's hair.

"Do you have any time between appointments?" he asked. This wasn't a discussion to squeeze in between hair jobs, but he had to leave for a rodeo early the next morning and he wanted some answers before he left.

"I'm pretty booked this afternoon," she said as she folded the ends of a foil. But when she glanced over her shoulder at him and saw his expression, she added, "But why don't you come back at one?"

"See you then."

He left the shop, hearing the usual burst of noise as the door swung shut and the patrons said what they wouldn't say while he was there. He was glad he couldn't hear what it was, having hung around the shop enough as a kid to know that no subject was sacred. He pulled out his phone, called Francisco to tell him he'd be back later than expected and wouldn't be able to help move the bulls then crossed the street to his truck.

AFTER A MORNING of wearing her professional hat, making phone calls, touching base, contacting companies she'd once consulted with, Ellie needed a break. A long one. As soon as Walt had disappeared across the pasture on his four-wheeler, she'd spent time communing with the horses, who enjoyed having their ears and necks rubbed, then decided to tackle house-shopping phase one: the small stuff. She'd have to travel to Bozeman or Butte to properly shop, but the long distances to and from the major Montana cities were more than she wanted to take on at the moment, so she'd settled for exploring Glennan.

The town boasted the chain grocery store and a smaller market, a couple hardware stores, two restaurants, an antiques/thrift store that was closed and a few boutiques aimed more at tourists and travelers than locals.

She wandered in and out of the boutiques as she made her way down the main street, thinking that she might at least find something decorative. She found a couple colorful throws, some pillows and a set of dishes she thought Angela would like in the funky gift store next to the café. Then she wandered on, planning to return and make the purchase on her way back to the car. She went into the fishing shop just because she'd never been in one and was happily ignored by the two elderly gentlemen in deep conversation over a tray of fishing flies. She left the store, paused at the tiny art gallery, then moved on to the last store on the street: a children's store. Ellie hesitated before going inside.

She still felt like a stranger to this baby business.

She stopped inside the door and was overwhelmed by cuteness. There were bunnies and chicks, giraffes and hippos emblazoned over bibs, overalls, Onesies. Ruffled dresses and tiny motorcycle jackets.

Ellie reached out to touch the jacket, marveling at the details. It was a work of miniature art. But then so were the amazing smocked dresses. Boy or girl? Which was she having?

The doctor said they'd do an ultrasound the next visit. Try to see what's what and hear the heartbeat. An overwhelming idea. This child would be in the world before she acclimated herself to the idea of being its mother.

"Shopping for a gift?" the young woman behind the counter asked as she pulled pale pink thread through a piece of cloth stretched in a small embroidery hoop.

Ellie shook her head, pulling her hand away from the smocked dress. *Just coming to terms with reality.* She wandered over to the quilts, feeling ridiculously self-conscious even though the proprietress was busy with her embroidery and politely letting

Ellie shop. Feeling a bit dazed, Ellie left the boutique a few minutes later, calling a quick thank-you to the woman behind the counter. She stepped out into the sun and then headed for her car.

"Ellie."

Her heart skipped as she turned toward the direction of Ryan's voice. He was halfway across the street and coming toward her, looking way too good for her peace of mind. He also looked stressed—maybe even more stressed than he'd looked when he'd realized the calves were out. Not that the picture of him standing on the porch bare chested in his jeans was burned into her brain or anything. Or that she'd ever thought of him kissing her before they parted company.

"Hi," she said, for want of anything else to say. "I hadn't realized you were already in town." By seemingly mutual agreement she and Ryan had avoided each other over the past several days, but she was always aware of where he was. She'd assumed when she'd seen him take off with Walt earlier that morning in the ranch truck that his business was taking place later in the day.

"I am," he said simply. "But I'm heading back as soon as I talk to my mom."

"She's here in town?"

"Owns that shop over there," he said, pointing at the black-and-gold sign that read Crowning Glory. "She's in the middle of a foil job."

Ellie couldn't help smiling. "Familiar with beauty procedures?"

"Lived with them all of my life. Kids came to me to find out what was going on around town. Anyway, I was waiting in my truck for her to get done and saw you wander down the street."

And into the baby store. She shouldn't feel self-conscious, but she did. If she'd planned to get pregnant, she would have embraced baby shopping, but having it happen the way it had… She was uncomfortable embracing it—at least publicly.

"I needed to get out of the house," she said.

"Cabin fever?"

"Depressing job search. Tight market. A lot of 'I'll let you know if I hear of something' type of stuff."

"I can see where you'd want to take a break from that." He looked down at his boots for a moment, then back up at her. "You busy tomorrow?"

The question startled her. "No," she said cautiously.

"Want to go to a rodeo?"

A day alone with Ryan?

Her first instinct was to say no, to protect herself, but the word died on her lips as she took in his taut expression, the tense lines around his eyes.

Something's happened to him. Something bad. She'd have to be thickheaded to not pick up on it.

"I've…never been," she said, even though it wasn't an answer.

He gave a too-casual shrug. "I wouldn't mind some company on the drive and I figured that you might like to get off the ranch for a while."

"Company?" she echoed.

"Yeah," he said, his mouth tightening an iota. "Just…company."

"When would we leave and when would we get back?"

"Early tomorrow morning and we'd get back tomorrow night."

For a moment she studied his face, trying to pinpoint what it was that made her feel so strongly that he was dealing with something other than waiting to talk to his mother. The breeze blew her hair across her cheek and she pushed it back.

"All right," she said quietly. "I'll go to the rodeo."

The corners of his mouth lifted slightly, almost self-consciously, before he said, "Can you be ready to go at four-thirty?"

"In the morning?" Again she brushed back the hair that drifted across her face. She really needed to stop clipping it up and go with the unprofessional ponytail. "If I sleep in my clothes I ought to be able to make it."

"Great." He lifted his chin, looking over the top of her head at his mother's shop. "Her client just came out. I'd better get over there if I'm going to catch her." He looked down at Ellie and she could see from his expression that he needed to get over to that shop. Now. "See you at four-thirty?"

She hoped. "I'll meet you at the truck…but feel free to knock if I don't show." She rubbed a casual hand over the side of her neck, remembering the last time he'd gotten her up with a knock. "I'll, uh, take extra care with my buttons if you do have to get me out of bed."

"And I'll tell you if you don't," he promised wryly, his mood a touch lighter than when he'd flagged her down. "See you then."

LYDIA WAS WAITING for Ryan at her chair. "Is this a backroom talk?"

"Of the highest order," he said. His mother's face instantly sobered and then she turned to lead the way down the narrow hall to the most private room in the place—her minuscule office.

Ryan closed the door after them and got right to the matter at hand. "Mom, has Montoya offered you some kind of deal?" Lydia's chin went up and he saw color stain the tops of her cheekbones.

"Why?"

"Because he offered me a deal."

"Take it," she said.

"You don't know what it is."

Lydia raised her eyebrows an iota. "I imagine it's a lot of money."

"Yeah."

"That's money he owes you. Take it."

"He threatened you a couple weeks ago, didn't he?"

"He thought I was the reason Matt knew about you." She gave a soft, disgusted snort. "And that really aggravated me. I spent all those years being quiet because I didn't want to hurt people. His wife. His other son. They were innocent." She rubbed her fingertips across her forehead as if erasing a memory. "And that's how he rewarded me. Threats. He said he'd ruin my business if I talked."

Ryan felt his blood pressure rise, but he remained silent.

"As if he could," Lydia said with another snort. "No one does a weave in this town like I do." She tilted her head as she regarded her son. "But I'd had it. I called him a few weeks ago, told him that if he paid the child support he owed you growing up, he'd never have to worry about either of us saying anything."

"You're blackmailing him?"

Anger flared in her eyes. "I wish I was. That would be fun, but my conscience won't let me. The confidentiality agreement makes it all nice and legal. We keep quiet, you get what he owes you." Lydia's shoulders drooped. "I should have done it a long time ago, but I didn't want to share you. I was half-afraid that if I pushed him, he'd take you away just to show me who's boss. I was young and dumb and intimidated."

Ryan leaned his palms on the desk. "Did you ever think about what might happen if I didn't want to sign the agreement, Mom?"

Lydia blinked at him. "Are you ever going to tell anyone he's your father?"

"I seriously doubt it." He had nothing to gain by hurting Charles's wife.

"Then sign and get what's coming to you. What you should have had all along."

Ryan pushed off the desk. "I need time to think," he said.

"I figured you would," Lydia said quietly. "And since I didn't raise no fool, I assume you're going to make the right decision."

CHAPTER TWELVE

ELLIE WALKED OUT of the house at exactly 4:25 a.m., yawning as she stepped into the cold Montana morning. Her hair was in a low ponytail instead of a French twist, her shirt fully buttoned. She had a thermos of tea and a pocketful of granola bars. Ready to roll and nervous as hell.

She wasn't even sure why she was so nervous, but it had to do with Ryan. With the unknown. After kissing her that night, he'd backed off as promised, but she still felt uneasy. Something to do with a gut-level attraction, no doubt—and the fact that part of her couldn't help thinking how much she wished she'd met him before she'd hooked up with Nick… which was kind of dumb. If she'd met Ryan before, she wouldn't have hung around the ranch long enough to get to know him to any great lengths. She would have found him attractive, maybe even slept with him and then gone back to her own world.

She was *still* going back to her own world. The ranch was a good hideaway, but it held nothing for her in the long run.

The trailer was hooked to the truck, which was

idling in front of the barn, the scent of diesel exhaust heavy in the damp early-morning air. The lights went out in Ryan's house as she stepped off the flag-stones onto the gravel drive, and a few seconds later he came out carrying a cooler. He looked her over, then said, "You might want a more substantial coat."

Ellie set the thermos on the front seat and headed back to the house. By the time she came back out, Ryan had turned the truck and trailer around and was waiting at the end of the walk.

"Have you ever been to a rodeo?" he asked after she'd stowed her coat and fastened the seat belt.

She shook her head. "Last night I watched some YouTube videos to get an idea as to what to expect, however, the rules escape me."

He smiled a little. "I can explain a few things."

"That'd be nice," Ellie replied, without looking at him. The sun hadn't yet topped the mountains and the rolling meadows were still a dark bluish-gray. They drove through the gate the calves had escaped through, down the road, past Walt's place, past the Garcias'. Ellie sat stiffly in her seat, her head turned slightly away from Ryan as she stared at the scenery, telling herself it was just a two-hundred-mile drive followed by a day at the rodeo.

"Relax," Ryan said.

"I'm relaxed," Ellie replied, her clipped tone belying her words. She let out a breath. "All right. I'm nervous."

"It's just me. What's to be nervous about?"

You. "I'm just kind of stressed," she said, glad that she had a truthful reason for being tense—a reason besides her overwhelming awareness of him. "I had my first OB appointment, and the job search turned up practically no leads."

Ryan kept his profile to her, but she could see his frown. "Did you apply for anything?"

"Several things." Long shots every one. Most of the companies she had connections with were reducing forces, not hiring.

He nodded, his eyes still fixed on the road. "How long do you think it'll take to hear?"

"There's no telling. It's not the best market."

Ryan nodded, frowning slightly as he focused on the road. He was listening to her, but he was also deeply preoccupied.

So what's up with you? She wanted very much to ask the question, to find out what had put that troubled expression on his face when he'd asked her to come with him yesterday, giving her the impression that he didn't think he'd be able to stand his own company.

Instinct told her that now was not the time. Ryan was holding tight to whatever it was that was eating at him and she wouldn't pry. It was his business… just as her problems were hers. He'd asked her along for company, so the least she could do was be decent company.

"Explain to me some things about the rodeo," she finally said, choosing the safest subject she could think of. She pulled out her phone and settled deeper in her seat as she turned it on to see if she could stream any of the video that had made little sense to her the night before. "I'll ask questions and you tell me what you know."

He glanced over at her and a second later a half smile formed on his lips. "Sure. Fire away."

RYAN PULLED HIS trailer into a space at the edge of a field filled with trucks, horse trailers, horses and cowboys. Lots and lots of cowboys—none of them as good-looking, or probably as patient, as the man who'd just spent most of the long drive going over the various events with her while she looked up video on her phone when the connection was available.

She opened the door, the smell of damp earth, crushed grass and fresh horse manure hitting her nostrils as she stepped out into the crisp air. Instantly she thought of the early-morning dressage lessons at boarding school. She hadn't been as nuts about horses as Kate had been, but she'd grown fond of her mount and had enjoyed the discipline of dressage. Horses simply hadn't been part of her big plan.

"Breakfast is that way," Ryan said, pointing toward a food truck. "I'd go with you, but I have to check in."

"Want anything?"

"No. I'll meet you back here in ten or fifteen minutes."

Ryan got back to the trailer at about the same time Ellie returned with the coffee and doughnuts. Many doughnuts.

"The line was brutal," she said, setting her foam cup on the truck's running board.

"Are you sure you got enough to eat?" he asked with a half smile, nodding at the bulging white bag she carried.

"I'm good for an hour or two." What could she say? She liked doughnuts and living at the ranch had not allowed her to indulge herself. And she was eating for two. "I'll share."

"That's all right, but thanks." She stepped back as Ryan opened the rear trailer door and led his big black horse out. The animal stopped as soon as all four of his feet were on the ground, raised his head high and let out a long whinny that flared his nostrils and made his entire body vibrate. An answering whinny soon came back.

"He has lots of buddies he sees on weekends," Ryan explained as he tied the horse to the trailer.

"I didn't know horses made friends."

"Herd animals," Ryan said. "They hate to be alone."

"You have a lot of horses. How do you decide which one to bring?"

"PJ here is my rodeo horse. Most of the other horses are for practice."

"Don't you have to practice on him, too?" Ellie asked.

"Only enough to keep him tuned up. I can't afford for him to go sore or lame on me." Ryan ran a hand over the horse's neck, smiling a little as he said, "He likes what he does and I want to keep it that way."

"Makes sense. The only time I've hated my job was when I had to do the same thing too often."

"And the only time I've hated mine is when it's forty below and I have to feed. But I like it again once I get inside."

"I don't know that I'd do well with forty below."

"Nobody does well at those temps…except maybe Walt. He seems to be impervious to cold."

Somehow Ellie wasn't surprised.

Ryan tied the gelding to the trailer and Ellie perched on the trailer fender, sipping coffee as she watched him first brush then saddle his horse, his movements quick and automatic. Cowboys rode by, many of them nodding at him as they passed. Ryan nodded back and Ellie reflected on the fact that not many words were exchanged, but there was a sense of camaraderie one didn't normally find in her line of work.

"I have to warm up," Ryan said after stowing the brushes. "I rope in the last section, and then I can join you, but by that time the rodeo will be almost over." He turned toward the rapidly filling stands and scanned the crowd with a slight frown. "I was hoping to find somebody you could sit with."

"I'd rather sit alone," Ellie said as she slid off the fender. She wasn't in the mood for chitchat. She wanted to watch Ryan do his thing, to figure out the rodeo by herself.

"You sure?" He seemed surprised that she'd prefer to watch without company.

"I do a lot of things alone." She'd thought that was fairly obvious.

"But do you like it that way?" he asked. "Alone?"

Ellie frowned at the unexpected question. "I'm okay with it," she said, although truthfully sometimes she wasn't so okay with it.

"If you're sure." Ryan mounted the black gelding as he spoke. He gathered the reins, then frowned as something behind her caught his attention. Ellie looked over her shoulder to follow his gaze, which was fixed on a couple standing near a trailer fifty feet away. The man was balanced on crutches, his leg in a blue cast that extended up to his hip. The woman, who was busily grooming a small bay horse, wore a dazzling pink-sequined shirt, making Ellie wonder if it was the woman or the man that had Ryan staring so intently.

"Someone you know?" she asked.

"You could say that," Ryan said, tearing his gaze away. "You asked about Matt Montoya. That's him."

Ellie brushed the hair back from her face. "No longer your fiercest competitor, I see."

"Not in the traditional sense," Ryan agreed. He smiled tightly. "I'll catch up to you later. In the stands."

"All right." Ellie tugged up the zipper of her sweatshirt against the breeze. "Good luck."

"Thanks." He trotted away and Ellie glanced back at the couple, noting from their body language that they were just that. A couple. And truth be told, even though it wasn't in her future, Ellie felt a twinge of jealousy.

RYAN TROTTED PJ to the warm-up area, barely aware of his surroundings. Matt's girlfriend was wearing a mounted-drill-team outfit, so that was probably why his brother was there. And he'd be okay with that if he hadn't seen the Montoya Ranch pickup driving into the parking lot a few vehicles ahead of him when he'd turned off the highway.

It might not be his father. One of his ranch hands could have been driving the rig. It didn't mean that Matt and Charles were meeting, plotting against him...although he could see where Matt would be in favor of Ryan being bought off. The payoff wasn't worth what a third of the Montoya Ranch might be worth if he could challenge the will. And Matt was superprotective of his mother. Yeah. No doubt he was fully in favor of Ryan signing away all rights.

Damn.

Had he known he was going to run into these ass-holes, he wouldn't have brought Ellie to the rodeo. But he had, and he was going to have to muscle through. Roping hadn't felt all that important to him of late, what with worrying about Walt's future and lawyers and shit like that, but today...today he felt his focus coming back. There was no way his father and brother were going to steal this win away from him.

"Hey, Madison." Ryan glanced over at Tommy Walking Dog, who had urged his horse up to canter beside PJ as they circled the arena. "Buy me another coffee this morning? Seems to give me good luck when you do that."

"You're going to need more than luck today," Ryan muttered.

Tommy laughed. "If you say so."

"I know so."

RYAN, AS IT turned out, didn't need the luck Ellie had wished him. When the last section of roping began, just after the second section of saddle bronc, he came blazing out of the box on his black horse and to Ellie's untrained eye, it appeared as if he was off his horse and running toward the calf almost before he'd finished throwing the rope. He tossed the animal onto the ground and after a few sweeps of his hands, three legs of the calf were tied and Ryan stood, hands in the air.

"Shee-it!" the guy seated in front of her in the crowded stands said. Ellie silently echoed his sentiments. So this was why Ryan practiced so much. To dominate. And somehow, seeing him do what he did so well made him seem even sexier.

Just what she needed.

Ellie shoved the thoughts aside as she stood and made her way through the crowd to the steps. By the time she approached the trailer, he was already there tying his horse. PJ's chest was covered with glistening sweat, but Ryan was the picture of cool detachment. There was no air of victory about him, even though Ellie was certain he was going to win this event. None of the cowboys that had gone before him had even come close to his time. He patted the black gelding's neck and started to unsaddle him, his expression oddly distant, as if he was going over things in his mind, and Ellie didn't think it was roping.

"Hey," she said softly when he didn't seem to realize she was there. His gray gaze snapped up, met hers, making her breath catch with its intensity.

"You're missing the rodeo."

"I saw the best part," she said.

Ryan smiled but it didn't reach his eyes. Didn't come close. If anything he looked even more stressed than he'd been the day before.

"You want to talk about it?" she asked.

"What?" he asked on a note of surprise, dragging the bridle off the gelding's head, expertly catching the bit with one hand as it slipped out of the horse's mouth. Ellie barely refrained from rolling her eyes. Why did guys always think they were so inscrutable?

"Whatever's on your mind?" He frowned more deeply and she abandoned her mission. "Never mind." She wasn't going to push. She didn't like it when people did it to her and she wasn't going to do it to him.

RYAN REGARDED ELLIE for a long moment before buckling the halter and tying PJ to the trailer. A slight frown pulled her eyebrows together, as if she was seriously trying to read his mind, and maybe she was. He hadn't realized he'd been so transparent. He'd figured she'd be busy with her own problems and wouldn't notice that he wasn't quite himself that day. Hell, he'd hoped having her along would make him feel more like himself.

Ryan leaned his shoulder against the trailer. What could he say after she'd shared her situation?

Nothing. He hoped she could understand that.

"Okay, I do have a few things on my mind, but the truth is…there are confidences involved." He hated answering like that, but didn't know what else he could say. "I really can't talk about it."

Ellie considered his answer for a moment, her green eyes narrowing slightly. "So you asked me to come along with you as a distraction from…whatever?"

Ryan let out a soft snort. "Sounds kind of crummy put that way."

"I don't think so. In fact, I totally understand."

He smiled slowly, and for the first time all day, it felt genuine. And a moment later Ellie smiled back. They hadn't shared one damned confidence, but somehow it felt as if they had. And he was grateful that she could let the matter alone.

"You want to grab something to eat before we head home?" he asked. "There's a steakhouse at the edge of town where we can grab a late lunch. Or we could stay for the rest of the rodeo."

"Let's get out of here." He wanted to leave and she saw no reason to stay. But she really, really wanted to know what was eating at him…. She hoped it wasn't a certain old man back at the ranch, because she had a very bad feeling about his future.

WHILE THEY WERE at the restaurant, Ryan was able to do the impossible and push his father and his brother to the back of his mind and focus on Ellie.

"You're kidding," she said, grimacing at the menu after he'd explained that Rocky Mountain oysters were not freshwater shellfish. "Testicles?"

"An acquired taste," he said.

"Do *you* like them?"

He considered the question and then said, "I don't think I'll answer that."

"You *do* like them," she said, pointing her finger at him. "What do they taste like?"

"Chicken?" he said, and Ellie laughed. "Order them. Find out."

"I don't think so," she said primly as the server approached. She smiled up at the kid, dressed in Wrangler jeans and a checked shirt. "What do you recommend?"

The kid stared at Ellie for a moment, seemingly lost in her rather dazzling smile...as was Ryan. "Uh..." Ryan knew it was coming, had experienced the phenomenon himself, and sure enough, the kid's voice broke as he answered. "The, uh, chicken-fry steak is really good and so is the, uh, pork-chop sandwich."

Ellie raised her eyebrows at Ryan over the menu. "I'll have the chicken fry. Half portion."

"You can take the rest home," Ryan pointed out.

"Full portion," she amended. "With salad. Blue cheese dressing."

The kid wrote furiously, apparently spelling out each word in its entirety. "And for you, sir?"

Rocky Mountain oysters? Ellie mouthed silently.

Ryan smirked at her before saying, "I'll have the same as the lady."

"I don't know about you Westerners," she said as the kid walked away. "Testicles on the menu?"

"No worse than heart, liver or brains. The organ meats have their own special charm."

"If you say so." Ellie grimaced before she smiled at him again.

Ryan noticed that since arriving in Montana, she'd developed a few freckles across her nose, making him wonder how much time she'd spent indoors in her old life...the life she was going back to.

"Speaking of charm, when is our boy George showing up?" he asked.

"Within a week. His contract got extended at his previous job."

"Once he got extended for a year, I hear."

Ellie's eyebrows rose. "Really? That must have been lucrative."

Ryan lifted his beer. "George is industrious...and he likes to fire people."

"So you've said."

Ryan debated about continuing, then figured he had to do what he could when he could. "I'm worried about Walt. It would kill him to get fired, and you could do something about that."

The look that crossed Ellie's face told him that she'd expected him to mention Walt once George's name came up. So she'd been thinking about the old man, too. And apparently not in a hopeful way, judging from her expression. She shook her head. "I can't. And neither can you. It's up to Walt."

"He's an old man. All he wants to do is to die on his property someday."

"It's not his property, Ryan."

His mouth tightened. There was no logical argument he could make, but the fact was that in Walt's mind it was still his and it would destroy him to have to leave.

"Is there any chance you can be merciful to an old man?"

"It has nothing to do with mercy, Ryan. It has to do with reality."

Ryan set his beer down. *Way to destroy a mood, Madison...* Not that the mood was important. It wasn't as though it was going anywhere. He met Ellie's eyes and she smiled that cool smile that told him fun and games were over. She was a woman who'd made decisions about hiring and firing for a living—she wasn't one to be swayed by sentiment, but that didn't mean he wasn't going to try.

"I really care about Walt."

"I know, Ryan."

And that was that. Subject closed. The server came and plopped salads down in front of them. Ellie picked up her fork, met Ryan's eyes then put her fork down again. "I won't make promises I can't keep," she said. "It's not something I do."

Ryan took in a long breath, then exhaled slowly. "And I guess I can't ask you to."

DAMNED WALT. EVEN when he wasn't there he managed to inject surliness into the moment. But maybe it was for the best. Maybe she'd been enjoying her time with Ryan just a little too much.

No, she'd definitely been enjoying it too much.

They solemnly finished the dinner that had started out so well talking about the rodeo and Ellie's garden. Safe topics. Boring topics. Good old Walt. If anyone was going to keep her grounded in reality, it was that old coot.

After dinner they walked silently out to the truck. Ellie put her take-home box in the cooler, then a few minutes later Ryan put the truck in gear and pulled out of the parking lot onto the highway that led back to the ranch in a two-hundred-mile straight shot. They rode for long moments in heavy silence and Ellie wondered if it was better to stay locked in her own thoughts or to make some kind of mindless conversation. It was Ryan, though, who broke the silence.

"What happens if you can't find a job in your field?"

"Good question," Ellie murmured, thinking this was her punishment for holding the line with Walt.

"Do you have geographical considerations?"

"Excuse me?"

"Will the father be involved with your child?"

Ellie laughed before she could stop herself. "Hardly." When he looked over at her, she said, "He's married." Ryan's expression instantly shuttered and he turned his eyes back to the road. "That was a quick judgment," she murmured.

"I'm not judging you."

"Yeah. I think you are, but it's my fault for dropping the information like that. Although I don't know how to pretty it up."

"Did you know he was married?" Ryan asked after several silent miles.

The sudden question surprised her, as if he was looking for a way to exonerate her from whatever judgment he'd made. "Would that matter?"

"No."

"No, as in there's no excuse for getting involved with a married man?"

"No, as in I understand that things like this happen."

"Do you?" she asked in a disbelieving voice.

He glanced over to meet her eyes and she could see how very serious he was when he said, "Yeah. I do. Better than you might think."

"Has it happened to you?" she asked.

"Not to me, personally."

Ellie let out a sigh and let her head fall back against the headrest. "He wasn't married at the time. He was engaged and got married two weeks later. We lived in different cities. I didn't know about his fiancée."

"Sounds like a stellar kind of guy."

"He had a few positive traits," Ellie said. If he hadn't, she wouldn't have slept with him, but the negatives far outweighed the positives now. "And I didn't do due diligence." She looked out the window. She would never make that mistake again.

ELLIE FEEL ASLEEP about fifty miles from home. There hadn't been much to say after the explanation of her situation—it didn't seem like the time to shift awkwardly into chitchat about the rodeo or the scenery.

When he'd asked her to come along with him yesterday, his hope had been that they could distract one another. Well, it'd worked. He was now distracted, wondering what kind of an asshole would sleep with a woman while engaged. No, wait. He knew the answer to that because he was closely related to a guy like that.

Did the jerk's bride know that he'd knocked up another woman? Ryan's hunch was no. Which left Ellie in the same position as his mother—raising the kid alone. Except that Ellie had more financial resources than his mother had had, and he sincerely hoped that she had demanded child support from the father.

Ryan's fingers tightened on the wheel and he made an effort to relax them. He'd bet that Charles had never once thought that lack of paying child support would come back to bite him in the ass as it was now, thanks to Lydia having had enough. Maybe he should take the deal…except it would kill him to take money from the Montoyas. And again he wondered if his brother was somehow involved, egging Charles on, making certain that he would receive his full inheritance.

Ellie stirred in her sleep, the coat she'd draped over herself slipping into the seat beside her. Ryan automatically reached over and pulled it back over her. The gut-level attraction he felt toward her was subtly shifting into protective mode now that he knew her circumstances, which was a good thing… if he could keep it there.

She was sexy. She was off-limits.

She was probably going to fire Walt.

ELLIE WAS AWAKENED the next morning by the land-line ringing in the living room. She glanced at the clock and groaned. Eight o'clock. After lying awake last night for most of the night, fighting regrets while telling herself she'd done the right thing, all she needed was a blasted phone call a few hours after she'd fallen asleep.

She cleared her voice, picked up the phone, said hello.

"Hello?" The voice was deep, pleasant, masculine. "George Monroe here. I wanted to let you know

I'm available to start work immediately. I'd like to discuss preliminaries with you today after I set up, then start my observations day after tomorrow, if that can be arranged."

"Set up?"

"I bring my own mobile home to the ranches. That way I have a base to operate from without putting out the owner."

"Then I guess I'll see you later today, Mr. Monroe."

"George."

"George. See you then."

Ellie hung up and then ran a hand through her hair as she wondered how this evaluation process was going to play out. If Walt was fired, then Ryan was going, too, and regardless of what was happening between them, Ellie hated to think of him leaving the place he'd put so much into. He was qualified and adaptable. Francisco was staying no matter what. He did his job well and he had an attitude of quiet professionalism that Angela would respect. Ellie was personally going to see to it that he still had a job when George was done. But Walt... He was his own worst enemy. He was also providing quite a decent—and perhaps necessary—block between her and Ryan, who'd barely said a word to her after she'd confessed the paternity of her child. He said he wasn't judging her, but she definitely felt judged.

All for the best, really.

George arrived two hours after his call, pulling a sleek travel trailer behind his shiny black dual-wheeled pickup truck. He pulled to a stop in front of the house, where Ellie met him, and indicated with an engaging smile that he thought the best place for his trailer was in the shade of the bunkhouse. Ellie agreed, although she'd actually have preferred to not have him so close to the main house. It was interesting how living on the ranch for only a matter of weeks had changed her perspective on privacy. Just having him here gave her the uncomfortable feeling that her space had been invaded.

As George set up, Ellie retreated to the privacy of the backyard where she watered her flowers and pulled the newly sprouted weeds for nearly an hour as she convinced herself that she was being unfair to Milo's consultant, swayed by Ryan's obvious distaste for the man. Okay, so his teeth were overly white, but even Ryan had admitted that the guy knew his stuff, he just had a tendency to make sweeping changes. She'd do what she could to counteract that tendency. Being in a field that was loaded with specialists, Milo had high regard for experts, so George's recommendations might ultimately trump hers, but Ellie could be persuasive, so hopefully—

"Hello?"

Ellie's head jerked up at the sound of George's

voice. He stood on the other side of the garden gate, smiling at her. "All set up," he said. "I was wondering if you might have a few minutes for some preliminaries. I have iced tea if you'd like to sit in the shade while we talk."

Ellie considered his invitation for a moment as she gathered her gloves in one hand, thinking it was odd that she had the instant impression that he was the one in command here—or at least the one who thought he was in command. She met his eyes, smiling slightly as she said, "I'd like to clean up first. Shall we meet in the main house, say in half an hour?"

George's expression remained congenial, but Ellie sensed a shift in his demeanor as he processed her response. "Certainly," he said. "See you then."

Ellie stayed where she was, damp gloves in hand, as George turned and made his way back down the path leading to the drive, wondering if she'd misread him or if charismatic George liked to run the show. It probably wouldn't take long for her to get a true read.

Almost exactly half an hour later, George knocked on the front door and Ellie let him in, smiling coolly at him before closing the door. She waved at the kitchen table and he walked past her, setting his laptop on the table.

"I just got off the phone with your uncle," he said.

"I'm surprised you caught up with him," Ellie said mildly. Usually, Angela confiscated his phone when they went on vacation.

"It wasn't easy," he admitted. "But I thought it best to touch base with him before starting."

So George was making it clear she wasn't his boss. "I see. Well, what did you two decide?"

George leaned back slightly in his chair, more comfortable now that she was following his lead. "I have to meet with a former client tomorrow in Butte, and then I officially start my evaluation here day after tomorrow. Milo wants me to meet with you and keep you updated. If you have any concerns, I can address them and I can make you aware of any issues that crop up."

"That sounds reasonable," Ellie agreed.

George pressed some keys on his laptop, pushing the machine away from him so that Ellie had a clear view of the screen. "These are the areas I'll be evaluating after doing my general observations the first couple days…"

He went on to describe how he would tackle each area, and Ellie had to admit that his plan seemed efficient and logical as he moved from the general to the specific in the areas of livestock and pasture management, irrigation, infrastructure and business operations.

"The first day will just be general observations,

then I'll meet with you and we can discuss which aspects deserve the most attention during the time I'll be here."

"How long does it usually take to do an evaluation?"

"I've done everything from two weeks to a year."

"A year?" Ryan had said something about that.

"I moved onto the property and managed it until I could hire and train a new manager and crew who could run the place right." George smiled reminiscently. "I had to basically tear everything down and build it again from scratch. The breeding program, the haying, the pastures and forage. Hell of an undertaking."

"Mmm," Ellie said politely.

"It's still doing well. The owners were the ones that recommended me to the Kenyons, who in turn recommended me to your uncle."

"Hopefully this ranch won't need such a thorough overhaul," Ellie murmured.

"Hopefully," George agreed, closing up his laptop. "Time will tell. I have to tell you, though, usually properties with older managers need a lot of rehabilitation."

"Shouldn't the older managers have more experience?"

"In methods that are outdated and often ineffective. The problem is that they don't want to change, and if that's the case, then they are detrimental to the property."

"Again, I hope that's not the case here," Ellie said, knowing full well it was.

"And again, time will tell," George said.

CHAPTER THIRTEEN

RYAN GOT BACK from repairing the irrigation in the north hayfield, wet, dirty and in dire need of a beer, only to find a fifth-wheel camp trailer with a pop out parked next to the bunkhouse. George Monroe sat in a chair outside, tapping away on his laptop.

He set the laptop aside on the wooden folding table next to him—the one with the tall glass of iced tea on it—and got to his feet. "Ryan. Good to see you." He flashed a lot of teeth as he shook Ryan's hand. "I see that you're doing well in the roping this year. Looks like you have a trip to Vegas in your future."

"I hope so," Ryan said, although frankly he was beginning to care less and less about it.

George gestured toward the computer. "I'm jotting down some preliminary notes today, going over the personnel information before I meet with Ellie again."

"Yeah?" Funny thing, but even though he'd come to the conclusion that it would be best for both he and Ellie if he kept a healthy distance, he didn't like hearing George call her by her first name. Didn't like it one bit; didn't like George one bit.

"So here's the plan," the king of consultants said congenially. "I want to go out with you guys for several days, watch operations and then we'll have a sit-down and discuss what I've observed, your perspectives and possible changes."

"All right." Possible changes such as changing out the entire crew if the Vineyard was anything to judge by.

"You seem hesitant," George said, a slight frown marring his good-natured expression.

"I'm just naturally cautious," Ryan said.

"If you're doing your job well, you have nothing to be cautious about."

That wasn't what he'd heard, but he wasn't going to challenge the guy. Walt would do that. Ryan had already started looking for small parcels of land nearby that Walt could purchase, but there was little that wasn't close to the road and the traffic Walt hated so much, yet in Walt's price range. And then there was the matter of convincing Walt that he wasn't going to die on this land. The last time he'd tentatively brought up the matter, over beer a few days ago, Walt had shut down, refused to speak.

Oh, yeah. The next weeks were going to be fun.

"I think you'll be satisfied with the jobs we do."

George smiled, a fake smile not unlike the one that Ellie had given him upon first arrival. Although

George's seemed to hold a hint of quiet malice, reminding Ryan of his mother's assessment of the man—George was a bully.

Half an hour later Ryan was sitting at Walt's table, on the receiving end of the older man's fierce glare. There'd been a time when Walt didn't glare. He'd been stern, but not angry.

"I will jump through hoops for this guy, but don't think it's not pissing me off."

"I wouldn't think that for a minute," Ryan assured him, and then he leaned forward, got serious. "You've alienated Ellie and you can't afford to do that with George. Hell, you couldn't afford to do it with Ellie."

"If she can't handle straight talk—"

"What? She can fire you?"

Strong emotion played over Walt's face and Ryan could see that he still stubbornly clung to the idea that no one knew the ranch like him and no one was qualified to run it but him. He'd lost the place due to a mix of bad circumstances, but he saw those now as things that had been beyond his control—and in some ways he was correct. That didn't change the fact that Ellie—and probably George—could fire him in a heartbeat.

"I can't stand the idea of justifying my job to that guy," Walt grumbled, "but I'll do it. At least he knows something…unlike the princess."

"Don't underestimate her," Ryan said smoothly.

Walt cocked an eyebrow at him, studying him as if ascertaining whether or not he'd gone to the dark side. "No," he finally said. "Maybe I shouldn't."

WALT MADE MORE noise than necessary early in the morning—particularly when Ryan was at a rodeo, which he was today. Thanks to his revving of the four-wheeler, she was wide-awake and could get an early start on the day. Ellie walked to the window just as Walt, who must have finally figured out he'd annoyed her enough, put the ATV into gear and started across the pasture. The sound of the engine faded and Ellie went to put on the kettle.

Blessed peace.

Walt was gone. George was gone, off meeting with his former client in Butte. Of the two, she'd rather have Walt there revving his motor. She found it unsettling having George on the property, even though he'd been there less than twenty-four hours, which was probably exactly how Walt felt about her. Ellie gave a small snort—hard to believe, but she and Walt had something in common. They were both territorial.

Ellie had never thought of herself as being that way; if anything, she'd always felt like a drifter, because her home had never felt like home. She hadn't lived there for more than a few months at a time during middle school and high school and when she was there, it felt temporary because she knew she'd be leaving again soon. But she was definitely feeling territorial about the ranch. Maybe she could blame some pregnancy nesting instinct. Or maybe she was simply feeling protective toward the crew.

The phone rang in the late afternoon while Ellie was working some horse manure into the flower beds, following the directions from a gardening forum. Her flowers were doing well, but were nowhere near Angela standards. Well, Angela would either have to make do or hire a professional.

Ellie wiped her hands on her jeans as she crossed the back patio, wondering if it was George touching base. Or—speak of the devil—Angela. It turned out to be Kate, checking up on her.

"Are you dying of boredom out there in the wilderness?" she asked.

"I'm doing better, but it was touch and go for the first few weeks," Ellie replied with a smile, going to sit on a leather chair.

"I envy you being there," Kate said. "The location, not the circumstances that sent you there," she clarified.

Kate always had liked the outdoors. "Someday you'll have to visit," Ellie said.

"Are you *staying* there?" Kate asked, horrified.

"I'm looking for a job," she said simply. "I know it might take a while and I know I'm not going to get any smaller as time goes by, but I have to give it a shot."

"I'm glad to hear that."

"Me, too. I just…needed some time to accept the reality of my situation. Work through some issues. I think I'm there and now I know what I have to do."

"You are sounding more like yourself…. Is there anything I can do to help?"

"Keep your ears open."

"You know I will."

Ellie hung up a few minutes later and headed out to the garden, where she continued to work outside until the sun went behind the mountains and the air grew chilly. If she went back to apartment life, which was a given until she'd reestablished a career, she wouldn't have much opportunity to get her hands dirty, and she was going to indulge while she had the chance.

Ellie snapped on the lights as she walked into the house, then went to the kitchen to dig out something frozen to eat. George's truck was still gone…and Walt's was still there.

Ellie frowned. It was late for Walt to still be there.

Probably just doing ranch stuff she was unfamiliar with. The chores changed with the days and the seasons. But as it began to grown darker, Ellie's concern also grew. The guy was a total jerk toward her, but he was getting up in years and Ryan cared for him.

Ellie, knowing how quickly it could change from cool to freezing, pulled on a sweatshirt and a coat, then headed out the door. One of the barn cats trotted out from the tall grass, then crossed over to meet Ellie, who bent to stroke his orange-striped back before walking on to the pasture gate and staring off across the field in the direction that Walt had disappeared.

She had a bad feeling about this. Pulling her cell phone out of her pocket, she dialed Francisco and got no answer. Okay. She was on her own.

Ellie headed around the barn to the ranch truck and, as she'd hoped, the keys were dangling from the ignition. She hated doing this, hated to think of what a hearty laugh Walt was going to get when he caught her out looking for him, but on the other hand, what if he was in trouble?

Because of the recent rain it was easy to follow the four-wheeler tracks and Ellie drove along slowly, losing the tracks every now and then, only to pick them up a little farther on. She drove past the pond where she and Ryan had rescued the goose, past the place where he'd dumped the tank on the second-to-last day they'd worked together. Shortly after that she lost the tracks.

Had he turned off somewhere? Left the property?

Ellie reversed the truck and returned to the stock tanks where the last vestiges of ATV tracks were clear. She turned off the truck and got out, standing in the growing darkness, listening. Nothing.

"Walt?" In the distance she heard a cow. "Walt!"

Still nothing.

Frustrated, she got into the truck and was about to put it into gear when she saw movement in the brush across the meadow. She popped on the headlights and a man put his arm up in front of his face to ward off the glare.

Walt. On foot, his dogs trailing behind him.

Ellie turned the lights off and got out of the vehicle, wondering if Walt was going to be stubborn and walk on past her. The thought probably crossed his mind, but as he got closer she could see that he was limping badly enough that even he had to see the benefit of being driven home.

But it had to be killing him.

He walked straight to the passenger side of the vehicle and got in, groaning as he pulled his weight onto the seat. The dogs clamored up over the sides of the back of the truck without so much as an invitation.

"What happened?" Ellie asked in alarm.

"Four-wheeler rolled."

"Your ribs?"

He nodded, and in the dim light of the cabin she could see sweat beading on his upper lip and forehead.

Ellie didn't say another word. She turned the headlights back on and swung into Reverse.

"Watch the stock tank," Walt muttered.

Ellie stopped, jammed the gearshift into Park and turned toward Walt.

"You're welcome." Her tone was low and harsh.

"What?"

"You said, 'Thank you for coming to look for me so I didn't have to walk home,' and I said, 'You're welcome.'" Then she threw the truck into gear and started toward the ranch, taking care, in spite of her instincts to the contrary, to miss as many ruts as possible. Walt very likely had broken or bruised ribs, and having once survived a bruised rib herself after a nasty fall from a tree, she knew what he was dealing with.

The old man sat in stony silence, staring straight ahead, or at least Ellie assumed he was because she refused to look at him. *Watch the stock tank.* She'd been well aware of the stock tank. She'd helped put it there!

When they got to the pasture gate, Walt made to get out and Ellie snapped, "Stay put." With a surprised look, he acquiesced and Ellie got out to open the gate. After driving through she got out again and closed it, then drove the two hundred yards to where Walt's truck was parked.

"Thank—hey!" he said as Ellie drove past his truck and on down the driveway. "You don't have to take me home."

"I know," she said serenely. She was more than

aware that she didn't have to do anything for Walt. He didn't want her to do anything for him. Tough.

She drove over the small hill and Walt's and the Garcias' places came into view. She continued on, past their driveways.

"What the hell?" Walt demanded. She cut him a sideways glance, saw the shocked and angry look on his face. And confusion. For once he was the one out of his element.

"You're going to the doctor."

"The hell I am."

"The hell you are, and the ranch is footing the bill."

"No!"

Ellie didn't bother to respond.

"Now, listen here, Miss High and Mighty, you can't just kidnap me and take me to the doctor."

"Yeah. I can," Ellie replied calmly. "You've been injured on Rocky View property and I'm not risking a lawsuit."

"A law—" Walt let out a ferocious breath followed by a colorful curse—one that Ellie made a mental note to remember. Not that she would use it, but Kate would find it amusing.

Walt grabbed for the door handle. "Really?" she asked. "You'd throw yourself out onto the road?"

"No, I wouldn't *throw myself out onto the road,*" Walt said, mimicking her.

"Then what are you doing?"

"I'm… I'm…" Another long exhale and then Walt tilted his head back, squeezing his eyes shut. "Pissed off!"

"I understand, but nevertheless, you're going to see a doctor." She glanced sideways to see that Walt's eyes were still closed and his face was set in harsh lines from both mental and physical anguish. "I'm not doing this to piss you off and show you who's boss. I'm doing it because I'm concerned."

He made no response. Didn't speak. Didn't move. Once they hit the outskirts of Glennan, Ellie said, "Are you going to tell me the easiest way to get to the hospital, or am I going to have to use my phone?"

It took two blocks for Walt to say, "Turn at the next stop sign."

That was his only instruction and proved to be the only one necessary because six blocks down the street was a red-and-white sign that read Emergency Entrance.

Ellie drove into the lot. Walt tried to get out of the truck almost before she'd taken the key out of the ignition and again he groaned as his weight shifted. Ellie waited, then followed as he limped toward the entrance, bent over to keep the pressure off his damaged chest. And it occurred to her as she walked past him to open the door that if she could deal with this guy and win, maybe she did have what it took to deal with a toddler.

WALT'S HOUSE WAS dark when Ryan drove by. It wasn't until he got to the main ranch, found Walt's truck by the barn, the ranch rig gone and all the lights off in the house that was usually all lit up, that he suspected something was off.

He unloaded PJ, turned the big gelding loose then pulled the phone out of his pocket and tried to call Francisco. Nothing. He called the bar. They hadn't seen Walt, knew nothing—not that he'd expected them to, with Walt's truck still being there. Then he noticed that the four-wheeler was also gone. None of this made sense, because he was pretty certain that Walt and Ellie hadn't gone four-wheeling in the dark.

But what if…

He dialed the hospital, which was easy, since Jessie had insisted he put the number on speed dial when she was pregnant with the twins.

"Hi, this is Ryan Madison. I was just wondering if Walt Feldman might have checked in."

"Hey, Ryan." Whoever was on the other end obviously knew him, but Ryan wasn't asking for names. "Walt was here, but he's on his way home now."

"Was he alone?" Ryan asked.

"Nope. Good-looking woman with him. He got all snarly with her when she handed over a credit card to cover the bill, but she just ignored him."

"Thanks," Ryan said, not bothering to ask why Walt had been at the hospital. If he'd left, he was ambulatory. He pocketed the phone and then set about parking the trailer and unhitching it, his movements automatic. He hadn't eaten since lunch and had planned to get something in his stomach as soon as he got home, but he wasn't hungry now. Once the trailer was taken care of, he got into his truck and drove down to Walt's house, getting there only a few minutes before headlights appeared from the opposite direction.

Ellie pulled the truck to a stop close to the front of the house. She got out as the dogs scrambled from the back and came around, probably to open the door for Walt, who pushed his door open, almost hitting her, and then painfully eased himself out of the truck.

"What kind of wreck did you have?" Ryan asked, startling both of them.

"Rolled the four-wheeler, cracked some ribs," Walt muttered, heading for the steps—steps he was going to have a hard time negotiating with cracked ribs.

Ellie stayed where she was next to the rig, her eyes first on Ryan and then on Walt who grimaced as he raised his foot to the first step. Ryan knew better than to offer help. Once Walt was on the top step, his breathing shallow, Ryan opened the door and snapped on the lights.

"Thanks," the old man muttered as he shuffled past. Ryan looked past him, waiting for Ellie to follow, but she'd already gotten back into the truck and through the evening shadows he couldn't see her. A second later the truck was in gear and heading off down the road.

Ah, Walt.

"What happened?" he asked, turning his attention back to Walt.

"I lost control on the side hill just past the granite knob."

"What were you doing out there?"

"Looking for the blasted cows," Walt grumbled, ripping into a white paper pharmacy bag.

"I told you, those cows are long gone. We'll find them with someone else's herd in the fall if they haven't been stolen."

"Whatever," Walt muttered, shaking out a couple pills. Ryan took the bottle and read it, then handed it back, ignoring the look of outrage on Walt's face. "I'm not some kind of kid. I can take my own medication."

"How did Ellie come into this? Did you ask her to drive you to the hospital?"

"She found me."

"Found you? Like…came looking for you?"

"I guess. I don't know why else she'd be driving around the pastures at night."

"You owe her," Ryan said matter-of-factly.

"Yeah. I know. Probably thousands of dollars for this little visit and follow-up."

"That's not what I meant."

Walt just shook his head. "I don't want to talk about it." He raised pain-filled eyes to Ryan. "This stuff is supposed to knock me out, so if you don't mind, I think I'm going to take care of some business, then settle into my chair for the night."

Ryan knew better than to ask if Walt wanted him to stay. "I'll check in with you in the morning."

Walt grunted and slowly made his way down the hall to the bathroom. Ryan waited until he came back and slowly settled into the recliner. Gently he raised the footrest. Walt grimaced, then seemed to relax. The drugs were taking effect. Fast.

"Call if you need anything."

Walt raised a hand off his lap in what was probably supposed to be a wave without opening his eyes. It fell limply back to his lap. Ryan turned on a lamp near the door, then turned off the overhead light. By the time he'd shut the door behind him, Walt was probably asleep.

And he should probably have gone directly into his house after getting back home. He was hungry and exhausted. It was the sane thing to do. But there were a couple lights on in Ellie's house, so he did the opposite of sane and started up the flagstone path to the front door.

ELLIE FROZE AT the sound of the knock, her stomach doing a small flip-flop. Ryan, of course, wanting to know the story about what had happened with his surly mentor. She started to pull her hair back with an elastic, then stopped and came out of the bathroom to answer the door. Ryan had only knocked once and by the time she opened the door, he was halfway down the front walk.

He stopped, turned back. Without thinking, she pulled the door open wider and he started back to the house. Neither of them said a word until Ellie quietly closed the door behind him.

"You rescued Walt?" he asked.

"Somebody had to," she muttered, eyeing him warily, as if afraid that he was going to take up where they'd left off the last time.

"Do you have any idea what happened? If it rolled over him or what?"

"Walt doesn't talk to me."

"But you went looking for him."

Ellie crossed over to the counter. When she turned back toward him, she felt a wash of exhaustion. Walt was enough to exhaust anyone when he was being stubborn. "Again," she said softly, "someone had to. It was getting dark and he hadn't come back, so I drove to the stock tanks and he came out of the brush just before I was about to leave."

"I wonder how far he walked."

"Don't know. Enough to weaken him to the point that I was able to get him to the hospital. It was a bit touch and go, though. For a minute I thought he was going to throw himself out of the truck."

Ryan's eyebrows went up. "He didn't ask to go to the hospital?"

"Are you kidding?" Ellie blew out a derisive huff of breath. "And when I paid, I thought he was going to have a stroke." She turned a frowning glance his way. "Does he not understand insurance?"

"He said you used your credit card."

"Deductible. Walt didn't have his wallet on him."

Ryan slowly nodded. "You don't have to pay when you go in."

"I wanted to take care of matters right then."

She felt him walk around her, closed her eyes, listened to the tread of his feet, wondered why he made her feel so grounded. He came to the opposite side of the counter, leaned his arms on it. "I know he was probably an ungrateful bastard, and I'll apologize for him—" his gray eyes held hers "—and I'll thank you from me. I've worried about him getting hurt while I'm gone, but figured that Lonnie or Francisco would be there."

"They weren't," Ellie said, unable to tear her gaze away from his.

"But you were and you went looking for him."

She shrugged one shoulder. "What can I say? I'm a masochist."

He smiled, just enough to curve his perfect lips, making them look more perfect.

Pretty faces. What have you learned about pretty faces?

Except Ryan also had substance. He was steady. Dependable. Father material.

Ellie took a mental step back as the thought slammed into her. She was not trolling for father material.

"Something wrong?" Ryan asked.

"It's been a day," Ellie said casually. "Or rather, a night." She rubbed a hand over the side of her neck, surprised at how stiff her muscles were. "How'd you do at the rodeo?"

"One step closer to finals." Although he felt none of the excitement he'd felt last year at this time.

"What are we going to do about Walt?"

"Maybe we can keep him sedated," he said, making Ellie smile.

"Maybe we can slip a little to George, too."

Ryan laughed and Ellie felt her insides go liquid at the low, sexy sound.

She swallowed. "It's getting late."

Ryan's gaze didn't waver as he said, "Totally late." He pushed off from the counter and started for the door, Ellie trailing behind him, her hormones crying, "No, don't let him go...."

She held the edge of the door as he walked outside. He turned, his expression half smiling yet intense.

"Thank you for rescuing Walt."

"Anytime," she said lightly. And then it took everything Ellie had to close the door behind him.

CHAPTER FOURTEEN

THE NEXT MORNING, George's official first day of work, the man commenced making himself a pain in the ass. He strode around the property with a clipboard, watching, waiting, notating. Today was apparently machinery day. He spent a long time in the shop evaluating and inventorying the equipment. He grilled Francisco for more than an hour on his mechanics training and practices, where he bought his fuel, his oil, his filters. Did he consider online sources?

And this was only the beginning. Ryan had thankfully been busy moving cattle from one pasture to the next, stringing new temporary pasture fencing—which he was certain he'd soon have to justify—and generally laying low. He was so damned glad Walt was out of commission. He felt for the guy, but if he'd had to get hurt, this was the best possible time. If they played their cards right, George may have to write his final report and make his recommendations without a lot of one-on-one with Walt. And his general crankiness could be blamed on the pain of healing ribs.

George stopped evaluating in the early afternoon when Ryan broke for lunch, and retired to his mobile home, where he sat outside and tapped away at his laptop, looking official. Ryan went back to work after a quick sandwich in his house. Ellie came out of the house, shook a rug then went back inside. George watched her in a way that made Ryan feel the need to connect his fist to the man's nose. Was he going to start hitting on her?

Ellie was quite capable of holding her own, but all the same he couldn't help but think that fist plus nose equaled satisfaction.

GEORGE KNOCKED ON Ellie's door at a quarter to seven, an efficient fifteen minutes early.

"How'd it go today?" Ellie asked as she ushered him to the kitchen table where he set up his laptop.

"I did inventory, talked to the crew. Generally got a feel for the place. Some of the equipment is sadly outdated and would best be replaced. The initial investment is steep, but it'd pay for itself in more efficient operation and fewer repair costs." Ellie sat and he proceeded to go over his inventory, explaining which pieces of equipment should go, which were still cost-efficient.

"Of course, it doesn't all have to be replaced at once," he said, closing the laptop. "I'll prioritize and offer different strategies for replacement."

"Sounds good."

"I also talked to the crew," George said. "With the exception of Walt Feldman, of course. Were you aware that Francisco Garcia has no formal training in the field of mechanics?"

"He seems to know what he's doing," Ellie said.

George smiled tightly before continuing. "Ryan Madison has a college degree in range management, which is a plus. Walt also has a college degree." Ellie's eyebrows rose. She had no idea. "However," George continued on a cautionary note, "one of the biggest detriments to forward-thinking management is lack of technical knowledge and a refusal to learn new skills."

"You mentioned that," Ellie said.

George laid his palm flat on the table in front of him to emphasize his point. "So much of what we do now is computer oriented, and I can't tell you how many of the old guard refuses to learn technical skills."

"Do you have any reason to believe that Walt doesn't have computer skills?" Ellie asked reasonably.

George shook his head before he slowly admitted, "No. However, it's not uncommon for men of his generation."

"Well, let's not make unfounded suppositions," Ellie said mildly, although she'd be quite surprised if Walt was computer literate.

"That's the furthest thing from my mind," George

said easily. "I simply want to make certain that the crews on the ranches I've evaluated are the best and most effective employees possible."

"Of course," Ellie murmured.

"I want to make certain my employers get what they pay for, and so far I've had no complaints."

Except from the former employees, according to Ryan. "I'm sure you do an excellent job or Milo wouldn't have hired you." This was unfortunately true. Ellie got to her feet as she spoke, signaling the end of the meeting. She'd had enough of George.

The consultant took the hint and picked up the laptop. "Would it be convenient to meet again tomorrow at around seven p.m.?"

Tomorrow? What had happened to every few days? "Yes. That would be fine," Ellie said, walking him to the door.

Once he was gone, she reached up to pull the pins out of her hair and let it fall around her shoulders. Despite his charming exterior, there was something about George that she really didn't like. His track record was impeccable, employers did sing his praises—she'd researched him online, found a few testimonials. He'd successfully turned more than one failing operation around, but Ellie was getting a vibe from the man that she didn't particularly care for.

And Walt… What to do with that cantankerous old coot?

Not that long ago Ellie had also thought that

replacing him was a given. She pictured the new manager as someone college-educated, articulate. Someone who could deal with Angela and someone that Milo could trust to run his ranch.

The problem was that now that she'd lived here for a while, she couldn't shake the idea that Milo and Angela had no idea what they were getting into. They had good friends at a neighboring ranch and, as Angela had once stated with tolerant amusement, Milo had always wanted to be a cowboy. But the new was going to wear off. They were going to, in all likelihood, spend less and less time at the ranch and eventually the manager would run the operation and they would visit one or two weeks out of the year.

For this they were going to kick an old man off his property?

Ellie walked down the hall to the office and started the computer. Her laptop sat on the chair next to the desk and when she bent to move it she had an idea. It might torture Walt a little, but she wasn't totally against that. The more she thought about it, the more she liked her rough plan, so she went to the freezer to take out a casserole she'd recently bought, slipped on shoes and a coat, popped her laptop into the case and took off for Walt's house.

"Come in," Walt called when she knocked five minutes later. Ellie pushed the door open and came inside, juggling the casserole and the laptop bag. After kicking the door shut behind her with one foot, she looked up to see Walt gaping at her. A frown quickly formed when she met his eyes, but she ignored it and walked past him into the kitchen, setting the laptop on the kitchen table as she went by. There was, thankfully, a small microwave oven next to the refrigerator, so Walt would be able to heat his meal.

She placed the casserole into the fridge and then walked back into the living room, where Walt was craning his neck to see what she was doing.

"I know Jessie is probably taking care of you, but I brought you food," she said as she took the laptop out of the case.

"I don't—"

"You're welcome," she responded, cutting him off. She unfastened the Velcro wrap that held the cord together, unfurled it and plugged it into the laptop. There was a good-size end table next to the old man's chair, so she turned on the wireless mouse and set it there.

"What's that?" Walt demanded.

"I think you know what it is," Ellie responded.

"Okay, why is it here?"

"Because you need to learn computer skills."

"I have the TV." Walt dug the remote out of his lap and waved it at her.

"This isn't about entertainment. This is about keeping your job. George doesn't think you have computer skills. You have the time it takes you to heal to learn some."

"I'm not—"

"Yeah. You are."

Walt grunted, looking as fierce as she'd ever seen him, which was saying something.

She opened the laptop and booted it up before setting it gently on his lap and stepping back. He pulled his chin in and stared down at it as if it was a poisonous snake and he was afraid to move for fear of startling it.

"Have you used a laptop before?"

He gave his head a sullen shake. "And I don't see why I should start now."

"Because you can shop for bulls online. And semen." She had to fight to say that with a straight face. "You can check out the competition. You can read husbandry articles. You can take online courses if you want." She settled a hand on the arm of his chair and leaned closer. Walt shrunk back a little. "You can use the time that you're trapped in this chair doing something worthwhile instead of jonesing to get back outside and hurting yourself by doing too much, too soon."

"Look—" He started to lift the machine, then caught his breath and let it settle back on his lap.

"And there's more. George Monroe is going to meet with you and he's probably going to try to tell my uncle that you're hopelessly out of touch with modern whatever it is you do. But if you can develop a few computer skills, research information and generally look like you're tech savvy, then I can go to bat for you and say, 'No. Walt is on top of things.'"

"Why would you do that?"

"Because I like Ryan." His eyes narrowed slightly and Ellie leaned closer. "Walt," she said sternly. "For once in your life, think about other people." That got his attention. "If you go, Ryan's going. This place probably needs both of you." She inhaled a deep breath as she straightened. "Play. Ball."

Walt's eyes widened for a moment, as if he couldn't quite believe she was talking to him that way, and then he quickly dropped them back to the computer.

"Have you used a mouse?"

He nodded as he reached out to put his gnarled fingers over the small blue device. Ellie frowned slightly. Those swollen joints had to hurt. No wonder he was cranky all the time.

"The laptop is the same as any computer. When you close the case, it goes to sleep. Try not to move it too much when the case is open, because the hard drive is spinning and—" Walt's eyes started to glaze over. "Just close the lid when you set it aside. Open it and shake the mouse when you want it to wake up. That there—" she pointed at the internet icon "—will put you into a search engine. Type in *Gelbveih* or *bulls* or whatever and then start exploring."

Walt breathed deeply, his eyes squeezing shut for a moment, telling her just how badly he was hurting. She was so glad she'd forced him to go to the hospital. Otherwise Ryan or Francisco would have had to have done it.

"Do you want me to heat up some casserole or anything?"

"No. I'm good," Walt said, his hand still on the mouse, even though he hadn't yet used it to move the cursor.

"All right, then. I'll, uh, come back and check your progress." Hopefully without George, but no telling.

Walt nodded without looking at her and Ellie had mercy on the guy. She headed for the door without looking back. She'd done what she could. The rest was up to Walt. If he'd let her teach him a few things in the coming days, great. If not… Well, she'd done her best—and maybe she could solicit some help.

Ellie drove the half mile to the Garcia house and walked to the open front door. Two nearly identical and adorable faces peered through the screen door at her, then one little girl giggled and ran for the kitchen while the other continued to stare.

"Mama!" Jeffrey called from where he was racing cars on the sofa. "That lady is here."

"What lady?" Jessie asked as she came into the room, wiping her hands. "Oh," she said, meeting Ellie's eyes through the screen. "Hi. Come on in."

"Thanks," Ellie said, pulling open the door. Jessie scooted some toys aside with her foot as Ellie walked into the room, letting the screen door close behind her. She smiled at the closest twin, who put her hands up to her mouth, but smiled back. "You have such cute kids," Ellie said.

"Thanks," Jessie said wryly. "Cute but messy."

"Something I need to get used to," Ellie said.

"Yeah?" Jessie asked on a note of bemusement.

"I'm pregnant."

Jessie's eyes widened at the confession. "Congratulations."

"Thanks," Ellie said, somehow feeling better, stronger, for having announced her condition. She was pregnant. She was fine with it. She was going to be a mom. "But that's not why I'm here. I need help with Walt."

A look of patient confusion crossed Jessie's face. "Walt?"

"I just gave Walt a laptop. Our consultant wants the ranch to have a computer-literate ranch manager. I'm not holding out a lot of hope, but maybe you can help Walt get a bit more comfortable with the computer."

Jessie pointed at her four-year-old son. "If I can't, he can." Her smile faded a bit as she idly folded the dish towel she held. "You're trying to help Walt."

"I…I think he should be given a chance."

"That's a turnaround," Jessie said candidly, making Ellie like the woman even more.

"Hey, I'm not saying he'll survive my aunt and uncle, but I want to give him the opportunity to change."

Jessie's mouth curved back up again. "I'll do what I can."

"Thanks," Ellie said, leaning to admire the doll that one of the twins was holding up for inspection. "Pretty," she said to the girl, who beamed as she hugged the baby closer to her. "I should get going, but I really appreciate your help."

Jessie walked to the door with her. "So…were you able to get the orange juice out of your pants?"

"I was."

Jessie grinned as her daughter leaned her head against her leg. "Welcome to motherhood."

ELLIE DIDN'T SEE much of Ryan over the next week. In fact, she never got closer than fifty yards from him. Whenever he saw her, he seemed to change course, go in the opposite direction. According to his schedule, he'd gone to two rodeos and she looked up the results later—one first, one second—but when he was on the ranch, he continued to avoid her. And even though Ellie should have been relieved that the matter was taken out of her hands and she didn't have to deal with an attraction that realistically could go nowhere, she felt empty when he wasn't around.

As though she'd missed an opportunity, which was crazy. What opportunity? How well did she know the guy?

Well enough to know that he had integrity. That he was loyal and did everything in his power to protect a cranky old mentor.

That he made her want to get busy despite being pregnant.

Maybe it was best that one of them was behaving sensibly.

So Ellie spent her days for the most part alone… except for George, the other man in her life.

As near as Ellie could tell, the purpose of George's nightly meetings with her were to gain her support in convincing Milo that his current contract was not long enough to tackle all the work that needed to be done. What the ranch really needed was George's expertise for an entire year, during which time he'd assist in hiring adequate help, find suitable equipment, revitalize the pastures and infrastructure and help purchase new cattle.

Walt would hit the ceiling on that one.

George might have control issues, but he was too slick to be condescending. In fact, he spoke to Ellie as if she was a seasoned landowner, phrasing things so that it was possible to follow his explanations and recommendations easily, thus allowing her—if she so chose—to pretend to be familiar with whatever he was discussing. No wonder the Kenyons had loved him. He made people feel smart. The guy was a master, and Ellie was familiar with the tactic.

A couple times she'd innocently said, "But Ryan says…" just to gauge his reaction.

George did not like Ryan. In fact, Ryan might have a college degree, but his rodeo career was obviously interfering with his dedication to the property, as Ellie was no doubt aware. Right?

Right, George.

"And when exactly will your aunt and uncle arrive?" he asked before parting company on their fifth meeting.

"Next week, unless they get hung up in Belize," which Ellie half expected since Angela loved it there, "or my uncle gets called back to the hospital."

"Hard to run a ranch long-distance," George said.

"Guess that's why we have a manager."

George frowned slightly. "That's why we need to make sure you have the *best* manager."

"Of course." Which was why she hoped to keep him away from Walt for as long as possible.

After that meeting, Ellie picked up the phone and was lucky enough to connect with her uncle who'd just finished a phone conference concerning a hospital emergency. But did he sound exhausted, as well he should, having dealt with business at 9:30 p.m. on his vacation? No. He sounded energized and eager to discover how the consultation was going. After all, George was one of the best in the business.

After giving Milo all the positives—George was charismatic and gung-ho, et cetera, she broached the possibility of George not knowing everything. What would Milo do if she disagreed radically with the consultant's recommendations? Milo grew silent at her suggestion that George might not be omnipotent.

"There are differing schools of thought on ranch management," she ventured. "And I have reason to believe that ultimately George and I will not agree on the matter of personnel."

"I can't see that happening," Milo said in a surprised tone. "Surely if a man is good for the operation, you two would be of the same mind."

"Not necessarily."

"George knows ranching," Milo said.

"I know people."

There was a brief silence before her uncle said, "If it came to an impasse, I'd take both sides into consideration, even though I would *hope* my two experts could come to a consensus and I wouldn't have to choose."

"Hopefully it doesn't come to that," she agreed. "Have you nailed down your arrival date yet?" She wanted to get Walt as gussied up as possible before Milo and Angela arrived.

"Nothing firm, but trust me, we'll be there as soon as I can get away. Angela is anxious for a little peace and quiet."

Oh, yeah. Ellie was certain she was. For maybe a week.

"Well, give me a heads-up so I can have the place ready." And prepare for battle.

"Will do, Ellie. Everything else all right?"

"I have an appointment next week, and yes, everything seems to be fine."

"Great. I'll see you in a week or two."

Ellie hung up feeling both depressed and frustrated. This wasn't her battle, but she'd become attached to the crew of this ranch. This was their home, and in a way Angela and Milo were interlopers…who'd happened to buy the place. Okay, saviors and interlopers.

Now what could she do to keep George from screwing with the crew? Endure really long unnecessary meetings so that she knew what tack he was taking in his quest to temporarily take over the ranch.

But on George's seventh night there, she broke. She'd just come back from checking on Walt—mainly to make sure he hadn't thrown her laptop against the wall—and saw George typing away in his usual spot outside his mobile home, getting ready to read her his assessment for the day. He looked up as she pulled into the drive and waved. On the opposite side of the barn, Ryan was loading his horse. Tough choice.

Ellie parked the SUV and headed straight to the barn.

"Take me with you," she said to Ryan. His eyes narrowed slightly at her point-blank request and she couldn't really blame him. They'd had next to no contact since she'd rescued Walt. "Don't make me beg," she said.

"George?"

"Who else?" she snapped.

"He probably likes you," Ryan said with a touch of sarcasm.

"No. He wants me to tell my uncle that the ranch can't survive without him."

Ryan jerked his head in the direction of the travel trailer. "Even if I take you with me, he'll probably wait up."

Ellie glanced over at the consultant, who was watching them closely, then back at Ryan. "I'll take my chances."

Ryan shrugged. "Climb in."

CHAPTER FIFTEEN

"WHERE ARE WE going?" Ellie asked, settling into her seat as they drove through the gate.

Ryan shot a quick look into the rearview mirror, as if checking to see if George was following them. "Idaho."

Ellie's heart jumped even as she realized he was kidding. "Beats a George meeting," she said mildly, leaning her head back against the headrest.

"You're no fun," Ryan said.

"Where are we really going?"

"Practice at the Glennan arena. We should be home around eleven."

Surely George would be asleep by then. Tomorrow she would not shirk her duty; tomorrow she would fight the good fight. But today had been stressful and she simply didn't want to deal with the man. She really wished that Milo wasn't so taken with the guy, or that he'd made it so clear that while he trusted her insights, she wasn't a ranch specialist like George.

"How's it going?" Ryan asked after several silent miles.

"George is driving me crazy," she said, without looking at him. She hadn't missed the undertone of irony in his polite inquiry.

"And everything else?"

Ellie put her hand on her abdomen, assuming he meant her pregnancy. "I feel great." Physically, anyway.

"And the job search?"

Ellie rolled her head on the headrest to look at him. "Still on it. Had two depressing phone interviews today. Anything else?"

"Yeah. What's the deal with giving Walt a laptop?"

"Surely Jessie filled you in." That was part of the reason why she hadn't sought him out—it also would have been hard to pin him down the way he'd been avoiding her.

"George has a problem with lack of computer skills."

"Doesn't that work for you?"

"How so?" she asked with a frown.

"It seems to me that that would be a perfect excuse for firing him."

"Maybe I don't want to fire him," Ellie said quietly, knowing she'd have to explain her about-face and not certain she wanted to.

"Why?"

Ellie exhaled, studying the glove compartment for a moment before saying, "Because of you, okay?"

Ryan gave a slow nod, his eyes still on the road as he pulled up to the highway stop sign. "Care to expand on that?"

"No."

HE PULLED OUT onto the highway, and ten way-too-silent minutes later they pulled into a group of trailers parked near the small arena. Ryan turned off the ignition. "Feel free to wear my jacket if you want to watch from the stands. It gets cold out there."

"Thanks," she said.

"Ellie?" She raised her eyebrows at him. "I want to talk. About Walt and…other stuff. If not tonight, then sometime." He waited to see if she had a re-sponse, and when she said nothing, he opened the door and got out of the truck.

Ellie sat where she was. The truck rocked a little as he opened the trailer door and unloaded his horse, then a few minutes later he rode toward the arena on the brown practice horse he called Skipper. Ellie let her head fall back against the headrest again.

Yes, they were going to talk. There was simply too much unfinished business between them, and if she didn't get a job, who knew how long they would be living together on the ranch? And it would prob-ably take a joint effort to keep George from ousting Walt and taking over the position himself.

Ellie got out of the truck and then reached in for

the heavy corduroy jacket as the cool night air raised goose bumps on her arms. There was a small cluster of people sitting in the stands watching the action in the arena but Ellie headed for a lone picnic table where she could see what was happening but didn't have to socialize. She had a few things to work out before the ride home.

Why had she gotten into the truck? To escape George? Or to force herself to hash things out with Ryan, to see if they could come up with a method of coexistence that didn't involve full avoidance?

The latter, no question about it. She prized being direct, but lately she'd been taking the coward's way out, avoiding George and avoiding Ryan as much as he was avoiding her. Avoidance wasn't working—not for her, anyway—so that left only confrontation. And perhaps a deeper examination of herself, her motives, her needs, her desires....

She pulled Ryan's jacket more tightly around her as cold air gusted over her, closing her eyes as his scent rose from the fabric. Ellie opened her eyes again as the chute clanged open and a rider charged out of the box, swinging his loop. This was so not her world, even if part of her was starting to think of the ranch as home. This was not her aunt and uncle's world, either. This was Ryan's world. Walt's.

Ellie sat huddled against the crisp Montana night as roper after roper swung their loops, caught and tied their calves. Ryan went twice, and both times she was aware of a surge of emotion as she watched him do what he did so well. The guy was spectacular. It was getting close to his turn again when the creak of saddle leather caught her attention and she turned to see Ryan walking his limping horse toward the trailer. She got off from the table and headed toward him.

"What happened?" she asked as she caught up with man and horse.

"Muscle pull," Ryan said with a quirk of his lips. "Second one this season. I think Skipper will be on pasture until next spring."

"Sorry to hear that." Although Skipper probably wouldn't mind eating grass and sleeping in the sun.

"I have other practice horses. He just happened to be one of the best." He handed Ellie the reins and started uncinching the saddle. "When I was young I only had two horses. My good horse and my practice horse. If one of them went lame, I was in a world of hurt."

"Did one of them go lame?" she asked.

"Of course. Walt loaned me the money to buy another horse, so I wasn't dead in the water."

"How much does a roping horse cost?"

"Many tens of thousands if they're good."

Ellie's jaw dropped. "Tens…"

Ryan propped the saddle on his hip. "Yep. Which is why I take damned good care of my horses."

THE LIGHT WAS on in George's trailer when they got back to the ranch close to midnight.

"A good consultant's work is never done," Ryan muttered as he pulled to a stop.

"There's a note on your door," Ellie said, pointing at his house.

"I'll be damned." Ryan got out of the truck and headed back to unload his horse. "George, no doubt," he said when Ellie joined him at the rear of the trailer. He led Skipper out of the trailer and into the barn, snapping on the light as he walked inside.

Ellie followed him, closing the door—and hopefully George—out. Ryan led the horse to a panel corral next to a stack of hay and then gestured to Ellie with his head. "Would you mind holding him while I work on him?"

"Not at all." He handed her the rope as he walked past her out of the corral and over to a cabinet from which he took a dusty brown glass bottle. Ellie wrinkled her nose as he opened the cap.

"Wow. I can smell it from here."

"Horse liniment. Cures what ails you."

"I would hope, smelling like that."

Ryan poured a good amount onto a piece of toweling and then bent to apply it to the gelding's foreleg. Skipper flinched when Ryan first touched him, but as he continued to massage the liniment into the horse's leg Ellie could see the animal start to relax. Ryan continued to work the muscle, and Ellie watched, fascinated by the strength of his hands and the gentleness of his touch.

She cleared her suddenly dry throat and asked, "How often do you do that?"

"A couple times a day. I'll leave him in the pen for a day so I can get to him easily and then assess." He glanced up then and Ellie felt a jolt as their gazes connected. Held.

Oh, dear heavens….

And that was when Ellie realized why he'd been avoiding her. And she him. Because they'd instinctively known what was going to happen if they spent any length of time together. It was happening right now…

Ryan looked away first, breaking the charged connection. He handed Ellie the bottle as he undid the horse's bridle. She took it and opened the gate, slipping out to return the bottle to the cabinet. Ryan latched the gate and walked to the barn door where he waited while she closed the cabinet. Neither spoke, even though there was so much that needed to be said. Issues to confront…or to avoid. At the moment Ellie didn't know which was the better tack.

They walked outside and Ryan closed the barn door. The evening was over and in a matter of minutes she'd be back in the safety of her house, away from Ryan and away from temptation.

But neither of them moved after the door was latched.

"Ellie?" Ryan asked softly after a long, silent moment.

She raised her chin instead of replying, knowing she should turn and walk away, and also knowing she wasn't going to do that. Not when he was looking at her that way…and she was looking back.

Ryan finally reached out to slide a warm hand around the back of her neck in a possessive caress, his fingers setting her nerves afire as they threaded through her hair. Ellie caught her breath and when he leaned down to take her lips, she met his kiss halfway. She kissed him back, wrapping her arms around him as he pulled her closer, pressing her body into his.

"I don't have answers," he said.

"I need answers," she said against his mouth. "I need answers and a plan."

"And I can't stop thinking about you," he said before kissing her again.

Likewise. Ellie stepped back into sanity, pulling in a long shaky breath as she eased out of his embrace. It would be so easy to simply invite him up to the house, but as she'd said, she needed answers.

"The note," she said huskily, grasping at an excuse to pull back from what she'd help start. "I want to know what's in the note."

Together they walked to Ryan's door, where he pulled the paper off the door and unfolded it. "Imagine that—it's from George and he'd like to start early tomorrow and take a long hard look at the forage and pastures."

"Good luck with that," Ellie said vaguely before meeting his eyes. "Avoidance isn't working," she said.

He had no difficulty following her meaning. "Obviously."

"I don't know what to do."

"Take our time? Meet things head-on?"

"I guess." She took a backward step, putting some distance between them.

"This may lead nowhere," he pointed out. "But at least we can be honest about it."

"I hate unfinished business," Ellie murmured.

"I won't hurt you, Ellie."

She smiled wryly for an instant. "Not on purpose anyway."

He gave a slow nod. "Not on purpose."

GEORGE WAS WAITING by the barn when Ryan walked out the door at five o'clock the next morning.

"I got your note," he said congenially.

George smiled. "I haven't seen a lot of you since

I've been here, so I thought I'd better nail you down if I was ever going to get your take on operations."

"Yeah. I've been working."

"And rodeoing," George added as he fell into step.

"I've cleared that with my boss. I work flex time," Ryan said.

"I've never really heard of such a thing."

"It's an innovative employee practice," Ryan explained.

"I meant on a ranch," George snapped.

Ryan opened the barn door and George followed him inside. Lonnie would show up in an hour to feed the animals there, so Ryan saw no need to delay the tour. And tour they did. Ryan had to admit that George was thorough. His questions were intelligent and showed an understanding—though not necessarily an approval—of what Ryan had been trying to accomplish with his lands-management strategy. Ryan knew his science was dead-on and he knew that the pastures were better than they'd ever been. There was still room for improvement, but grazing management was an ongoing process.

Walt came up several times. George wanted to meet with him and Ryan knew what a friggin disaster that could be if George indicated in any way that Walt's breeding program was off base. When they arrived back at the ranch just as the sun was setting, Ryan parked the truck and then turned in his seat to look at George.

"So how's this consultant gig working out for you?"

"I enjoy my work," he said cautiously.

"Pretty lucrative?" George frowned. "I was just considering future career possibilities," Ryan said. "And professional competition is healthy, you know."

"Why would you want to leave this place..." George cleared his throat meaningfully "...when it seems like you have a good thing going here?"

Ryan had no difficulty following his meaning— George had been spying on him and Ellie last night. "I've noticed a lot of job turnovers in the wake of your consulting."

"The Vineyard?"

"For one."

"The original crew wasn't up on current practices."

"Did you suggest that the owner give them training opportunities?"

"It was more cost-effective to hire people who were more innovative." George opened his door and got out. Ryan did the same. "You don't have anything to worry about. I'm not going to suggest they let you go."

"I don't think it'd matter if you did," Ryan said as he closed his door. Just so they understood each other. "What Bradworth needs from you is an overview of operations and ways to fine-tune. Not a crew overhaul, and I think we both know that."

"Last I heard you weren't in charge."

"But Ellie trusts me." Probably the last thing George wanted to hear.

"Ellie's not making the decisions."

Ryan merely smiled. "If there's nothing else, I have a few things I need to catch up on."

"Nothing else," George muttered. "For now anyway."

"Just let me know if anything pops into your head," Ryan said congenially. He walked away gritting his teeth, glad his day with the consultant was over. He didn't know if he could ever shape Walt up to be the manager Milo Bradworth would want, but he was going to go down swinging.

His phone, which he'd left on the table in the name of professionalism that day, was lit up when he walked into the kitchen. He picked it up, then cursed when he saw the number. The lawyer. Shit.

He pushed the play button, listened to the voice mail, cursed again.

Had he come to a decision? Yes, he had. Ryan had chased this particular problem around for days now and his gut instinct was still to tell Charles to take his money and shove it. The only thing stopping him was his mother. Lydia would be pissed. She wouldn't take the money herself, but she damn well wanted Ryan to have what she considered to be his.

His mother was going to have to learn to forgive him. Ryan dialed the law offices and wonder of wonders the receptionist picked up, even though it was five minutes to five. "I'd like to talk to Mr. Myers."

"Who's calling, please?"

Ryan told her, waited on hold and less than a minute later Myers came on the line. "I have made a decision," Ryan told the man. "I'm not signing anything."

"I'll relay that information," the lawyer said, and Ryan hung up, hoping that was that.

Opening the fridge, he stood for a long moment studying the contents, wondering if beer was going to do the trick. A shot or three of bourbon sounded good, but in the end he reached for a can.

Drowning his problems in hard liquor never worked for him. They just popped up again once his head had cleared. He settled on the sofa, propped his feet on the old coffee table and opened the beer. Through the window he could see the main ranch house; he wondered what it was going to be like when Ellie's aunt and uncle took residence. She'd probably be gone by then, and he didn't like thinking about that. She'd gotten under his skin in a big way.

Did it matter that she was pregnant?

He could deal with it…if she'd let him.

SOMETHING WAS OFF with George. His report on the condition of the pastures and forage, as well as the rundown of the strategies he was going to research, was less verbose than usual. Ellie half wondered if he'd already given his report to Milo and was therefore giving her the condensed version.

When he was finished, George stored his bullet-point printout in his eel-skin folder, which he tapped on the table. But he didn't leave.

"Is there something else?" Ellie asked, dreading the thought that there might be and she'd be trapped here listening to it, when she was thinking about finding Ryan.

George exhaled loudly. "This is a touchy matter," he said.

"What's a touchy matter?" Ellie asked as a nasty prickle went up her spine.

George hesitated for a moment, as if debating the pros and cons of professionalism, then said, "How long have you known Ryan Madison?"

"How is that any business of yours?" she asked, instantly sensing this was personal, not professional.

"I don't want to seem—" He broke off. Started again. "I have concerns…"

"Let's just put it this way, Mr. Monroe. I've known him long enough to know that I don't want to see any crew changes here at the Rocky View. I was going to discuss this with you further at the end of your sojourn, but perhaps I may as well make myself clear now. Feel free to offer suggestions for staff improvement, but this crew will not be fired and replaced by another."

George went red to his roots. "If I've made recommendations such as that in the past, they were warranted by the situation."

"No doubt. And I'm telling you that this situation doesn't."

George leaned forward. "How well do you think Walt Feldman is going to do working for your uncle?"

"You've met with Walt?"

George leaned back. "I went to his place late today. He was not congenial and he smelled of alcohol."

Damn. Ellie pressed her lips together for a moment. Debated. "Do you ever consume alcohol on your days off?"

George all but sneered at her. "Somehow I don't think my alcohol consumption is the same as Walt's."

Neither did Ellie, but she had yet to see Walt inebriated on the job, which made her believe it wasn't a problem and made her wonder why George was so immediately certain it was…almost as if he was looking for something to latch on to.

"I think you're jumping to a conclusion," she said reasonably, deducing from his subtle shift of expression that George took exception at being challenged. "You have no reason to assume Walt is an alcoholic because of one meeting."

"He has a reputation in the ranching world," George said witheringly. "It's common knowledge that the man drinks to excess."

"Common knowledge is akin to rumor," Ellie said, noting that George was doing his best to stare her down. She'd been dead eyed by the best in the course of her job and George was going to have to try harder. "I don't believe rumors and I want my uncle to keep Walt on. I want you to recommend he do so."

"That would go against my professional ethics. The man is a menace."

"This crew stays in place," she said.

George stood. "You make your recommendations and I'll have to make mine."

Ellie paced through the house a few times after George had left. She wanted to see Ryan, tell him what had happened, but she didn't want to add ammo to George's arsenal by going to his place late in the evening.

Screw George.

She let herself out of the house and walked across the gravel yard. Ryan opened the door almost as soon as she knocked, ushering her inside with a quick glance at George's trailer. Ellie took a quick look around as he closed the door and pulled the small curtain on the window closed.

He definitely lived in a guy place—sparsely furnished with ropes and boots and horse gear scattered about—but it was still relatively neat considering the fact that he didn't have much free time for house-work.

"What's up?" he asked as soon as the door was closed.

Ellie crossed her arms over her chest, wishing she wasn't so intensely aware of him. "I made a stab at getting George to recommend keep Walt."

Ryan's gaze sharpened. "And?"

"George went to Walt's place today. I think it left a mark."

"Damn. He must have snuck down there after we parted company. I was hoping to be there."

"Well, you weren't." Ellie leaned back against the door. "If George recommends that Walt stay, then Milo will believe that the guy has merit, even if he is cantankerous. That's the way Milo works—he believes his experts. If, however, George says Walt should go, but I insist he stay, then he'll stay…" Ellie was fairly certain of that, despite Milo's assertion that George was the expert.

"But…"

"When he has his first run-in with Angela, and he will, because everyone does, they'll have it in the back of their minds that George said he should go. And eventually he will, because there'll be another run-in and another and I won't be here to save him."

"Is there any chance your aunt and uncle won't take up residence?"

"That would be the one thing that *would* save him," Ellie agreed. "But right now Milo is set on living here." Her fear was that they'd fire Walt, live on the ranch for two years and then move back to California. A very real scenario.

"Will your uncle last here?" he asked, reading her mind.

Ellie met his eyes candidly. "My gut tells me that he might, but Angela won't."

"That's what I'm afraid of. Walt's old," Ryan said. "I want him to stay on his land."

"Me, too," Ellie said softly. But it was more for Ryan than for Walt. Ryan, who appeared stressed to the max. Was all that stress due to George? She pushed off the door. "I should be going."

"Wouldn't want to scandalize George," he agreed.

Ellie gave a small smile. Truer than he knew.

"I assume you know that I have to leave tomorrow."

"Overnighter," she said.

Ryan closed the space between them. He didn't touch her, but her body responded almost as if he had. "You want to come along?"

Ellie shook her head. "Someone has got to keep an eye on George." She took a backward step. She still hadn't categorized exactly what was developing between them—but it felt more serious than she had anticipated, and for the moment, she was going to bide her cautious time.

For as long as she could anyway.

I can't stop thinking about you. His words that night outside the barn had burned themselves into her brain.

She took another step, smiled at him then turned and started back to the safety of her house.

I'm pregnant. I have no job…. I can't handle more complications…but I can't stop thinking about you, either.

CHAPTER SIXTEEN

RYAN LEFT EARLY the next morning, leaving Ellie alone on the place with George and Francisco. Ellie spent her morning as usual, working her way through the job postings for which she was qualified, sending out another barrage of applications. She had plenty of experience, but the competition for the few jobs out there was fierce. What was going to happen if she didn't land something? Would she continue to be a charity case here on the ranch?

That wouldn't do. She needed to establish herself in a job before the baby was born, so she could afford child care, health care…. It was enough to put a permanent knot in her stomach. The only thing that seemed to still her growing anxiety on the job front was working in her garden, tending the plants, celebrating new life, new growth.

Over the past weeks she had started to think that the calves running roughshod over the backyard may have been the best thing that could have happened—because of it she'd discovered that she liked tending plants. Having never in her life grown anything except for an avocado plant in science class, she was amazed at how much satisfaction she got from playing in the dirt. Angela still had nothing to speak of to make her house more homey—Ellie had truly failed on that front—but she thought that her aunt was probably going to be quite happy with her flowers.

She'd bought several daisies on her last trip to the town, which were going to look perfect scattered near the base of the pine trees, and had just started to work the soil to plant them when a scream brought her up to her feet—an honest-to-goodness man scream.

What was that...?

Heart pounding, Ellie dropped her trowel and ran to the side gate in time to see George take hold of the shovel she'd leaned against the post newel the night before and start marching toward her.

"Stand back," he commanded as he brandished the shovel. In front of him Hiss slithered through the grass, trying to get to the safety of the cracks between the rock steps before George attacked.

"No!" Ellie said, racing through the gate and jumping over Hiss to take a stance between George and the snake. "Don't you dare touch my snake!"

George stopped dead. "*Your* snake?"

"My snake," she growled. "He's harmless and he eats rodents." *Which makes him more useful than you.* Ellie looked over her shoulder just as the last bit of Hiss's tail disappeared into a crack. She looked back at George, who was staring at her with a be-mused expression. "Do we understand each other?" she asked in a deadly tone. "Leave my snake alone."

"Ellie…you don't want a snake around the house," he said, lowering the shovel. "Even if they seem harmless."

"I don't want you around the house, either, but here you are," she retorted, still shaken by Hiss's near miss. For one long moment, she held George's stunned gaze, before turning and walking back through the side gate, thinking that tonight's George meeting should be very, very interesting. She couldn't wait.

RYAN WAS IN the last section of roping, but he was not in the mood for mingling or socializing prior to his run, so he stayed close to his truck, listening to the scores and focusing on the event ahead of him.

This was definitely going to be his last season of trying to make Nationals—and if he didn't make it, he could live with it. He was a better roper than his brother as far as natural talent went, but he lacked the resources to pursue world standings year after year, and maybe it was time to face that reality.

He was just about to open his tack room door when someone came up behind him. He turned to find the last guy on earth he wanted to see. His father.

What the hell?

"Are you holding out for more money?" Charles demanded in a low voice. His face was red, contrasting vividly with his silver hair, and he seemed to have maybe lost some weight since the last time Ryan had seen him, not much more than a month ago.

"No." Ryan shouldered by the man to get his saddle.

"Bullshit. Your mother set this…extortion…up and now you refuse to sign. What the hell's the deal?"

Ryan squared his shoulders. "The deal is that I'm not signing. I don't want your money."

"But you do want something to hold over my head," Charles blustered.

"I want you out of my life," Ryan said. "Now would be a good time."

His father gave him a long, hard stare. "I tried like hell to talk her into terminating, you know. I should have tried harder."

The admission shouldn't have stunned him, shouldn't have hurt, but for some reason it did. Ryan sucked in a breath, trying to come up with a response when Charles growled, "You have one more week to come to a decision and I need to warn you, you can try to hurt me, but I have influence in more areas than you do. I can make you and your mom wish you'd signed. Do the smart thing, boy."

Ryan stood staring at his father, blood pounding

in his ears, willing himself to keep his mouth shut and not give Charles the satisfaction of responding to his threat. Then, with a throaty snort, his asshole father turned and walked away.

THE PHONE RANG late in the afternoon as Ellie was washing mud off her hands in the kitchen sink. She'd started out with gloves, but they'd gotten so wet that she'd abandoned them and gone au naturel as she planted some pansies. Now she was dealing with some serious dirt-under-the-fingernail issues.

"Hey, Milo," she said, recognizing the hospital number and then recalling that he was supposed to be on vacation. "Why are you at work?"

"Something came up—a staff issue, and it's kind of gnarly, so we came back a few days early."

"So when will you be arriving here?"

"I don't know when I can get away. There's a potential lawsuit brewing here. I wouldn't feel right leaving until a few issues are settled."

"George will be upset. He's planning a long face-to-face with you next Tuesday." Emphasis on *long*.

"Actually, I'm calling about George." Milo cleared his throat. "Mr. Monroe thinks that Ryan Madison is trying to, as he put it, ingratiate himself to you."

That son of a bitch. Well, maybe this was what she got for indicating she'd liked a snake better than him.

"Really?" Ellie asked wearily, pushing her hair back from her forehead. "This is his business how?"

"He thinks the guy is trying to sway your opinion by romancing you."

Ellie felt as though steam would be coming out of her ears in a few seconds. "Damn, Milo. Do you really think I wouldn't be able to figure out if a guy was coming on to me in order to sway my opinion?"

"Well," Milo said gently, "you kind of missed the boat on the last guy."

Ellie closed her eyes at the touché. "Does Angela know about this?"

"I thought I'd talk to you first."

"Thank you. Trust me, there is nothing going on that George needs to concern himself about. And, Milo...if I do get involved with someone, as much as I appreciate your concern, I'm quite capable of looking out for myself, despite what happened before."

Ellie hung up and leaned back against the counter, debating whether or not to walk over to George's trailer and throttle him. She ultimately decided against it. Too hard to hide a body. But she would be taking a different tone in their meetings from now on.

When Ryan arrived home later that evening, Ellie put her coat on and headed out of the house, wanting to share what had transpired between her and Milo...and George. She knocked on the door and when Ryan opened it, she took one look at his set expression and said, "You lost."

"Family issues," he said, stepping back.

Ellie came in without an invitation and he closed the door behind her, walking over to the fridge. "You want something?"

"I'm good," Ellie said as Ryan grabbed a beer out of the fridge. He popped the top and poured a great deal of it down his throat.

"Must be some family issue," Ellie said, taking a seat on the edge of the sofa.

He nodded. "Families can be rugged." Then he sat beside her on the old sofa, sprawling his long legs out in front of him, staring off into the distance.

"I can leave," she said softly.

"Don't."

For a long moment they sat in the semidarkness, Ryan still seemingly lost in whatever had happened.

"Your mom?" she finally asked.

"My dad."

"Want to talk?"

He slid his hand along the sofa so that his fingers rested lightly on her shoulder and shook his head. "The last thing I want to do is talk."

Ellie didn't press matters, but moved closer. Seconds later Ryan brought his arm around her, pulling her against him, and she rested her head on his chest. And there they stayed, Ellie feeling the steady beat of his heart, breathing in the scent of arena dust and man. She closed her eyes, wondering how something she'd been unfamiliar with a few months ago could now make her feel like she was somehow at home.

"George tattled on us," she finally said. "I think he did it because I wouldn't let him attack Hiss." She cleared her throat. "I might have indicated I liked the snake better."

Ryan moved his head so he could look down at her, a wry smile twisting his lips. "Good for you, and who did he tattle to?"

"My uncle. He told Milo you're trying to romance me into letting you keep your job."

"Of course that's what I'm doing," he said, a touch of amusement finally lighting his eyes. He set the beer on the end table and brought his fingers up under her chin. "What other reason could I have for making out with you?"

"Are you going to make out with me?"

He brought his lips down to hers in the lightest of kisses. A delicious tremor shot through her. "I'm thinking about it."

"Mmm." Ellie smiled against his lips, her hand sliding up around his neck, thinking how differently she reacted with him than with other men. Even with Nick—her wild fling—she'd *planned* to be impulsive. With Ryan, she went with the flow. And right now the flow was carrying her deeper into his arms, bringing her mouth up to meet his in a kiss that started out soft but became hungry in a matter of seconds.

The next thing she knew she was being hauled up onto his lap and was curling into him as he kissed her again. Then his mouth left her lips to trace a trail down the side of her neck to the V of her blouse. Ellie gave a soft moan and he kissed the fullness of her breasts.

She put her hands on his face, brought his lips back up to hers. "I told Milo what I do is none of George's business."

Ryan wrapped his arms around her, holding her close as he pressed his face against her hair. Ellie let out a long breath and snuggled against him. She could feel how aroused he was, but this was new territory for her. Making love while pregnant.

But damn, she wanted to in the worst way. She wanted to feel close to a man. This man.

Ryan continued to kiss her, his hands traveling over her, caressing, exploring, making her want to strip his clothes off. She started undoing his shirt, releasing the buttons one at a time until she could get her hands on his broad chest and flat, hard abdomen.

He sucked a breath in from between his teeth when her fingers trailed down his chest to the curl under the edge of his jeans.

"Are you honestly good with this?" he whispered.

"If I wasn't I wouldn't have my hand where it is right now," she said. Slowly they undressed one another, tossing the clothing on the floor beside them, reveling in the touch of skin against skin, and she was thankful that Ryan had enough respect for her to believe that she was doing what she wanted when she'd chosen to make love to him.

He gently laid her down, kissing her deeply as he slowly pressed into her. He stilled once he was inside and then, when she closed her eyes and let out a deeply satisfied sigh, loving the way he filled her, he started to move.

Ellie came before he'd stroked more than a dozen times, shattering against him and then clinging as he finished his ride, burying her face against his damp chest until he gave one final shuddering thrust.

"That was so fast," she murmured, then raised her head to meet his eyes. "I mean me, not you." Apparently there was an upside to pregnancy hormones.

"Thank you for clarifying," he said with a half smile. He rolled to the side, gathering her in his arms and taking her with him. Ellie cuddled against him, feeling well loved. Satisfied. She smiled against his chest and thought about telling him about how much she'd enjoyed feeling like herself again, but instead she closed her eyes, only for a minute.

That was the last thing she remembered.

RYAN KISSED ELLIE before getting out of bed the next morning. She opened her eyes lazily and watched as he picked up his clothes, dressing as he went. He was so gorgeous with that hard roping body. Eye candy of the highest magnitude.

"Awake?" he asked with a half smile as he buttoned his shirt.

"A little," she murmured. "I'm never going to be a morning person."

He came to sit next to her on the bed, smoothing the hair back from her face. "Go back to sleep." She smiled at him, happy to comply. He bent to kiss her cheek. "Thanks for helping me through a rough evening."

"Anytime." And maybe, if she played her cards right, he'd tell her what had made it such a rough evening in the first place. "Do you really have to go?" she asked as she pushed herself up on one elbow. The sheet drifted down and Ryan's gaze followed the movement. "Right now—" she arched her eyebrows "—as opposed to later?"

"Do not make this harder than it is," Ryan growled. "Walt's waiting, and pretty soon he'll be hammering on the door."

"We don't want that," Ellie agreed, getting out of bed. She crossed the room to where Ryan stood near the door, took his face in her hands and showed him what she'd love to be doing if Walt wasn't about to hammer on the door.

"Go to work," she said against his lips as his hands slid down to caress her ass before pulling her against him.

"You make it so easy…" he said with a smile.

Ellie couldn't keep Ryan out of her thoughts that day. He was a tender lover. Caring. Giving. Toward the end, demanding. She'd enjoyed all the many facets.

And she still wondered what had happened at the rodeo, which was why she spent a good chunk of time at the computer that day trying to find a guy with the last name of Madison who might qualify as Ryan's dad, who was giving him trouble. Trouble he didn't want to talk about.

The doorbell rang late in the afternoon and Ellie rolled her eyes as she got up from the computer and walked into the living room. She was getting tired of George, but it wasn't George at the door. Walt stood on the step with her laptop case in his hand.

"Are you sure you're done with it?" Ellie asked as he handed it to her with a quick thanks. His eyes were relatively clear and there was no scent of alcohol. Maybe broken ribs and a computer had been good for him.

"I, uh, bought one of my own. It came today."

Ellie smiled widely. "Good for you." Walt nodded and started to turn when Ellie said, "Want to have a cup of tea?"

"No."

A few weeks ago she would have been insulted. Now she just shrugged it off. "Then could you tell me something before you go? Do both of Ryan's parents live around here?"

"Ryan doesn't have a dad."

She distinctly remembered Ryan saying last night that his problem was with his dad. "Is he dead?"

"He's unknown," Walt said abruptly.

"His stepfather, then."

"He doesn't have one."

"Oh." Ellie instinctively knew she'd asked one too many questions and that she wasn't going to get any more information out of Walt. "Too bad," she said.

But Walt surprised her again. "Why the question about his father?"

"I guess I misunderstood something he said. None of my business, really." But she hadn't misunderstood. She was certain of it.

Walt's expression was a touch gentler than usual when he said, "Lydia's the daughter of my best friend. She ended up pregnant shortly after he died. I tried to do what I could to help her out, what with her having no family and all, but she never would tell me who the father was." He scowled at Ellie then. "That goes no further than this room."

"I understand," she said, touched that he trusted her with this bit of information.

"Ryan's a good kid. He's accomplished a lot."

"Agreed."

"He tried to save my ass when the ranch went tits up. He tries to take care of people. Gets that from his mom." Walt's eyes narrowed thoughtfully. "And I notice that now he seems interested in taking care of you."

He was a caretaker, Ellie would agree with that. He'd been watching out for everyone on the ranch since the day she arrived. And now he *was* watching out for her.

"I would be obliged," Walt said grimly, "if you didn't go stomping on his heart."

"Trust me, Walt. That's the last thing I want to do."

CHAPTER SEVENTEEN

EVEN THOUGH HE had other issues to deal with, his father for one, Ryan spent most of the day letting his thoughts drift toward Ellie. It'd been so long since he'd felt close to someone, truly close, and he and Ellie had seemed to know instinctively what the other wanted. Needed.

Hell, from the moment he'd realized there was more to cool Ms. Ellison Hunter, human-resources specialist, he'd been drawn to her. He'd enjoyed discovering the aspects of her personality that she kept hidden behind that professional exterior; enjoyed the natural way they were able to interact once she dropped her guard. Even discovering she was pregnant hadn't slowed him down for long, but that had been because he'd focused on Ellie as a woman, not Ellie as a pregnant woman. He'd thought about sleeping with her, but hadn't expected it to happen. Well, it had, and could well happen again before she left. And something deeper *could* develop if things continued on as they were....

Was he getting ahead of himself here?

Yeah, he was, but this was not something to go

into lightly. If a deeper relationship developed between them, there was a huge life change involved
not too far down the road. Was he ready for that responsibility? To just dive in on short notice?

What did he know about fatherhood? Only what
he'd learned from Francisco—it filled your heart,
wore you out and made you crazy protective. Would
he feel crazy protective over a child that wasn't his
own? He was starting to feel that way about Ellie,
so yeah, it seemed possible. And Walt seemed to
have maintained a soft spot for him, even through
those rotten teen years. But there were so many unknowns, so many things to consider, and it was way
too early for that.

So for now he'd follow Ellie's lead. It seemed the
gentlemanly thing to do.

AFTER WALT LEFT, Ellie put her laptop away and then
walked over to George's trailer, wanting very much
to tell him to mind his own freaking business. Not
surprisingly, after ratting her out to Milo, he had
not shown up the evening before to give his detailed daily report. Although Ellie had enjoyed the
reprieve, she decided it was in her best interest to
rebuild the bridge she'd burned. For now.

George smiled that congenial smile of his when
he opened the door to find her waiting on the aluminum step, but his eyes were not friendly. Well,
neither were hers, she was sure. Ellie faked a smile

back at him. "I missed our meeting last night. Would you like to go over the findings?" she asked politely, gesturing to the chairs sitting under the pine outside the travel trailer.

"I didn't get much new information yesterday," George replied, shifting his weight uncomfortably as he spoke.

You did according to my uncle, and you felt quite free to pass it along to him.

But Ellie wasn't going there just yet, because Milo still seemed to think George was the answer to all his ranching problems. Until she could convince her uncle otherwise, it made no sense to alienate the consultant, have him working against her. Thus the purpose of her current visit. Humble pie.

"I just wanted to drop by and apologize for what I said after the snake incident," she said smoothly. "I've grown fond of Hiss and spoke more out of emotion than common sense when I saw you threatening him. It was uncalled for and I, of course, did not mean it."

George's eyebrows rose in surprise at her apology, although he quickly overcame his reaction. He cleared his throat and said, "No apology necessary. I understand." He then worked up an engaging smile, once more falling into character. "I've never before met a woman with a soft spot for a snake."

"You have now," Ellie said with a sweet smile. "I'll talk to you soon, Mr. Monroe."

"Yes. Soon."

Ellie suppressed a creeped-out shudder as she walked away. To think that upon first meeting the man she'd thought him charming, accomplished and good-looking.

As soon as she got back to the house, Ellie checked her email, then instead of starting her daily, and usually dismal, job search, she jotted down a few notes on a legal tablet—just as she'd done when she'd first arrived and had been trying to get her life on track. After her job hunt that day, she wanted to find out a bit more about George's professional reputation, because no matter what Milo and the Kenyons thought, no one was as perfect as he was on paper.

She'd just opened a search engine when she got an email from Kate with a happy face in the subject box and a request to call when she had a minute to talk. Ellie called immediately.

"I have a job lead for you!" Kate said excitedly.

"You do?"

"Yes!" Her friend sounded tickled. "A pretty good one. Not the same caliber of job you had before, but one that might work with your…future…shall we say?"

"What kind of job?"

"It's in human resources, but more in the way of teambuilding as opposed to traveling around and evaluating."

"Great. Shall I forward my résumé?"

"No need. They have it and more than that, you already have an interview."

"I do?" That was a bit shocking.

"You're kind of in the middle of it right now."

Ellie's mouth fell open. "I didn't know your company was hiring."

"They're not, but my dad's is, and if you want the job, it's yours."

Ellie's stomach sank. Not what she'd been looking for. Kate's father ran an electronics firm that he'd built from the ground up, moving from transistors to computer chips as the times changed. It was a nice privately owned company with offices close to the company she'd just left. She could go home—where, she knew from chatting with her former coworkers, Nick now lived.

"Oh, wow." The chances of running into Nick might be slim, but it still made her grow cold inside thinking about it.

"Yeah. I know. Dad's always had a soft spot for you."

"Which is why I don't want him to create a job for me." In the same way that Angela and Milo had done by offering her the opportunity to stay at the ranch.

"He didn't create a job. He needs someone. The current person is leaving in September. She's going back to school to get a master's degree in psychology."

Ellie pressed her hand to her forehead. "So I'd start in September?"

"Yep. The pregnancy wouldn't be covered by insurance, since it's a preexisting condition, but other than that, I think it would work for you, Ellie. If you don't mind working for a tiny company instead of a Fortune 500."

Not the career path she'd envisioned, but she wasn't exactly following the life path she'd planned, either.

"When would you need an answer by?"

"I'm not sure," Kate said, sounding a bit taken aback. "I guess I thought you'd jump on this."

"I probably will," Ellie said. "I'm waiting to hear on a few other things, too." Not entirely true, but getting involved with a friend's family was a big deal. Ending up closer to Nick than she intended was a big deal. It wasn't something she wanted to jump on without thinking it through.

"I understand. Of course."

"Kate…you don't know how much I appreciate this. I'll let your dad know very, very soon. I promise you."

Ellie hung up, thinking that she should be more excited and feeling as if she'd let Kate down. The solution to her problem was right there, waiting for her to say yes, but she needed time to go through the pros and cons. Make her plan. Go at it as the old Ellie would, and that meant thinking things through before acting.

And unexpectedly, now that an escape route had

presented itself, flawed though it may be, Ellie realized she was going to have to get used to the idea of leaving Montana. Of leaving Ryan.

She had to leave. The summer was ending soon; Milo and Angela were no closer to staying on the ranch than they'd been when she first arrived. She could probably live there indefinitely, "overseeing" the place, freeloading off her relatives, having no particular plan for the future.

The thought froze her up even more than the risk of running into Nick.

The scenario ate at her all day, ruining her concentration until finally she retreated to her garden. She was in the backyard, planting the last of the flat of daisies, when she heard the ranch truck coming across the field. Her hands stilled in the damp earth, and then she plunged them back in again, making a hole to plant yet another daisy. Would she see Ryan tonight?

Without a doubt.

Would they make love?

She hoped. It wouldn't solve her job dilemma, but it would distract her from reality, give her a few hours of not having to think about her future and to simply be in the moment. And he seemed to need that as much as she did. In a way, they were lucky to have found each other at this point in time. She hoped that they still felt that way when she had to leave.

Ellie planted her last daisy, then went into the house to shower. George would no doubt want to meet now that she'd made peace, and then, after that—her lips curved in anticipation—she'd see if she could arrange a short meeting with Ryan.

ELLIE SHOWED UP at his door just after dusk. Ryan had promised himself that he would wait for her, let her make the moves since she had the most at stake. And move she did. He'd barely closed the door behind her when she reached up and started unbuttoning his shirt. He returned the favor, backing toward the bedroom as they shed clothing. He caught her to him and collapsed onto the mattress a few steps after they cleared the doorway, his body taking the brunt of the impact before he rolled over and trapped her beneath him. She laughed before reaching up to pull his head down to hers, and then they lost themselves in the business of pleasing one another, pleasing themselves. Twice.

Since he was spending the next day with George, discussing the possibility of mobile fencing—which he actually thought was a decent idea—he figured it was probably a good thing that Ellie had arrived fairly early and then, with a kiss that made him very much want to drag her back into bed, left. But he could still smell her subtle scent on his pillow. Damn, but he wanted her there, where he could hold her against him as they fell asleep.

THE DAY WITH George went better than any of the others they had spent together. For some reason the guy was on better behavior than usual and for most of the day he spoke to Ryan as a peer instead of acting like an asshole expert—right up until the subject of Walt came up as they were driving back to the ranch. That was when George asked Ryan pointblank how long Walt had been an alcoholic.

"Define alcoholic," Ryan instantly responded.

"I think you know the definition," George replied.

"Walt isn't an alcoholic." He simply had a binge every now and then.

George smirked at him and Ryan knew that Milo Bradworth would receive a tip that the current manager had a probable substance-abuse problem. This guy never let up. He wanted to extend his contract for a year, pulling in a hefty salary and throwing his weight around, and Ryan didn't think either he or Ellie was going to be able to do anything about that.

That night he'd joined Ellie in her garden where she'd proudly showed him the improvements she'd made. There were flowers everywhere. Banks of petunias, rows of daisies and snapdragons and pansies. She beamed up at him, making him want to kiss her yet again.

"I don't know," he said slowly, wanting to smile at the instant frown that formed on her face. "Don't you think a pie-shaped bird feeder would add something?"

"Jerk," Ellie muttered, but she had to bite her lip to keep from smiling back.

He didn't leave until sunrise.

They stayed awake for most of the night talking, sharing experiences, laughing. Bonding. Ellie, he discovered, had a profound sense of whimsy that she rarely expressed. Why? What would people think if she wore lime-green heels to work? He'd suggested that it didn't matter what they thought, only what she thought. "In other words, screw 'em," he advised.

Ellie laughed. "You have *no* idea of what my world is like."

"Probably not," he agreed, tracing the line of her hip with his fingertips.

She propped up on one elbow. "I admit that I don't even own lime-green heels, although I do admire them. But think about it… Would you want the person who made the decision as to whether or not you got to keep your job wearing frivolous heels?"

"I'm having a hard time imaging George in heels, frivolous or not," he replied.

"George isn't making that decision," she said, her expression sobering.

"Are you sure?"

One corner of her mouth lifted. "I'm doing what I can to make sure of it."

Ryan didn't ask for details. With Ellie he found that if he waited, she let loose with what she wanted him to know. She simply wasn't one to be pushed and he, fortunately, was patient. It worked out.

"I like it when you stay," she finally murmured as her eyes drifted shut.

He idly stroked her hair. "Maybe I'll stay more often."

She nodded against his chest and a moment later her breathing became steady and deep. Ryan put a protective arm over her and closed his own eyes. Tomorrow was coming all too soon, so it felt good to be so at peace right now.

RYAN HAD NO rodeos that week, so in seven days they made love at least seven times, enjoyed more than one sunrise before Ryan slipped out of the house and discovered that, for having grown up in such different environments, they valued many of the same things. Peace and quiet, a good beer, now off-limits to Ellie, old movies and goofy TV reruns. But there was an undercurrent, a sense that as good as things were at the moment, it couldn't last. Not without taking a hard look at some hard issues. At some point they were going to have to either face those issues or go their separate ways.

Ryan was in favor of the former. He was falling in love with Ellie, and unless there was a radical shift in their dynamic, he saw no reason he couldn't be there for her. It wouldn't be an easy adjustment. He was more than aware of that. The thought of fatherhood, if their relationship went that far, was intimidating to say the least, but he could handle it. One day at a time, as with everything else in life.

And if Ellie wanted to avoid commitment for a while, take things slow as, knowing Ellie, she'd probably want to do, he was good with that, too. But he didn't want to end the relationship just because Ellie had this idea drilled into her head of what her future had to be. Circumstances shifted and changed and so could life paths. One simply needed to be aware of the choices.

ELLIE HAD NEVER been in a relationship where she'd felt so…connected. She'd always dated the career driven, which, she now realized, had protected her from having to connect in a more intimate way. She'd never had to bare her soul, let the other person know her real fears, her real heartaches. She'd always held those things close out of lack of trust— fear of having someone else know too much about her—and had replaced that closeness with a more superficial bond, a shared drive to succeed. The need to put a career first.

She hadn't yet told Ryan about the traumas of being raised by a distant mother, but when she did, she knew he'd understand, even though his relationship with his own mother was tight. She had the feeling she could tell him anything, which, while drawing them closer, also frightened her—as did the fact that she suspected Ryan felt as strongly about her as she did about him. It was evident in the way he looked at her, treated her. The way he'd sometimes splay his hand over her abdomen, as if silently telling her that he accepted her—all of her.

But still she didn't know if she was ready to take a chance. To jump in with both feet, only to find out it wouldn't work, and then have to scramble to deal with the emotional fallout…and at the same time be there for a child.

Serious stuff.

It would be so much simpler to just go it alone… if it wasn't for the fact that they seemed to be doing so well together, and that she had a feeling that Ryan was falling in love with her.

Or that she was quite possibly falling for him, too.

She went to roping practice with him several times, sitting on the rough bleachers, a little apart from the others as usual, but the people there still smiled and said hello and she answered back in kind. Kids raced by, squealing and clamoring up and down the stairs, and it struck her more than once that in a year from now she would have a kid and in two years' time her child might be toddling up and down the stairs. It was a sobering thought.

After Ryan's last run, she made her way off the bleachers and slowly walked through the sea of horse trailers, wondering if this was the last time she'd be doing this. She had to contact Kate's father, give him her decision. She also had to make a logical decision, not an emotional one.

As she approached the trailer, she could see that Ryan was talking to a man who seemed out of place in his pressed khakis and corduroy sports jacket. Ellie stopped, not wanting to walk in on the conversation, but a split second later the guy gave his head a grim shake and stalked off toward a BMW parked at the edge of the fairground lot.

Ryan watched him go, then turned back to his horse, catching sight of Ellie as he did so. She started toward him again as he unsaddled his horse, his expression taut.

"More trouble with your dad?" she asked impulsively.

"Yeah."

She cocked her head. "Walt says you don't have a dad."

His movements stilled, then he met her eyes. "Walt's wrong," he said simply before lifting the blanket off the horse's back and carrying it to the tack room.

The ride home was silent. Ellie had expected Ryan to ask her why she'd been discussing him with Walt, but he didn't. By the time they pulled into the ranch, her jaw was aching from holding it so tightly. After Ryan parked, he pulled the key out of the ignition and finally spoke.

"If you have a few minutes, I would like to tell you what's going on."

Ellie's lips parted. She hadn't expected that. "Sure," she said, her heart beating faster for no real reason.

"That guy I was talking to... He was a representative of my father."

"And Walt has no idea that you have a father?"

"I'd appreciate it if he never did know it." Ryan fiddled with the keys he held for a moment, before saying, "My father was married when my mom got pregnant. She never named him on the birth certificate. No one knows."

His father was a married man who never claimed him? For a moment all Ellie could do was to stare at him. She hadn't even realized that her hand had traveled up to cover her belly protectively.

"No one?"

"Only my mom, my brother and now you."

"You have a brother?"

"That would be my father's legitimate son. My father's wife doesn't know, and that's why I'm being paid to keep my mouth shut."

"Why are you telling me this?" Ellie asked.

Ryan stared down at the steering wheel for a moment, as if straightening out the reasons in his mind. "Because if I sign that agreement, I can't tell you and if we ever...you know...I want you to know."

"If we ever what, Ryan?"

"If we ever move beyond what we have now."

"Do you see that happening?" she asked cautiously. There'd been times during the past few days when she'd thought about her and Ryan and her child making a life…but she never let herself think about it for long. Didn't allow herself to fantasize about happily ever after because reality had a way of kicking fantasies like that to the curb, to make a person feel foolish for ever thinking that way.

He reached out to take her hand, turning it over in his, caressing her palm with his thumb. "I see us taking one day at a time."

She tried to smile, though it wasn't easy as she was still feeling the aftershock of discovering that his mother's situation was so similar to her own. "Good answer," she murmured.

He squeezed her fingers. "I'm not trying to add to your stress level. I just wanted you to know the truth."

The truth…that until he'd told her, only four people in the world knew. Now there were five. Not even Walt, who Ryan looked at as a surrogate father, knew. A twinge of panic crept up on her at the thought, but she pushed it down.

THE CALL ELLIE had been dreading came the day after she found out about Ryan's father. She hadn't meant to make Kate call, but each day she thought that she needed just a little more time to make the proper decision—a decision not based in avoidance. She wasn't yet at that point.

"It's Nick," she told Kate. "I don't want to be anywhere near him."

"I hadn't thought about that," Kate said. "So are you thinking of staying in Montana?"

"That may not be the best choice, either. I—" she hesitated, then made a blurting confession "—might be in over my head."

"How so?"

"I got involved with a guy." Ellie rubbed a hand over her face, wondering how much to tell…or even how to tell. "It was just supposed to be a two-ships-in-the-night kind of thing. He was dealing with issues and so was I and together we could just kind of forget them."

"And then it got serious."

"It seems to be."

Kate was quiet for a moment. "You want to get out before it gets more serious?"

Ellie cleared her throat. "I don't want to make a mistake and be an emotional wreck when I have my baby. I need to be strong, not vulnerable." She couldn't bring herself to tell Kate that her biggest fear was that Ryan saw too much of his mother's situation in her own. That he was compensating for past wrongs without even knowing it. She wanted to be his lover, not his project.

"Valid."

"Rotten timing on my part," Ellie said. "I need a job. I need autonomy."

"You have a job. All you have to do is say the word," Kate said gently. "As long as it's in the next ten days. If you don't want it, then Dad will have to fly it."

"Understood," Ellie said. "I'll get back to you soon."

"Yeah…and in the meantime, don't do anything I wouldn't do."

"Not helpful," Ellie said with a choked laugh. Kate was notorious for getting herself into man trouble.

"Okay," Kate said. "Do the opposite. And call. Anytime."

"Will do. Thanks."

Ellie hung up and let her head fall back against the cushion of the leather chair. She needed some distance, some space. Something that would allow her perspective. She needed to be where she wasn't tempted by a hot, caring cowboy whose motives she wasn't sure of. He made her feel so good, so safe and at the same time so unsettled. What if she loved him and he only thought he loved her?

SOMETHING SEEMED OFF about Ellie. She smiled and laughed and made love, but there was an air of preoccupation about her that made him feel edgy. Something was up.

"Have you heard on a job?" He was guessing as they walked to the pond one evening after dinner.

"I did get a job offer," she said slowly, watching his face as she spoke. "I haven't made a decision yet. It's not an optimal situation, but I'm not in a position to be too choosy."

Ryan had the oddest sense of the bottom falling out of his world, even though he'd known this day was coming. He wanted to ask her questions about the job, but instead followed his gut and let the matter be. She reached out and took his hand and they walked in silence.

It wasn't until they were on the way back that she said, "I'm working on getting George kicked off the place."

"As a going-away present?" Ryan asked, surprised to hear the touch of bitterness in his voice. Ellie heard it, too, and slipped her hand free. "I didn't mean to be snide," he said, glancing over at her. "I just hate to see you go."

Her eyes held his for a moment, and then she put her hand back in his and they walked on. But somehow it didn't feel the same.

GEORGE, APPARENTLY SENSING that Ellie was never going to be an ally, had given up on the nightly meetings shortly after trying to take Hiss out with a shovel. Ellie was fine with that, but now that she'd finished looking into George's consulting track record, she requested a meeting. Her original intent had been to see if she could find any ranchers who did not sing his praises and to discover what his actual percentage of employee retention was. The employee retention rate was every bit as dismal as Ryan had indicated, but the information from the lesser-known ranches that he'd "turned around" had been even more telling.

But it was only fair that George have a chance to answer the charges.

The one question he seemed to resent most was when she asked him to recount his time on the Bear Creek Ranch just south of the Canadian border.

After some digging and assurances of anonymity, she found that George had worked his way into the good graces of the new owners, fired the crew, brought on several of his cronies to fill the vacancies and left the ranch no better off than when he'd started the job—except that he'd been able to spend nine months in a beautiful area with world-class fishing and his friends had gotten lucrative employment.

George made noises about not all changes being evident on the surface, and Ellie had nodded in an understanding way…. But she wasn't fooling George and he wasn't fooling her.

At the end of her three days of research, Ellie understood exactly why George had been so over-the-top in his instantaneous assessment of Walt. He wanted Walt's job, at least for a while, and then he probably had a friend who could slip into the position when it was time to move on. Ellie sent the file she'd compiled on George's not-so-successful ventures to Milo and waited for the call. It was better that he call her and she was surprised at how fast she heard from him.

"What's this file about, Ellie?"

"Have you had time to read it?" she asked patiently.

"I've been locked up with lawyers."

"That is a file on some of your consultant's not-so-stellar jobs."

"Meaning…?"

"I know that it appears that George did a fantastic job of turning around some properties," Ellie said carefully, "and those were properties that were in dire need of turning around. I've done some research and come up with a few properties that he's 'turned around' that actually only needed some minor tweaks."

"What's your point, Ellie?"

"As you know, George wants his contract extended for a year here while he shapes things up… but I don't think the place needs a year's worth of George. The people who work here are doing a decent job."

"He knows ranching, Ellie."

"I'm not saying that George isn't good at what he

does. What I am saying is that sometimes he works things out so that a property *needs* him, whether it actually does or not."

Milo didn't answer immediately, so Ellie said, "He's like a surgeon that, once the patient is opened up, does a lot of extra stuff, whether it's necessary or not, because he has the opportunity. He's not only addressing the actual problem, he's doing what he can to invent problems—on paper anyway."

"Are you certain about this? Or is this that Madison guy talking?"

Ellie put a hand on her forehead. "That Madison guy has no idea I've been looking into this, Milo. I checked with ranches George has worked with—the ones that don't have testimonials on his webpage. He's notorious for shaking up personnel."

"Sometimes that has to happen."

"But not always, and after making some calls, I can tell you that he always fires at least half of the crew. Every single place he's consulted. You should keep that in mind."

"What about the manager at the Rocky View— that Walt character? I couldn't get any information out of him without prying it out and George indicated he had a drinking problem. Are you saying he should stay?"

"He's good at what he does," Ellie said. "He's a cattleman, and from what I understand and what the ranchers I've talked to say, his breeding program is top-notch. My suggestion is that he step down from the management position, concentrate on cattle breeding and that Ryan Madison step in as manager. He has a college education and he's the one who started turning the place around financially."

Milo gave a small humph of acknowledgment, so Ellie went on. "If you and Angela aren't going to move here immediately, my recommendation is to leave things as they are. These people care for this place is if it was their own. It'll be in good hands. Its profitability is increasing every year and after taking into account the unfortunate setbacks suffered, it's on par with other working operations in the area."

Milo was quiet. Ellie had known going in that he wouldn't want to believe his expert was trying to milk the situation and she didn't want to push things.

"You have George's first report," she said. "And I imagine you've been too busy to look at it. Read it now with a critical eye, Milo. You're good at discerning smoke and mirrors. Seek a second opinion if you need to, but right now my gut reaction is that the Rocky View doesn't need George Monroe. It's in good hands."

"And if the report looks good?"

"I'd still get a second opinion. And I would not extend his contract. If you hired me to consult about this matter, that would be my answer."

"All right, Ellie," Milo said on a sigh. "I'll take a

look at the report. If I have questions, I'll get back to you."

"Thanks, Milo. Talk to you soon."

And now all she could do was hope that her uncle believed her and not the specialist. If George stayed a year, it was possible that he'd even drive patient Francisco away.

Two days later, when Ellie returned to the ranch from her OB appointment, George's travel trailer was gone. No big shiny black truck, no lawn chairs, no consultant.

Ellie sent up a silent prayer of thanks. Hopefully this meant Milo was putting ranch management back into the hands of the current crew, where it belonged. Walt might carry the title of manager, but Ryan was the actual push behind operations and he was good at steering the ranch activities in the proper direction.

She'd have to touch base with Milo, but for the moment she was hopeful and relieved. She could leave knowing she'd done some good…and she was leaving. All she had to do was call Kate's dad. Let him know.

FRIGGIN GEORGE WAS gone. Ryan got out of the ranch truck and for a moment simply stared at the place where the trailer had once been as a slow grin formed on his face. Good riddance. Ellie's Land Rover was parked in front of the house with the rear compartment door open. He walked over and saw that in addition to a box of groceries there were two flats of daisies. He pulled them out and carried them to the side gate where she met him.

"I had my second OB appointment today," she said as she opened the gate for him.

"And bought more flowers?"

"I can't seem to help myself, although there aren't too many left in town."

"The growing season is close to over," he pointed out as he set the flats down on the table where the jays had once eaten Jessie's pie.

"It's August."

"And we'll probably get our first killing frost sometime in September."

Ellie turned to him, a horrified expression on her face. "I'm doing all this and the flowers are going to die in a month?"

"Just means you get to do it again next year."

Ellie's gaze shifted then from horrified to...wary? Or was that flat-out fear? All because he'd mentioned next year. That was telling, and so was the knot in his stomach at her reaction. He reached out to take her hands. "Is next year out of the question? I know this isn't the life you used to lead, but it's a good life and you fit into it well...and if you stayed, well...you wouldn't be alone. So...you might consider that a possibility."

Ellie did not look reassured by his not-so-slick speech. "What exactly are you saying, Ryan?"

"You don't have to go through this alone," he repeated patiently.

Ellie pulled back. "*This* meaning my pregnancy?"

"Yes."

She took a step back, pulling her hands out of his. "Don't do this, Ryan."

"What?" he asked with a bemused frown.

"Don't be my white knight."

Okay, that floored him, as did the adamant tone in which she spoke. Obviously this was something that had been weighing on her mind. "I'm not trying to be your white knight, whatever the hell that means." He set his hands on his hips. "What the hell does that mean?"

Ellie let out a breath before saying, "It means that I wonder if there aren't so many similarities between what happened to me and what happened to your mom that you're, well, compensating."

"You think I'm trying to rescue you?"

"I think it's a possibility," Ellie said, folding her arms over her chest.

"And I think that's damned insulting. Do you have any feelings for me at all?"

"You know I do."

"Are you in love with me?" he asked in a low voice.

"I don't know."

She didn't meet his eyes and even though he felt as though he'd been sucker punched, he thought that it was quite possible she was not being truthful. Why? It had to be fear.

"This thing between us has been moving fast. We need some time to slow down, take a look at things," he said.

Her eyes flashed up at him. "The one thing I don't have is time, and I can't compromise my stability," she said. "Not now. I have to make a life for my kid, and that means I can't go into a relationship wondering about the motivation of my partner."

Sucker punch number two. "You could give me a chance, Ellie. Believe in me. Believe that I'm not righting any past wrongs at your expense."

"I'm not in a position to take chances," she said stubbornly.

Ryan's head dropped, and when he looked up again his expression was one of extreme frustration. The words came out slowly as he said, "Do you *want* to believe I'm being a white knight so that you can leave more easily?"

Ellie didn't answer, which was in itself an answer.

"If you have to leave, you do," Ryan said.

"I have to do what's best for me and my baby," she said quietly.

"How do you know I'm not best for you and your baby?"

She had no answer to that except for the same

one she'd given before. "I'm not in a position to take chances."

Third time was a charm. "And I have to accept that." He started for the side gate, leaving Ellie standing next to her daisies, an unreadable expression on her beautiful face—back behind her barriers, protecting herself from the world.

And he'd been stupid enough to think he'd broken through.

He turned back toward her before opening the gate latch. "Make no mistake, Ellie, when I made love to you, it had nothing to do with anything in my past. It had to do with you and how I feel about you. You may not know how you feel about me, but I'm pretty damned certain I'm in love with you."

CHAPTER EIGHTEEN

ELLIE WOKE UP to find Ryan's truck gone, then remembered he had the first of three rodeos in a row after his long break, many hundreds of miles away. She put on the kettle, then walked to the window and looked out over the pastures. Skipper grazed quietly with two of Ryan's other horses. Walt's dogs were snuffling around the barn and the four-wheeler was idling nearby. A few seconds later, Walt walked out of the barn and got on the vehicle, revving it loudly. The dogs shot into position on the back and off he went. She let her forehead touch the window.

And off she would go, too.

It had been a long, lonely night, but she'd convinced herself that things were working out the way they had to. She needed security. A job. She had to go with the sure thing. If she took a chance now and screwed up her life, then she also screwed up her baby's life. The child was already starting life with only one parent—why make things worse?

Ellie tidied up the house, threw her few belongings into her suitcase and booked a flight.

A day later, after returning her rental and spending the night in a motel, she landed in Santa Barbara. Angela met her at the airport, swooping her into a hug that involved an air kiss or two.

"Back from the wilds," she said on her husky laugh, stepping back to eye Ellie's midsection critically. "You're a little thicker."

"Thanks," Ellie said drily, smiling even though she didn't want to.

"Are you sure you can only stay two days?" Angela said.

"Yes. I told Kate's dad that I'd start work early next week. He found a house I can rent, so I need a few days to settle."

"It seems that things have fallen nicely into place," Angela said, sounding as if she was responsible for Ellie's happy ending.

"Yes." Except for that part where her heart felt like it'd been stomped into the ground.

"Milo won't be home for dinner," Angela said, "so I booked us a nice restaurant."

"Is Milo ever home for dinner?" Ellie asked as they approached the baggage claim.

"He loves this job."

Ellie walked toward the carousel that had just started moving. "He's losing interest in the ranch, isn't he?"

Angela cut Ellie a look. "I believe so, but that doesn't mean it won't resurge. Being chief of staff was such a goal of his for so long. He wants to revel in it for a while."

Ellie saw Milo briefly that evening, but he was too tired to talk ranch matters, so she'd taken a rain check. The next day Angela took her shopping, loading her up with loose silk tops that she'd need "soon enough" and promising that the next trip would be for the baby. Ellie didn't mind being spoiled a bit. She and her mother had exchanged a few emails over the past week, and things felt better there—she'd actually inquired about the pregnancy—but Mavis was never going to be an indulgent grandmother.

"I'll have this stuff shipped to you as soon as you have an address," Angela promised. "And Milo swears he'll be home on time tonight, so you can talk to him before you leave."

Ellie did get her time with Milo, sipping a club soda as he had his brandy after dinner. Her message was short and to the point. She didn't care what the ranch consultant had written in his report before leaving, Ryan Madison was more than capable of running the ranch, as was Walt—but don't plan on communicating with him.

"I, uh, believe you made that point a couple weeks ago," Milo said.

"Just wanted to make certain it struck home," Ellie replied. "Those guys know what they're doing with the pastures, the forage, the cattle. They'll take care of your ranch."

"You learned a lot in two months," Milo said, swirling the last of the liquid in the snifter he held.

"More than I ever anticipated," Ellie said.

"Did you like it there?"

"Eventually, yes." Ellie sucked in a breath, took the leap. "More than Angela ever will."

Milo gave a small nod.

"I wouldn't move her there, Milo. Even for half the year. Take your vacations there."

"You don't think two weeks would be too much?" Milo asked ironically as he continued to warm his brandy between sips.

Ellie smiled. "I think it would be pushing it." She smoothed her hair, once again in the twist instead of the ponytail. "The ranch is good for your taxes. A decent investment. Leave it at that."

"Was George that bad?"

"George knows his business, but he takes advantage of people who don't." She raised her eyebrows at her uncle. "He was talented that way."

DURING THE TIME she spent with her aunt and uncle, Ryan called her three times, leaving messages since Ellie kept her phone shoved deep in her suitcase for the two days she was there, checking only to see if Kate or her father had called. The first two times Ryan asked her to call him back. She didn't—she wasn't yet ready. The last time he'd left a message telling her that he wouldn't bother her again. And that was it. A click and it was all over.

All but the memories and the stubborn intrusion of "what if…" every time she thought of him.

She had to deal in reality now, not what-if. Besides, what-if worked two ways.

What if she gave up this job and went back to the ranch only to discover things weren't working between them?

What if she couldn't find another job because heaven knew how hard it'd been to get this one and she'd only gotten it because of Kate—which wasn't great for the ego, but she could live with it?

What if she lost an opportunity to provide for her child? She couldn't take a risk like that.

"So what's put you in such a black mood?" Lydia asked as Ryan carried his dishes to the sink. "A horse, a woman or a rodeo?"

"None of the above."

"What about the ranch owner's niece?" Ryan shot his mother a quick look. "Walt stopped by. Said you've been hell to work with because of her."

"That's not why." Now he was lying to his mother. Well, it beat discussing the matter with her.

"What about Charles?"

"What about him?" Ryan snapped. She gave him the eye and he shook his head. "I haven't answered him yet. I hate letting him win."

"If you take the money, you win."

"If I sign the agreement, he wins."

"I don't see it that way."

"Fine," Ryan said as he picked up his hat. "I'll figure out a way to deal with it."

"What are you going to do?"

"I'm going to call a guy who knows him."

"Take the money, Ryan."

Ryan shook his head and then kissed his pissed-off mother goodbye before driving home. Once there, he poured a shot of whiskey, neat, then got out the phone book and made a call he never thought he'd make. A kid answered. He asked for Matt and then said, "Tell him it's Ryan."

"Madison?" Matt said a few seconds later.

"Yeah. I would like to get together for a sit-down. It involves you. And your mom and mine."

There was a beat of tense silence and then his brother said, "So it obviously also involves my—our—dad."

"In a big way."

Another pause and then Matt said, "Yeah. I'll meet with you. Do you mind coming here? To the house? Traveling is still kind of hard on me and my chauffer is fourteen."

"That'll work," Ryan said.

"Tonight? Say seven o'clock?"

"I'll be there." Ryan jotted down the directions, figuring it'd take him an hour to get there. An hour to debate about whether this was a stupid thing he was doing or a good thing.

Ryan pulled into Matt's driveway a few minutes before seven. The house was fairly modest yet well kept, but the indoor arena next to it spoke of just how lucrative it was to be the son of a rich man with a championship roping career.

A teenage boy with sandy hair and glasses answered the door. "Hi, I'm Craig," he said, holding the door open.

"Ryan." He stepped into the house, noticing that it looked as if the housekeeper had just left. It was crazy clean.

"Matt's in the kitchen. He's not getting around too good."

"So I hear."

Feeling even more awkward than he had when he'd stopped by his brother's hospital room, Ryan went into the kitchen where Matt was sitting at the table.

"Thanks for seeing me," Ryan said as the kid disappeared.

"If I hadn't, I don't think I could have slept at night wondering what it was you wanted to talk about." Matt gestured at the seat across the table from him and Ryan sat.

"How long until you're out of the cast?"

"Way too long from what I understand," Matt said wearily.

"Competition isn't the same without you."

"Kind of you to say," he replied with a half smile. "But you're going to have to get used to it. I can still throw a rope, but try as I might, I don't seem to be able to mount and dismount." Ryan smiled as Matt placed his palm flat on his cast. "On the other hand, your season seems to be going well."

"It's my last," he said.

Matt's eyebrows went up. "Why?"

After Ellie had left, he'd done a lot of thinking about what was and wasn't important to him. "My heart's not in it anymore. I may do the Montana circuit again next year, but my Nationals days are over. My job is tenuous and I want to focus on something steadier."

"Tenuous how?"

"Urbanites bought the ranch. A doctor. I have this feeling that they're eventually going to sell again, since they haven't spent a day there in over a year, and if so, who knows if we—my mentor and I— will have jobs?"

"Rough one," Matt agreed with a nod.

They fell into silence then and Ryan knew that the catching up was over, so he laid out exactly why he came in one quick sentence. "The reason I'm here is because the old man offered me a lot of money to sign a confidentiality agreement agreeing to never claim paternity."

Matt let out a disgusted breath, which answered Ryan's first question—had he known? If so, he was a decent actor. "I'd, uh, kind of wondered if you were involved."

Matt looked shocked. "Why?"

"I saw you at the High Point rodeo and I also saw one of the old man's pickups."

Matt shook his head. "Didn't know one thing about it. I only went to that rodeo because my girlfriend rides in the drill team. I haven't seen the old man—" he tilted his back, narrowing his eyes "—since the hospital, I guess." Once again, he met Ryan's gaze. "Are you signing?"

"No. But he's not letting up. I told him no once and he came back at me with an offer of more money."

"And you're turning down the money why?"

Ryan snorted. "I don't want his money."

"Give it to your mother."

"She won't take it, but she wants *me* to have it."

"Take it."

Ryan leaned forward. "I kind of thought that you would understand why I don't feel right taking the money my mother should have had while I was growing up and using it on myself. And I know you understand why I'm not signing that damned agreement."

"Yeah."

"All I want is for him to back off. Never talk to me or my mom again. I thought you might have some ideas."

Matt leaned back in his chair, wincing slightly at the movement. "What's happened here is that the old man has opened a can of worms he can't control when he accused your mom of telling me about you." He thought for a moment. "Back when we were born, DNA wasn't quick, easy or affordable, so he probably never feared a paternity suit. If your mom claimed paternity, I'm sure he would have denied it."

"He felt safe."

"And never thought until recently he had a reason not to be safe since your mom never said a word." Matt's mouth turned up grimly. "Now he doesn't feel safe. He screwed up when he decided your mother told me about you."

"So all this is damage control?"

"More than you know. I love my mom and for some reason my mom loves my dad, but guess what? The ranch is in trust to her."

"No shit."

"Dad married the place."

"But he's wealthy, right?"

"Yeah. But he'd be less wealthy without the ranch that's his total identity. Not to mention being the object of public scorn. He's a proud, proud man. That would kill him. And—" Matt hesitated "—I think the old man really loves my mother."

Ryan tapped his fingers on the table. "Okay, I understand the why. Now, how do I make him believe I'm not a threat?"

"Take the money and sign the paper." Ryan opened his mouth to repeat his moral objection when Matt cut him off, saying, "Trust me. You have to take something or he'll never rest…but this doesn't have to be totally on his terms. Let's you and me have a sit-down with him and see what comes of it."

Ryan shook his head. "Do you think he could survive a sit-down?" he asked, recalling the last time Charles Montoya had been in the company of both sons, just before Matt had gotten hurt.

Matt laughed, but it had a harsh ring to it. "He's tough, and I think maybe it's time we got everything out into the open. Do you want to set up the meeting or shall I?"

"For the good of his heart, why don't you?"

CHAPTER NINETEEN

ELLIE'S NEW JOB wasn't particularly challenging, and it wasn't particularly engaging. It was simply an undemanding position that allowed her to go home every day and focus on her own life rather than plotting strategy for the next day. It was also a job she would have turned down a year ago because it didn't offer enough room for growth. She was no longer as concerned about growth as she was about security and longevity.

Her new rental was only a mile away from Kate, and now that they were once again in the same city, it allowed them more one-on-one time—which Ellie was beginning to see as a mixed blessing. Not because she didn't like to spend time with her friend, but because Kate was too intuitive for Ellie's liking.

"Do you miss it? The ranch?" she asked one evening after they'd gone to a movie and dessert.

Did she? Did she miss the ranch? Or did she miss Ryan? Both, probably. "It grew on me."

"It was beautiful?"

"Very, but more than that…" She tried to think of how to explain why her memories of the place were poignant without mentioning Ryan. "It's the place where I came to terms with being pregnant. Started to bond with my baby." Which she now knew was a boy, but she hadn't yet told Kate. Or her mother. Or Angela. She wanted to come up with a name before she started sharing.

"And the cowboy you hooked up with?"

Ellie gave her a startled look. "How do you know he's a cowboy?"

"I saw the photo you're using as a bookmark." The photo she'd snapped with her phone during that last roping practice.

"Just a reminder of good times."

Kate leaned across the table. "I don't think you would have taken a photo without him knowing it unless you had a reason."

"How do you know he didn't know it?"

"He's looking to the left, into the distance. His back's half turned." Kate settled back in her chair, giving Ellie a don't-try-to-bullshit-me look. "Did it go well when you ended things?"

"No." Ellie tried for matter-of-fact, but the word came out sounding choked. Kate pressed her lips together but said nothing, so in an effort to sidetrack her, Ellie said, "Funny, but the first time I saw him, I knew you'd like him."

Kate played along. "Then why didn't you introduce us? I have no problems moving to a ranch, burying myself in the country."

Ellie tried to imagine Kate rescuing a goose out of a pond and just couldn't do it, but to be fair, she couldn't have imagined herself doing the same thing a few months ago.

"Maybe I wanted to keep him to myself," Ellie said softly. *For a while anyway.*

"Then why are you here?"

"Because I'm a realist."

Kate nodded. "Yes, you are. Your greatest asset. Your greatest flaw."

Ellie wasn't going to ask why being a realist was a flaw. She didn't want to talk about flaws, or Ryan. Especially not Ryan, because her thoughts in that area were anything but peaceful. She'd done the right thing. The only thing. Why didn't she feel at peace?

"I'm enjoying work," she said, not so deftly changing the subject. "It feels like it's been years since I've been off, but really it's only been four months." Four months in which she found out more about herself than she'd thought possible.

"You'll love it. It's a great work environment. I should know, I interned there four years in a row."

"Only to go to work for the competition."

Kate snorted. "They pay more." Actually, her father had encouraged her to get experience in other companies before she came back to take over the reins of his company when he retired. Know the competition, he'd said, and what better way than to work for them? "So you're really happy to be back?"

"Of course. It's the place where I belong."

That night she unpacked the laptop Walt had borrowed from her, and in the case was the notebook where she'd written her three goals upon arriving at the ranch. Wondering idly if Walt had read her goals, she flipped the pages open and found the entry.

Had she succeeded?

Have a healthy baby. She was working on that, and it looked as though she was doing an excellent job. She'd found a doctor she liked. Her blood pressure was great; the baby's growth was right on schedule; she ate only the healthiest of foods…except for the ice cream, but the kid seemed to enjoy her lapses in that department. Mavis had started sending occasional brief emails inquiring about Ellie's health, and two days ago she'd received a surprise package in the mail containing a spectacularly impractical newborn designer coat with a fur collar—suitable for either boy or girl, according to the note. Ellie smiled at the thought. Perhaps her child would have a grandmother. Of sorts.

Present Milo with understandable overview of ranch operations to enable him to make future ranch management decisions. She'd done that, too. Milo was seriously considering selling the ranch, which Ellie thought would be best for everyone involved.

The yacht he had his eye on was a better fit for both him and Angela.

Use time at ranch constructively to prepare for personal future. So had she succeeded or failed there? Ellie told herself she'd succeeded. She was relatively satisfied with her life, focusing on the baby and her job, such as it was. Yes. She'd succeeded there.

Indeed she had.

She only wished it felt more like a victory.

CHARLES HAD AGREED to a meeting in two days' time, which gave Ryan more time than he wanted to think. And think some more.

Damn, but he missed Ellie. He'd thought Walt was stubborn once he set his mind to something, but he was a reed blowing in the wind compared to Ellie, who had it in her mind that the only reason Ryan wanted her was to undo some of the shit his father had done. To make up for her kid not having a father. He'd tried to contact her three times but she hadn't responded, which both pissed him off and tore him up.

After Ellie had pointed out the possibility that he was confusing love with the need to rescue her, he'd given the matter some serious thought. And decided her theory was bullshit. After two weeks away from her he knew that he didn't want to rescue her. He wanted to be with her.

He honestly had fallen in love with her—for all the good it did him now that she had a new job and was building a life for her and her baby in the world where she felt comfortable—not like on the ranch, where she'd been so sorely out of place.

Only in the beginning.... She'd changed after the first few weeks....

That didn't change the fact that there was nothing for her on the ranch, just as there was really nothing for her rich relatives who wouldn't be visiting this summer. Milo had arranged a teleconference with him and Walt two days ago and the three of them had hashed out ranch business. The end result was pretty much that Milo understood that he needn't have even hired George. Milo's ultimate message had been to carry on and not be surprised if within a matter of months potential buyers once again start touring the place.

Ryan's gut tightened just thinking about it, but this made it more important than ever that the meeting with Charles went well.

"I CAN GIVE you guys an hour," Charles said. He'd wanted his Billings attorney there when he met with his sons in the public library conference room in Glennan, but both Matt and Ryan had said they'd only meet privately this first time. After that Charles could bring in all the lawyers he wanted. And since Charles wasn't exactly in a position to draw any lines in the sand, which was clearly killing him, he'd agreed.

"Shouldn't take that long," Matt said, taking a seat. "You know Ryan, I believe."

Charles stood. "If that's the tactic you're going to take—"

"Dad. Sit down. Please."

Slowly, Charles lowered himself back down and Matt leaned forward. "My brother and I have some business to discuss that will benefit us all. Ryan and I have decided that now that our competitive days are over, we're going to become friends. People can make of it what they want, but if they haven't figured out by now that we're brothers, they never will."

"So you're friends," Charles said with a sneer.

"And brothers," Matt said in a low voice.

"What about your mother? I thought you'd give just about anything to keep her from finding out."

"She won't find out," Ryan said. "Not from me. Not from my mom."

"And I'm supposed to believe that."

Ryan's expression went flat. "Look. I figured out I was your kid when I was fifteen, after Matt, here, beat the crap out of me at a rodeo. I never said a word. My mom never told anyone, either, which was why it upset the hell out of her when you threatened her. She wasn't responsible for Matt finding out—maybe the furthest thing from it—and she was afraid that whoever had told would keep spreading the word and you'd follow through on your threat. What was it again? You'd see to it that her beauty shop didn't pass code?"

Charles started to turn red.

"I'm not signing the agreement," Ryan said.

"Then why are we here?" Charles asked.

"You know that money you offered to pay Ryan and his mom?" Matt asked conversationally. "I want you to loan it to Ryan. At three percent interest."

"Now, wait a minute," Charles and Ryan said simultaneously. They exchanged hard glances, then Ryan shook his head.

"No," he said firmly.

"Why not?" Matt asked. "It makes perfect sense to me." He looked at his father. "You were going to give him the money. Hell, you owe him the money. Did you spend a dime in child support?"

"He bought my braces," Ryan muttered.

"I know," Matt said, earning a sharp look from his father. "But like you said, you had to rodeo with a beat-up truck, a four-hundred-dollar horse and a single-axle trailer. I think he owes you this loan. And since it's a loan, I don't see why either of you would object."

"Maybe the source of the money?" Ryan said. This was not working out the way he had anticipated. He'd figured they'd meet with Charles, strong-arm him into backing down by offering a united front then he'd go home and do his chores.

He wasn't going to take money from Charles Montoya. His pride wouldn't let him.

"Which will help you keep that mentor of yours on the land he seems to love so much." Ryan shouldn't have told him his concerns about Walt on the drive over. "Think about it," Matt said. "You can make an offer on the ranch—see if the doctor will sell. It's not a huge place. I looked up the previous purchase price. Surely you have some money socked away from your winnings, and then with a loan from the Montoya Land Company...."

Ryan took in a long breath, then locked eyes with his father, holding Charles's steely gaze for a moment before saying, "I have a different proposal."

"Please don't tell him to shove it up his ass," Matt murmured from beside him.

"Tempting, but no."

CHAPTER TWENTY

Two months later

ELLIE RAN HER hand over her belly as she sat at the computer looking up tie-down roping results. Ryan had managed to hold on to his position in the top fifteen money winners in the world standings. There was a lovely photo of him with a gorgeous redhead standing next to his black horse. The redhead wore a tiara and sash, which would have made Ellie feel better about the picture, if only Ryan's hand hadn't been placed so low on her hip.

Not that it mattered.

"I hope you don't want to be a cowboy," she murmured to her belly. Because she no longer had the means to give him a cowboy life, or even a cowboy vacation, since Angela and Milo had gotten an out-of-the-blue offer on the ranch.

Walt had offered them purchase price plus three percent. Milo was still debating, but Ellie knew that the fact that he hadn't instantly said no meant that he'd finally come to terms with the fact that while his friends the Kenyons were loving life on the Vineyard Ranch, that didn't mean his bride was going to embrace life on the Rocky View. Angela had confided that he was *this close* to making an offer on a sailing yacht.

The big question to her was where had Walt come up with that kind of money? She hadn't noticed any Montana bank robberies in the news.

Soon her last tie to Ryan would be severed, leaving her with good memories and a dull ache in her heart. It wasn't even as though she could move back to the area and see what might happen between them. She had responsibilities. She had a job.

She had a prenatal class in fifteen minutes.

Ellie grabbed her bag and was on her way out the door when a text came in. She took a quick glance, then nearly dropped the phone when she read the first words. This is Walt...

Walt, who didn't own a cell phone and who'd just somehow made an offer on the ranch he'd lost? The man was full of surprises.

The message continued. Never underestimate the power of a second chance.

What the hell?

A second chance? Was he talking about his second chance with the ranch? Was he texting her because she was maybe instrumental in the place going up for sale?

Ellie turned around and went back into the house. She no longer felt like going to class.

What kind of second chance? she tapped into her phone.

Several minutes later, as she visualized Walt's arthritic fingers painfully clicking out letters, she received: If I have to tell you then you don't deserve it.

Typical Walt.

Ellie pressed her fingertips to her forehead and tried to remember what life had been like before she'd decided to have one impulsive fling six months ago.

Stop being stubborn, Ellie typed.

Me? Ha!

"YOU WHAT?" RYAN asked as he closed the tack door. He'd just gotten back from his last rodeo of the regular season. He was dragging-ass tired and Walt had met him with the happy news that he'd taken it upon himself to resurrect Ryan's love life.

"Well, you've been hell to live with since she left," he muttered. "So I sent her a text."

"Telling her what?"

"To give you a second chance."

Ryan's blood pressure redlined. "If she'd wanted to give me a second chance," Ryan said from between his teeth, "she probably would have answered my calls after leaving."

"She didn't answer your calls?"

"No."

"Then she's a fool, too."

"No. I think there's only one fool standing here."

"Yeah, you."

"Look, Walt. I appreciate the thought, but don't help, okay?" It was hard enough dealing with this alone.

"Fine. Be stubborn. I can't tell you how far that's taken me." Walt huffed off.

Ryan shook his head and went back to his trailer to unhitch it—right in front of the house, as he wanted to—comforting himself with the knowledge that Ellie had probably ignored Walt's text as well as his calls.

"Where are you going?" he called as Walt started to get into his truck.

"To pick up Ellie. She's at the airport. I asked her to come and consult on a personnel problem I'm having."

ELLIE WORE HER Christian Louboutins because she needed all the confidence she could get. After ignoring Ryan's farewell voice mail, he could well tell her to go to hell. If so, she'd turn right around and leave. At least she could tell herself that she'd made a stab at fixing the mistakes she'd made.

Ever since Walt had texted her about second chances she'd been floored by how much she wanted one. How afraid she was that due to her own stubbornness she wasn't going to get one.

Would Ryan even talk to her after she'd refused to answer his calls or even call him back? Did she deserve to have him talk to her?

She was about to find out, because there, working his way past a small group of people at the entryway, was the man who'd filled her thoughts for the past months. Looking better than she remembered and totally pissed off.

He hadn't forgiven her. He'd found out and he was there to send her home.

Ellie stopped walking and he instantly spotted her. It took all of three seconds for him to reach her, plant himself in front of her.

"I thought Walt was coming," Ellie said in a low voice.

Ryan scowled. "Look, I know Walt got you out here on some kind of pretext and I'm sorry about that."

He looked so distant, so totally put out that Ellie took a step back, nearly tripping in her trusty heels. Ryan automatically put out his hand, but she regained her balance without touching him. So much for second chances.

She lifted her chin, regret ripping through her at being so close to him and not being able to do anything about it. He was so…real. The angles of his face, the scent of his body… Everything was so much better than she'd remembered. And yet she couldn't touch him because he was so damned withdrawn.

Your fault.

"Walt didn't ask me out here," she said. "I came. I merely asked him for a ride from the airport."

"Why?"

"I was going to ambush you," she said candidly, holding his gaze even though it cost her. "I thought…" *Get a grip. You've made people cry in the course of your work. You're tougher than this.* "I thought…given a chance…despite the phone message…" She pulled in a breath that raised her shoulders even as she hunched them protectively. "I never expected this to be easy."

"What?"

"I miss you so damned much."

There. She said it.

Ryan cocked his head, narrowing his eyes as if he hadn't heard right. "Me, too."

For a moment Ellie stared at him before she realized that he'd given the very best of answers. She moistened her lips. "You missed me?"

"Yeah."

She broke into a breathless smile. Then before either of them could come to their senses, she launched herself at him and Ryan caught her, holding her so tightly against him that her feet left the floor.

"Don't want to hurt the kid," he murmured against her ear, easing her down to the floor.

"He's tough," she whispered back, placing a hand over her small rounded belly.

"He?"

"Joshua. I thought it was a good, strong name."

"Does he have a middle name?"

"Not yet."

Ryan pulled her back against him, burying his face against her hair. He leaned back a few seconds later to give her a wry smile. "I'm sure there's someone at the ranch who would think Walter is a decent middle name, since he's quite certain he's rescued me from decades of loneliness."

"Decades?" Ellie asked, not feeling one bit intimidated by the possibility.

He smiled that heart-stopping half smile. "I thought he was crazy…but now I have some hope." The smile faded. "How long *will* you be here?"

"I can stay for a week right now…and if everything works out… Well, I've started making a plan with my employer to transfer to a department where I can work long-distance." It didn't pay as much, but she wouldn't leave Kate's dad in a lurch. Thankfully, he understood the situation and was willing to work with her. She owed him—and Kate—in a big way. As to what she owed Walt… Words couldn't express what she owed Walt.

"I love a good plan," Ryan said before frowning as he seemed to realize she was close to looking him in the eye. He glanced down at her feet, then met her gaze with a sexy smile. "Those aren't lime-green… but I like them."

"They'll do," Ellie said, tucking her arm in his as they started for the baggage claim. At least until she could get into some boots.

* * * * *

LARGER-PRINT BOOKS!
GET 2 FREE LARGER-PRINT NOVELS PLUS
2 FREE GIFTS!

HARLEQUIN®

super romance®

More Story...More Romance

YES! Please send me 2 FREE LARGER-PRINT Harlequin® Superromance® novels and my 2 FREE gifts (gifts are worth about $10). After receiving them, if I don't wish to receive any more books, I can return the shipping statement marked "cancel." If I don't cancel, I will receive 6 brand-new novels every month and be billed just $5.69 per book in the U.S. or $5.99 per book in Canada. That's a savings of at least 16% off the cover price! It's quite a bargain! Shipping and handling is just 50¢ per book in the U.S. and 75¢ per book in Canada.* I understand that accepting the 2 free books and gifts places me under no obligation to buy anything. I can always return a shipment and cancel at any time. Even if I never buy another book, the two free books and gifts are mine to keep forever.

139/339 HDN F46Y

Name _____ (PLEASE PRINT) _____

Address _____ Apt. # _____

City _____ State/Prov. _____ Zip/Postal Code _____

Signature (if under 18, a parent or guardian must sign)

Mail to the **Harlequin® Reader Service:**
IN U.S.A.: P.O. Box 1867, Buffalo, NY 14240-1867
IN CANADA: P.O. Box 609, Fort Erie, Ontario L2A 5X3

**Are you a current subscriber to Harlequin Superromance books
and want to receive the larger-print edition?
Call 1-800-873-8635 today or visit www.ReaderService.com.**

* Terms and prices subject to change without notice. Prices do not include applicable taxes. Sales tax applicable in N.Y. Canadian residents will be charged applicable taxes. Offer not valid in Quebec. This offer is limited to one order per household. Not valid for current subscribers to Harlequin Superromance Larger-Print books. All orders subject to credit approval. Credit or debit balances in a customer's account(s) may be offset by any other outstanding balance owed by or to the customer. Please allow 4 to 6 weeks for delivery. Offer available while quantities last.

> **Your Privacy**—The Harlequin® Reader Service is committed to protecting your privacy. Our Privacy Policy is available online at www.ReaderService.com or upon request from the Harlequin Reader Service.
>
> We make a portion of our mailing list available to reputable third parties that offer products we believe may interest you. If you prefer that we not exchange your name with third parties, or if you wish to clarify or modify your communication preferences, please visit us at www.ReaderService.com/consumerchoice or write to us at Harlequin Reader Service Preference Service, P.O. Box 9062, Buffalo, NY 14269. Include your complete name and address.

HSRLP13R

LARGER-PRINT BOOKS!
GET 2 FREE LARGER-PRINT NOVELS PLUS
2 FREE GIFTS!

HARLEQUIN®

Romance

From the Heart, For the Heart

YES! Please send me 2 FREE LARGER-PRINT Harlequin® Romance novels and my 2 FREE gifts (gifts are worth about $10). After receiving them, if I don't wish to receive any more books, I can return the shipping statement marked "cancel." If I don't cancel, I will receive 4 brand-new novels every month and be billed just $4.84 per book in the U.S. or $5.24 per book in Canada. That's a savings of at least 19% off the cover price! It's quite a bargain! Shipping and handling is just 50¢ per book in the U.S. and 75¢ per book in Canada.* I understand that accepting the 2 free books and gifts places me under no obligation to buy anything. I can always return a shipment and cancel at any time. Even if I never buy another book, the two free books and gifts are mine to keep forever.

119/319 HDN F43Y

Name _____ (PLEASE PRINT) _____

Address _____ Apt. # _____

City _____ State/Prov. _____ Zip/Postal Code _____

Signature (if under 18, a parent or guardian must sign)

Mail to the **Harlequin® Reader Service:**
IN U.S.A.: P.O. Box 1867, Buffalo, NY 14240-1867
IN CANADA: P.O. Box 609, Fort Erie, Ontario L2A 5X3
Want to try two free books from another line?
Call 1-800-873-8635 or visit www.ReaderService.com.

* Terms and prices subject to change without notice. Prices do not include applicable taxes. Sales tax applicable in N.Y. Canadian residents will be charged applicable taxes. Offer not valid in Quebec. This offer is limited to one order per household. Not valid for current subscribers to Harlequin Romance Larger-Print books. All orders subject to credit approval. Credit or debit balances in a customer's account(s) may be offset by any other outstanding balance owed by or to the customer. Please allow 4 to 6 weeks for delivery. Offer available while quantities last.

Your Privacy—The Harlequin® Reader Service is committed to protecting your privacy. Our Privacy Policy is available online at www.ReaderService.com or upon request from the Harlequin Reader Service.

We make a portion of our mailing list available to reputable third parties that offer products we believe may interest you. If you prefer that we not exchange your name with third parties, or if you wish to clarify or modify your communication preferences, please visit us at www.ReaderService.com/consumerschoice or write to us at Harlequin Reader Service Preference Service, P.O. Box 9062, Buffalo, NY 14269. Include your complete name and address.

HRLP13R

ReaderService.com

Manage your account online!
- Review your order history
- Manage your payments
- Update your address

> *We've designed*
> *the Harlequin® Reader Service*
> *website just for you.*

Enjoy all the features!
- Reader excerpts from any series
- Respond to mailings and
  special monthly offers
- Discover new series available to you
- Browse the Bonus Bucks catalog
- Share your feedback

Visit us at:
ReaderService.com